Shady Palms

A CONDO CAPER

BY FRANK CERABINO

Editor: Bill Greer
Illustrator: Pat Crowley
Designers: Michelle Mazzone and Dan Neal
Publishing liaison: Lynn Kalber

The Palm Beach Post
The Maple-Vail Book Manufacturing Group

The Maple-Vail Book Manufacturing Group
Willow Springs Lane
P.O. Box 2695
York, PA 17405

Printed in the United States of America

1st printing 2000

ISBN: 0-9705026-0-5

This book was printed by The Maple-Vail Book Manufacturing Group.

Originally published in *The Palm Beach Post*
from February 27-March 31, 2000.

$7.95 U.S.

Preface

Don't try looking for Shady Palms.

You might think you have a pretty good idea where the condo is. A lot of people do.

You might think that if you drive far enough west on Boynton Beach Boulevard, you'll spot Hector standing next to the main gate. A lot of people do.

But Shady Palms isn't in one place. It's everywhere.

When this novel first ran in serialized form in *The Palm Beach Post*, readers asked me to divulge the real name of the condo I was writing about. Some were convinced that they knew the fictional characters I created. One went so far as to say he spotted Lois and Rose riding on an elevator at a local doctor's office.

Shady Palms is everywhere.

I heard from a guy who shouts, "Hi, Ricardo," when he sees a cyclist on A1A. A woman from out-of-state called to complain that her condo-dwelling Florida mother had begun to gossip not only about her real-life condo neighbors, but about the Shady Palms neighbors, too.

And another reader pointed to the fictional Bernie's ease at getting past gate guards as a real-life reason to increase security in his community.

One woman even asked for a character's phone number.

As I said, Shady Palms is everywhere.

Now it's in paperback form. And whether you're reading it for the first time, reading it again, or just passing it on to a friend, you'll know where to look for the real Shady Palms.

Everywhere.

Frank

1 An unusual situation in C Building

Bernie Hamstein knew he let his wife down. He could tell by the pace she was setting back to their condominium. It was nearly noon on a sticky September day, certainly no time to be striding so defiantly under the South Florida sun. Especially at his age.

But Bernie's wife was taking no prisoners, pumping her arms in that way she and the other Wonder Walkers did during their tromps through the Boynton Beach Mall. Power. Bernie was beginning to hate power. The cars leaving the Shady Palms clubhouse parking lot began easing by the Hamsteins, with friendly horn toots and fetid bouquets of air.

If Bernie had his way, he'd be among that line of cars, in his Toyota Camry, with the air-conditioner blowing hard on his face all the way back to his reserved parking space outside C Building. But no. As usual, Rose said they should walk to the board meeting, that the mile "stroll"— as she put it — would do him good, and that if only he would exercise more, he wouldn't be so grumpy.

But what really made him feel lousy was exercise, especially under these circumstances. Rose wasn't trying to strengthen his heart with this pace, she was trying to punish him for what he said at the meeting.

It's not easy being president of the board in your condo-minium building. You end up locking horns with people at every turn. To be a good condo president, you've got to relish the little skirmishes of your office. But the thrill was gone for Bernie, and at the age of 72, he had begun to wonder whether he was getting too soft for the job.

"For cryin' out loud, Rose," he shouted at his wife's back, between gasps. "Do we have to walk this fast?"

He got a grunt in return, a grunt of satisfaction, he imag-ined.

"Rose, I know you're angry, but that's no reason to ..."

Too many words. He had to catch his breath.

"Please, Rose."

Maybe it was the way he said "please" that had stopped her. They'd been married for 47 years. Enough time to decipher the many nuances a single word can carry, enough time to know when "please" really meant "I beg you."

He nearly walked into her when she stopped and wheeled around to face him.

"Are you stopping to apologize?" she asked.

"Apologize? For what?"

Bad tact there. Rose was off again, elbows pumping, nearly jogging away from him this time. Bernie didn't even try to keep up. He stood there for a minute, waiting for her to stop and come back, but she never did. Her little white tennis outfit just kept getting smaller and smaller. She was nearly three speed bumps down the road by the time Bernie heard the car that had pulled up beside him.

First there was a hum of automatic window as the glass on the passenger side door disappeared, then a frosty patch of refrigerated air washed over Bernie's face.

"What the hell ya doin' out here, Bernie?"

"Walking home."

It was Johnny Fox, the irrepressible force behind the Shady Palms Players, a group of wannabe actors, singers and dancers who rehearsed all year for the pleasure of inflicting themselves on their neighbors during clubhouse performances. The current production was a hodgepodge of show tunes called *That's Entertainment*. Rose, who had seen it with the Walkers, referred to it as You Call That Entertainment? Her capsule review was enough to keep Bernie away.

"It doesn't look like you're walking," Johnny said, leaning toward the open window. "Looks more like standing around. Keep it up and you'll attract vultures."

Bernie wasn't sure whether Johnny meant the bird or the people kind.

"Yeah, I don't feel too good, Johnny."

"Hop in."

Bernie gratefully sunk into the leather seat and took off his ball cap, letting it rest on his bent knee so that the words "My Grandkids Can Beat Up Your Grandkids" stared back at him. Bernie was happy for the ride but wished it had been somebody else who had picked him up.

There were thousands of residents in the 12 buildings of Shady Palms, and Bernie suspected that Johnny had a list of all of them who had yet to attend his latest production. It wasn't the five-dollar admission prices he was after, Bernie knew. Johnny just needed an audience to validate his obsession.

Bernie instantly felt guilty for being on Johnny's list, and he knew that before the car made the last turn into the C Building parking lot, Johnny would get around to letting Bernie know that his attendance at *That's Entertainment* had been missed.

"Heard you got some trouble in the building," Johnny said.

After six years, it still surprised Bernie how fast news traveled at Shady Palms.

"Where'd you hear that?"

"We were rehearsing next door to where you guys were having your meeting, and one of our actresses, Mrs. Gold — the one who does that Guys and Dolls number in the show …"

Then Johnny looked over at Bernie, paused a beat, and

said, "Oh, sorry, I forgot. You haven't seen the show yet."

"Yeah, I've been meaning to get a ticket, but ..."

"Next show's tomorrow night. How 'bout it?"

"Perfect," Bernie said, peeling off a five from his wallet.

It would have been cheaper to call a cab from the club-house, he thought.

Johnny waved off the five-dollar bill.

"Are you going to see Joe Loehmann?" Johnny asked.

"As a matter of fact, I am."

"Terrific, then can you tell him to put me down for a dime on Denver this weekend."

"A dime on Denver. Got it. You really think Denver's going to cover against San Diego?"

Bernie wondered how much advance ticket sales money for the Shady Palms Players went to cover Johnny's football bets with Joe Loehmann.

"I'll give you the other five tomorrow night after the show," Johnny said.

Bernie quickly lassoed the conversation back to its original course.

"So getting back to Mrs. Gold."

"Yes, so she's waiting for her number to come up, and she wanders from the auditorium and decides to kill some time by sitting in your little meeting."

Johnny called it a "little meeting" to emphasize his attitude toward the governing body of the condo complex. But to Bernie, this was the big meeting, the monthly gathering of all the building presidents, the feudal kings of the buildings, A through L. And it was at these monthly meetings that condominium regulations were thrashed out, and each building president's worth was measured. There was nothing saying that the building presidents had to be men, but that's the way it worked out at Shady Palms.

The 12 presidents, elected by the residents of their own buildings, formed the governing board for the entire complex, and every year, they elected one of their own to serve as chairman.

On paper, the chairman didn't seem to have much power. But in practice, the chairman ruled, shaping discussions that either ignored problems or made big deals of problems that may not have existed in the first place. He controlled the gavel, allowing some people to talk incessantly, while cutting off others before they even got a sentence out of their mouths. And he could make other building presidents look wise or silly, depending on whether he liked you or not.

Herb Troutman didn't like Bernie. Actually, Gilda Troutman didn't like Rose, and that animosity got passed on to the husbands, even though they had no first-hand problems with each other. The coolness had lasted for two years, ever since Rose accused Troutman's wife of cheating at cards.

It didn't seem like much of a problem at first. The Troutmans lived in H Building, which was on the opposite side of the sprawling Shady Palms complex. But within weeks of Herb Troutman's ascent to chairman, it became obvious that a score had yet to be settled. The residents of C Building wanted to know why the garbage dumpsters from B Building were moved closer to them.

Bernie's answer was simple: "Because Rose caught Troutman's wife cheating at cards."

For much of the past year, Herb Troutman had been doing his best to make Bernie unpopular. If there was a way to slight C Building or highlight a failure, Troutman did it.

"And so then, Mrs. Gold returns to rehearsal and says, 'You're never going to believe what I heard,' " Johnny continued.

Troutman waited for public comments to bring it out. Bernie was sure the man in the audience who raised his hand was a Troutman plant.

"I heard of an unusual situation in C Building, and I would like to ask Mr. Hamstein what he intends to do about it," the guy in the audience had asked. Troutman feigned surprise, but Bernie knew he had set up this ambush.

"I'm well aware of the situation," Bernie had said at the meeting, barely audible over the murmurs of surprise from the rest of the board and the audience. "But the question was," Troutman said, "what are you going to do about it?"

"I'm going to …" Bernie had no idea. "I'm going to conduct a thorough investigation and make a full report to the board at our next meeting."

"I hope you realize the seriousness of this," Troutman said, bearing down on Hamstein. Bernie just nodded, and he could see from the corner of his eye that Rose wanted him to say more. But he couldn't. He didn't have the fight in him anymore.

"So all the Shady Palms Players know about it?" Bernie asked Johnny.

"Not all of them. Mrs. Baxter wasn't there. Her bursitis was acting up and she left early."

Johnny's car made the final turn, slowed for the last speed bump and there it was, C Building, the three-story white cement-block condominium. Eighty units, each with a screened-in porch, piggyback washer-dryers and a kitchen that's almost big enough for a table. Home.

Johnny pulled into his assigned spot. He lived three doors down from the Hamsteins, living alone with his many toupees, dental appliances and Broadway musical CDs.

"See you tomorrow night, Bernie."

"Tomorrow night?"

"The show."

"Oh, yes. The show. Right."

Both men walked across the condo lot to the building's entrance.

"Thanks for the ride, Johnny."

"My pleasure," Johnny said, fishing for his door key. "And don't worry, Bernie."

"Worry?"

"Yeah, about your renter problem," Johnny said. "I mean it's not like you're the one who got her pregnant."

2 The Wonder Walkers step in

The four women sat around the table in the Boynton Beach Mall food court, picking at the last crumbs of pastries on their plates.

"Who wants another sticky bun?" asked Madeline Jones, pushing her chair away and creating a hollow screech in the near-empty mall.

"I could eat maybe a quarter," Jacqui Fisher said.

"Jacqui, dear, they don't sell them by quarters," piped up Rose Hamstein.

And besides, everybody knew that Jacqui could eat another whole sticky bun as fast as she could tell a touching story about her dearly departed husband, Phil. She never sang his praises until the day he died — hitting his head on the sneeze bar of an all-you-can-eat buffet during what may have otherwise been a non-fatal heart attack.

"If you eat a quarter, I'll eat a quarter," Lois Rodgers said.

"Listen, ladies, I'm not here to do the math," Madeline said to her chums. "I'm getting another sticky bun for myself, and I'm not ashamed to admit it. Now, if any of you want to step forward and …"

"Jacqui will have another whole one," Rose said.

"I will not," Jacqui said. "I told Maddy I only want a quarter."

"Yeah, and then you'll want another quarter and another quarter," Rose said. "For the first time in your life, just admit to wanting a whole of something."

"It's just that when poor Phil was alive, he'd always …" her voice trailed off.

Lois rolled her eyes at Rose. Lois was the one who took particular pleasure at pointing out Jacqui's newfound affection for her dead husband.

"OK, so we'll put down Phil for eating the other half," Lois said. "So, Maddy, we're up to two sticky buns."

"Lois, that was uncalled for," Jacqui said.

But the other two women were already laughing, and even Jacqui couldn't keep from smiling through her feigned indignation. She tried glaring at Lois, who only stuck out her tongue and then blew a kiss across the table.

It was hard to be mad at Lois, who sat there, wearing the T-shirt Jacqui had bought for her three years ago, the one that said "Chemo Babe" on the front. And after all, didn't Jacqui cry more when she found out about Lois' breast cancer than she did when she saw Phil stretched out on the restaurant carpet with shrimp scampi in his hair and the ladle still in his hands?

"I don't know what's the point in all this eating," Rose Hamstein said. "It defeats the purpose."

It was always like this. The Wonder Walkers would gather at the mall before many of the stores had yet to open their metal gates for business. The women would stride purposefully up and down the center concourse, puffing and working up a sheen of sweat. Then after about 40 minutes, they'd head for the food court, where they'd sit, eat and chat for hours.

"I'm getting two more buns then," Madeline said as she started to head away from the table.

"Get three," Jacqui said.

"Three? Who's eating the third?" Rose said.

"Lois, she'll have one."

"Lo, you having another sticky bun?" Madeline asked.

"Says who?"

"Jacqui said you're having another."

"Jacqui said that? Well, she's wrong. I only want a quarter," Lois said.

"I hope they lop off your other one," Jacqui said, looking at Lois.

"Oh, just make it four more, Maddy," Rose said. "They do seem extra good this morning."

The Wonder Walkers probably had 20 Shady Palms women who claimed to be members, but it was these four who could be counted on to show up nearly every morning. At first, the Walkers advertised for new members on the condo's bulletin boards, but after a while, it became clear to Lois, Jacqui, Madeline and Rose that they didn't really want anybody else.

The other women sensed it too, because one by one, they'd join, but soon find excuses to leave the four women to themselves.

It's not that the Wonder Walkers were all cut out of the same mold, either. Jacqui was a Rush Limbaugh Republican, much to the horror of the others. Rose was a militant environmentalist. Lois was just plain militant. And Maddy was black, the only black condo owner in all of Shady Palms.

But they were a unit somehow, bound together by the common geography of C Building and the shared habit of mornings inside the Boynton Beach Mall.

When Maddy returned with the buns, Lois was grousing about the notice she got in the mail, the one that commanded her to report to jury duty that afternoon.

"I'm just going to walk in that courtroom and tell them I'm not interested," she said.

"Lois, I don't think that works," Rose said. "They don't care if you're interested, only if you can be fair."

"In that case, you have nothing to worry about, Lo," Jacqui said. "They'll never pick you."

It wasn't until the second round of sticky buns disappeared that Maddy brought up the main topic of conversation that morning.

"So Rose, when you going to tell us about that pregnant woman?" Maddy asked.

"You know about that?"

"Rose, everybody knows about it."

"What pregnant woman?" Jacqui asked.

"Everybody except the socially retarded," Lois said.

"I didn't know about it until that meeting yesterday," Rose said. "Oh, I was so mad at Bernie over it."

"You mean, there's a woman who's pregnant in Shady Palms?" Jacqui said.

Rose nodded, sending Jacqui into fits of laughter.

"I find that hysterical. Is it one of those miracles?"

"No, Jacqui," Lois said, "Jacob isn't a suspect."

Jacob, Jacqui's gay son, moved in with his mother after Phil's sneeze-bar sayonara. Jacqui ignored the wisecrack and pressed on.

"I mean, how can this happen? Menopause is but a distant memory to the women at Shady Palms."

"C'mon, Jacqui. Haven't you seen the new arrival in 26C?" Maddy asked.

"In 26C? That's two doors down from you," Jacqui said. "How young is she?"

"Twenty-five, maybe."

"Twenty-seven," Rose said.

"Well, tell us about her, Rose," Jacqui said.

"I don't know much, except I told Bernie right from the start that it wasn't right. Something was wrong here. What's a 27-year-old attractive woman doing in a place like Shady Palms? But of course, Bernie didn't listen."

"Men are such pigs," Lois said. "They see a younger woman, and their brains start migrating south."

Three divorces, including the last guy who left Lois and her breast cancer for a younger woman, was enough to make Lois an outspoken authority on the subject.

"So, they have the usual selection screening committee for

renters," Rose said, "and Bernie comes back and says she's a wonderful person and will be no problem at all."

"And she's pregnant already?" Jacqui said. "After a little more than a month?"

"A baby in Shady Palms. That'll never do," Lois said. "Shady Palms only tolerates people in their second childhood."

"And so, how is she, Maddy?" Jacqui asked.

"Young, beautiful."

"I hate her already," Lois said.

"What does she do?" Jacqui asked.

"Beats me. She's got some part-time job, supposedly, at a clothes store around here. But mostly, she stays home a lot."

"Any man in the picture?"

"None that I can see," Maddy said. "She's all alone."

"Hooker," Lois harrumphed.

"What I don't know is how Herb Troutman found out she was pregnant," Rose said. "Bernie didn't know, and he's the president of the building where she lives."

"I didn't know, either, until last night," Maddy said.

"Yeah, well, word's all over the complex now after somebody at the board meeting yesterday brings it up, and then Troutman asks Bernie what he planned to do about it. And Bernie, like a fool, pretends he knows all about it and has the situation in hand."

"He's planning to do an abortion?" Jacqui said.

"He doesn't know what he's going to do," Rose said. "He's just petrified that Herb Troutman is going to make him look bad. So he says he's doing an investigation."

"It'll be nice having a baby around," Jacqui said.

"It'll never happen. It's against the bylaws," Rose said. "If she tries to stay, we'll have to get the lawyers and sue her."

"And then we'll get reassessed for attorney's fees," Maddy said.

"And then we'll hang Bernie and the rest of the screening committee from the third floor balcony," Lois said.

"Why can't we accept just one baby," Jacqui said.

"You want a baby, Jacqui? Get your son to stop dating waiters," Lois said.

"Precedent, Jacqui," said Rose, ignoring Lois. "You live in a condo. Make an exception for one person, and you have to make it for all."

"But it's not like all these 70-year-old women are going to start having babies," Jacqui said.

"But what will stop other young people from coming in and renting, if they know they can raise children here?" Rose said.

"She doesn't look pregnant," Maddy said.

"It's probably still early," Rose said. "We've got time."

"Time for what?" Lois said.

"Time to … I don't know … find out what we should do," Rose said.

There was silence at the table. Then Jacqui looked up.

"I've got an idea," she said. "Let's invite her to join the Wonder Walkers."

"Please, Jacqui," Lois said.

"Just to investigate, like Bernie said he was going to do."

"Walking is good for pregnant people," Maddy said. "I'll ask her."

"And if she likes it and wants to come every morning?" Lois asked.

"I wouldn't worry about that," Jacqui said. "You can drive just about anybody away."

"I've been working on you for years, and it hasn't worked," Lois said.

"That's because I know you're just a lot of talk, Lois Rodgers, and deep inside that little cancerous heart of yours, you really adore me."

And for once, Lois didn't have a snappy reply.

3 Margo gets a visitor

Hector took pride in saying he knew everybody who came and went from Shady Palms' main gate. But he didn't know this guy.

Hector walked out of his guard station, hitching up his uniform pants and clutching his clipboard. He eyed the red Corvette, suspiciously noting the little phone antenna and the dark tinted windows. The driver was tall, about 6-foot-3, Hector figured. Had a mountain man kind of beard, a gold necklace and those dressy sweatpants that middle-aged men wear when they start to get chubby.

Not your typical visitor.

"I'm here to see Margo Zukowski," the man said.

Hector consulted his clipboard, pretending to look up a resident by that name, which was completely unnecessary. Hector knew Margo was the young woman. The one in Number 26 in C Building. He had monitored her comings and goings with special interest even before he found out the previous day that she was pregnant.

"Your name, sir?"

"Bill Johnson."

"Wait just a minute, sir."

So this was the father, Hector thought. They had all asked

him who the father was, and it hurt Hector to say he didn't know. The young woman never had any visitors.

Hector walked back to his shack and dialed her number. As it rang, he concentrated on remembering everything about this guy. The people would want to know.

"A Mr. Bill Johnson here to see you, señora."

"Yes, let him in," she said.

She sounded happy. Hector made a mental note to tell the people that, too.

Margo was happy that Bill had finally thought it was time to stop by. It had been more than a month since they had sat in that Denny's restaurant, the longest month in her life.

"Here, this will help with your story," he had said, sliding a North Dakota license plate across the table.

Margo had laughed at the plate.

"North Dakota? I've never even set foot in North Dakota."

"Sorry, the only other one I had was New Jersey, and believe me, you don't want any state in the Northeast, or else they'd hound you to death about where you're from. You can get away with North Dakota. Nobody's from North Dakota."

She read the folder of information about her fictitious self, her alleged last address in Grand Forks and her references.

"These people," she said pointing to the names.

"Don't worry, Margo. They know what to say."

"And what about in the condo complex where I'll be living? Do any of them know who I am?"

"Are you kidding? Whatever you do, Margo, don't tell a soul. In places like Shady Palms, if you tell one person something, you might as well take out a full-page ad in *The Palm Beach Post*."

"But, I'll need to be chatty, right? To mingle."

"Oh, don't worry. You'll get your chance. Just don't rush things. If you're too forward, it might spoil things for us. But if you're patient, they'll come to you. You'll see. They won't be able to help themselves. They'll be dying to get to know you and include you in their circle. You're an exotic, Margo, a rare young flower."

"And what do I tell them about myself?"

"Anything but the truth about who you are and why you're there."

"And how will I get in touch with you?"

"You can't. I'll get in touch with you. I'll get you settled, and then in a month or so, I'll come by."

"In a month?"

"Margo, you realize this is going to take some time?"

"Yes, I guess I do …"

"And what about the job?" he had asked.

"I start tomorrow."

"Terrific."

"It's just part-time."

"That's all we need. You just keep your eyes open."

"I will."

"And learn the schedule."

"OK."

"You still sure you want to go through with all this?"

"Of course, Bill."

But a month after that conversation at Denny's, Margo was less sure. Bill had said to be patient, and she had.

The job was a bore. She kept notes. But that didn't stop it from being a bore.

Other than work, she sat around and waited. For what? Nothing happened. She watched soap operas, took walks around the complex and read spy novels in bed, gorging herself on tortilla chips and pretzels.

When she got bored, she went to see a movie. When she really got bored, she cleaned her gun.

The residents of Shady Palms had kept their distance, apparently still measuring her. Polite hellos, but that was it.

So she was happy Bill had finally returned. Maybe now, she'd get a better idea of the plan here.

"So, any problems?" Bill said, after parking his Corvette outside C Building and stepping inside her condo.

"Problems? No. I've been a little wallflower here."

"Good. Nobody suspects anything?"

"Nobody even talks to me. I'm a freak, Bill. You didn't tell me I would be a freak here. I think your words were 'exotic flower.' But I'm beginning to think I'm a freak."

"Patience, Margo."

"Have you been taking notes on our mutual friend?"

Margo nodded, pointing to the spiral-ringed notebook on the table.

"Did he ever say anything to you?"

"Nobody ever says anything to me," she said. "I don't think anybody even knows I exist."

By that time, C Building was in full alert. Soon after Bill's car had pulled away from the guard shack, Hector called Bernie Hamstein with the news. Bernie told Rose. Rose called Jacqui, who called the entire third floor, starting with Lois, who called Maddy down on two.

"Hey, girl. You talk to our knocked-up neighbor yet about coming for a walk with us?" Lois asked.

"Not yet. I was going to do it later this afternoon."

"If you get over there now, you can check out the side of beef in the red hot rod who's up there with her."

"She's got a visitor?"

"Or a customer. That's my guess," Lois said.

"Maybe I'll wait until he's gone."

"If you do, Maddy, we'll never forgive you. Now, listen. I'm going off to jury duty. When I return I'll expect a full report."

Margo had just finished telling Bill about how none of her neighbors showed the slightest interest in her when Maddy knocked on her door.

Startled by the knock, Margo looked at Bill.

"You bring somebody with you?" she asked him.

"Not me. I think you have a visitor."

Margo opened the door and was surprised to see a tall, black woman in her 60s, dressed all in white and holding four sticky buns in her hand. Margo had seen the woman before and assumed she didn't live in Shady Palms, but was part of the help, somehow.

For years, Maddy was help here, working as a nurse for a homebound resident who was in her final years. When the woman finally died, she had a mortgage-free condo and no relatives. So she left it to the only person who had been nice to her in the last years of her life, Madeline Jones.

Maddy's first inclination was to sell the condo and pocket the money as a little nest egg. But it was tough getting much for a unit in the aging Shady Palms complex, and the more time went on, the more Maddy realized that maybe this could be her home. After all, she had never owned her own home. Her brother in Riviera Beach laughed at the idea of her living among all those "cranky old white geezers." But he didn't know. People were all the same inside, Maddy knew, and she had come to know quite a few of the residents there. So instead of selling, she moved in.

Margo regarded the visitor at her door for an instant and said the first thing that popped in her head.

"I'm sorry, I don't need anybody. I clean my own apartment."

Maddy smiled.

"I'm glad you do," she said. "I clean my own apartment, too."

Margo still didn't get it. The woman at the door just stood there smiling.

"How 'bout giving me your card, and if I ever need you I can ..."

"I don't have a card," Maddy said. "I'm your neighbor. I live two doors down the hall."

"Oh, my," Margo said, putting a hand to her head and turning red. "I'm really sorry ..."

"Don't worry, you're not the first one around here who made that mistake."

"It's just that …"

"I know, I'm one of a kind," Maddy said, and then with a twinkle in her eye, she added, "and so are you. We don't see much of your kind around here, either."

It wasn't until Margo invited her visitor in that she remembered Bill, sitting there on her couch. Suddenly, there he was, standing for an introduction.

"Oh, and this is my …" my what? Margo asked herself. "… my boyfriend, Bill."

Maddy's instant reaction was that Margo could do better. Her boyfriend was older, not especially good looking, and she didn't like his smile, either.

"Congratulations," Maddy said.

Bill looked confused.

"On the new arrival," Maddy said.

"I don't live here," Bill said.

"No, I'm not talking about that," Maddy said. "I'm talking about Margo being pregnant."

"Margo's pregnant?"

Bill looked at Margo. Margo looked at Maddy.

"How did you …"

"Honey, you tell one person around here, and it's public knowledge," Maddy said. "Now I guess it's my turn to be sorry."

Margo looked back at Bill and shrugged her shoulders.

"I guess you're the last to know," she said, then quickly added a "honey" and squeezed his limp hand.

4 Stranger in a strange land

"Mom?"

"Jacob?"

Jake Fisher leaned his forehead against the cool metal of the pay phone and steeled himself for what he had to say.

"Can you come pick me up?"

He was 25 years old, he kept telling himself, old enough to make his own decisions, and yet he felt like a child again, her child again. Oh well, he had only himself to blame for moving back in with his mother, and for this.

"I just need a ride, Mom. I got myself stranded, sort of."

"Where are you, honey? I'll be right there. Did your car break down, Jacob? Are you all right?"

"I'm fine, and so is my car. I just need a ride to get back to where I left it."

Jake had thought he could avoid this call. He thought he could walk the distance between the Palm Beach County Jail and his car. It was only a few miles, not the most pleasant stretch of landscape to traverse, but it was certainly manageable.

But he had gotten only as far as Congress Avenue, which wasn't very far at all, when the purplish sky opened up, soaking him with the first fat drops of a long afternoon of rain.

He dashed across the street, looking for the nearest shelter, which turned out to be T's Lounge.

"What's all that racket from?" Jacqui asked.

The floor under Jake was throbbing with bass, and the song's lyrics, "She's got legs, and she knows how to use them," were muffled only slightly by the door.

"It's ZZ Top, Mom," he said. "I'm at a bar."

"Oh, Jacob. But it's barely the afternoon. What are you doing in …"

"Mom, it's not what you think."

It would take about 20 minutes to get from Shady Palms, he figured, so making the adjustment for his mother's driving, he had at least a good half-hour to wait. He might as well go inside. One drink might even do him a little good.

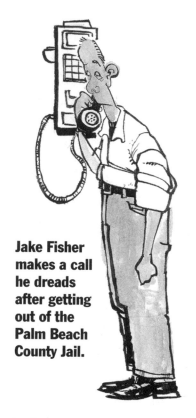

Jake Fisher makes a call he dreads after getting out of the Palm Beach County Jail.

He walked inside and had a seat at the bar. It wasn't until he refocused his eyes in the dark room that Jake realized what sort of place T's Lounge was. A topless woman was writhing on a stage, running her blood-red fingernails over her thighs.

A waitress pressed up against him from behind, digging her chest between his shoulder blades like a stick-up artist, while shouting in his ear, "Two for one well drinks, sweetheart. You interested?"

Jake wasn't interested. Not in the drinks, not in the silicone back rub, not in the woman on stage who was beginning to incorporate a chair into her dance routine.

Oh, if his friends could see him now, he thought. But then again, if he had real friends, one of them would be picking him up, not his mother. And he wouldn't have gotten himself in the fix he was in.

The truth was, Jake told himself, that coming back to live with his mother was a bad idea. It was an impetuous decision, made on the day of his father's funeral. For the first time in his life, his mother had looked so small and afraid, like someone who needed to be taken care of.

But after a year, he began to wonder who was taking care of whom. His mother was the one who seemed better adjusted now. He was withering in South Florida, living in that mausoleum of a place, working at a job far beneath his ability.

He was the guy sitting in a strip bar in the middle of the day, waiting for the ride. He looked around the bar, studying the other men, a couple of cops in uniform, a table of guys in short-sleeve dress shirts and bad ties, and two guys in some sort of uniform shirt that included their names stitched above the pockets.

He saw them staring back at him, probably measuring him in his pressed jeans, heavily starched cotton shirt and white tennis shoes. He curled up his hands a little bit more, tucking the manicured fingernails a little deeper into his palms.

He drained his beer quickly and decided he'd rather wait outside for his mother.

Jacqui Fisher followed her son's directions to T's Lounge, worrying all the way about what had happened to him. He had been so cryptic on the phone. That wasn't like him. Jacob was a sweet boy, and he knew that being so vague would only make her worry.

So Jacqui was prepared for a surprise as she turned onto Congress and looked for the address. But she wasn't prepared for what she saw. There was her only child, standing under the awning of a place that advertised "Girls! Girls! Girls! Triple X Dancers. Miss LottaBusta '96 thru Sunday."

She let out a little yelp, a yelp of joy, not of pain. Maybe, oh maybe, some prayers do get answered.

Even before Jacqui married her husband, Phil, nearly 40 years ago, they both talked about wanting to have a big family, a big house, a station wagon, a bunch of kids and a collie. They got the house first, a five-bedroom place in New Jersey. The collie came next. The children, however, never came.

They didn't give up hope until they were in their 40s and the collie died from old age. Jacqui finally turned to Phil one night and said, "Enough. It's not meant to be. Let's adopt."

"Do we really want to do that, Jac?" Phil had said. "I mean, you never know what you're getting when you adopt."

"I know what we've got now," Jacqui had said, motioning to the empty house. "And I know it isn't enough. Don't you want to have grandchildren some day, Phil?"

He did. They adopted a newborn and named him Jacob, because it sounded like a name of strength. The plan was to adopt a girl the following year, and maybe another, the year after that.

But Phil lost his manager's job at the car dealership, and suddenly money was tight. Other adoption plans were put on hold and eventually dropped.

Jacqui didn't suspect her son was gay when he was in high school. He even took a girl to the prom one year. It wasn't until one summer, when he was home from college. He dropped the news like a bomb at the dinner table, saying it was weighing on him and he thought they should know.

Phil didn't handle it well, pushing away from the table and throwing his napkin in his meatloaf gravy. Jacqui thought she reacted well, at least on the outside. She cried in her room for days, but she didn't let her son know that he had broken her heart, that he had denied her the dream of grandkids in her old age.

But Jacqui never stopped praying for something to happen, a miracle, maybe. She would scan the newspapers for those stories about scientific studies on homosexuality and what causes it. She kept searching for hope that one day a person's sexual orientation could change.

So when Jacqui saw her son standing under the awning of the strip joint, she let herself feel a new love for him. Dear Jacob, maybe he was giving heterosexuality a try.

He slid into the front seat.

"Thanks, Mom," he said, and from the way she was smiling back at him, he knew what she must have been thinking.

"No, it's nothing like that," he said.

"What are you talking about?"

"You know what I mean. I didn't come to this place to watch naked women, Mom."

Maybe he was just too shy to admit it, she told herself. She patted his leg.

"I'm just glad to see you're OK."

He directed her to Dreher Park, a meandering city park with a zoo and a science museum.

"Did you leave your car at the zoo, Jake?"

"Not exactly, Mom."

On the way, Jake kept wondering what made him think he could take care of his mother. It was he, not she, who was damaged most by the unexpected death of Phil Fisher. He never measured up again in his father's eye after that day he tossed the napkin in the meatloaf gravy.

Well, at least his father wasn't here now, Jake thought, to see this.

"There's somebody pregnant at Shady Palms," Jacqui said, filling in a silence that had begun to build between them in the car.

"A medical miracle."

"No. It's that young girl in our building. The renter. You've seen her, haven't you? She's in 26C."

He grunted and looked out the window. Poor Jacob, Jacqui thought. He could usually be counted on to enjoy the local gossip, but he was obviously preoccupied.

"Where do I go now?" Jacqui said, as she turned toward the park.

Since hearing the news of the pregnancy that morning, Jacqui had been fantasizing about her son being a closet heterosexual. Maybe he was just pretending to be gay all these years as some form of rebellion, or to stop her from playing matchmaker.

Yes, that just might be it. After all, she had never even seen him
with another man. If a baby could be born in Shady Palms, then
maybe her son could be straight.

Jacob directed her to drive past the zoo, past the museum
and into the winding park road that led to a blockhouse restroom
in a grassy field.

"Stop here," he said.

Jacqui's fantasizing came to an abrupt end when she saw the
restroom, a police car and a television news truck.

"No, Jacob, no," she said, before she could stop herself.

The TV news truck had its antenna telescoping into the sky.
The reporter, a young woman with a Hermes scarf flapping in the
wind, was standing under an umbrella a few yards away. Jacqui
had seen her before, that perky Asian-American woman on
Channel 5. What was her name? Suzie Ching. That's it.

The reporter was looking into a camera while she strolled on
the grass and motioned toward the restroom.

"It's nothing, Mom. Just a stupid thing . . . a misdemeanor.
It's not like . . . Oh, never mind."

What could he say? He had driven to West Palm Beach to
pay a speeding ticket. He had time to kill. He wasn't due for hours
at his job, and so he cruised through the park. He was lonely. He
thought maybe it was just what he needed.

Jake had come to the conclusion that morning that if he
didn't get back to San Diego soon, he would shrink into nothing-
ness — like some of the people at Shady Palms, the people who
seem to get smaller and smaller by the day. Pretty soon, they're so
small, you can't see them over the dashboards of their cars.

That's the way Jake was feeling. His soul was shrinking.

"Will you be on the news?" Jacqui asked.

"I don't know. I think they'd be more interested in the minister with four kids."

"Oh, there were others," Jacqui said.

"Yes, plenty."

"That's good."

"That's good?" he asked.

"Yes, you know. You won't be . . . singled out," she said.

They had pulled up behind his parked car, and he was waiting for the rain to ease up before he made a dash for it.

"Did you have to tell them about your job?" she asked.

Jake thought it was funny that his mother considered his job something worth saving. He was Señor Peppy at Kidz-a-Poppin', one of those cavernous halls full of video games, token-swallowing amusements and a huge piece of indoor plumbing with sliding tubes and netting to catch the sweaty kids who go rocketing around it.

"I told them I was an actor," he said.

"But they didn't ask you ..."

"No. We just moved right on to the next question."

When Jake moved to Florida, he had hoped that maybe the change of scenery could help him launch his acting career. He was waiting tables in California. Four years of college as a theater major, and his biggest role in the outside world was to push the blackboard specials every day, saying things such as, "Oh, yes. The mahi would be a great choice, and the risotto is to die for."

But Florida wasn't much different from California. After auditioning several times without success, he answered an ad in the newspaper. The classified said "Entertainer" in big letters. It was pretty vague, but it did say the company was seeking someone with acting experience.

It didn't say you'd have to dress up as a bandito and sing Happy Birthday all day in a fake Mexican accent to sugar-crazed children in the Kidz-a-Poppin' party rooms.

The funny thing was, his mother really did see Señor Peppy as a first step. Jake dismissed that possibility the first time a 7-year-old yanked off his sombrero while the little hellion's friend kneed him below the bandolero belt.

The rain kept pouring on the hood of his mother's car. It wasn't going to ease up, so there was no sense waiting there, imagining the words coming out of the TV reporter's lips and feeling the anxiety he was causing his mother.

"Mom, maybe this wasn't a good idea."

Jacqui thought he was talking about whatever happened in the restroom with the undercover cop. She didn't even want to think about the details, and she hoped her son wasn't about to explain.

But then she could see from his face that her son meant something else, something deeper than the day's events.

"Oh, my Jacob," she said, reaching across to hold his hand.

But a second before she did, Jake — her only link to the great, endless future — dashed to his car, lowering his head to the falling rain and fumbling with his keys.

She let the hand that would have held his hand continue on its course and fall gently on the passenger seat, resting on the warm spot he left behind.

5 Bernie's men-pen rendezvous

Bernie Hamstein parked his car at the Shoppes of the Shady Palms, a strip shopping center with a women's clothing store on one end and a Winn-Dixie on the other.

He headed for Loehmann's, the women's clothing store. He hoped he wasn't too late. The arrival of the pregnant renter's boyfriend had thrown his timetable off, and now he wondered whether he had missed his chance.

He walked through the door, not even looking at the aisles of clothing. First, he took a quick look at the waiting area in front of the store, and seeing that he wasn't too late, he walked to the restroom in the back.

He made sure nobody was there, then he walked inside the second stall, bolted the door and picked up the porcelain cover to the toilet tank. He pulled an envelope out of his pocket, taped it to the inside cover and replaced the lid.

He unbolted the stall, glanced at himself in the mirror on the way out and headed back to the men pen in the front of the store.

That's what Bernie called it. The men pen. It was that area Loehmann's had set aside for tag-along husbands. This was the place where men his age sat to read, sleep or commiserate while their wives swarmed through the store like fish feeding off a fabric coral reef.

The men pen had 13 seats, and on weekends it was nearly always full. But on a rainy Tuesday afternoon like this, there were seats available. Bernie wasn't looking for a seat, though. He was looking for the little round guy with the raincoat and the newspaper crossword puzzle on his lap.

Bernie sat down next to him.

"Joe, sorry I'm late."

"Bernie, I almost gave up on you this week."

"Thanks for waiting,"

It had been like this every football season for the past three years. On Tuesday afternoons, Bernie would meet Joe here.

Bernie knew very little about Joe. He had heard he lived nearby in one of those big houses at Lakes of the Village, but he wasn't sure.

He knew Joe was 72 and that he had a bad prostate, but he didn't even know Joe's last name. Neither did the rest of the small group of men who met him at the store on a weekly basis.

They all called him what Bernie called him: Joe Loehmann.

"What'cha got this week, Bernie?" Joe said, taking out his pencil and pretending to work on his crossword again.

As always, Bernie rattled off the names and numbers from memory, just like Joe insisted.

"Johnny Fox wants Denver for a dime. I'll take the Chargers for a quarter. Mike C will take the Eagles for 40. And Howard will do his usual 50 on the Giants."

"That's it?" Joe said.

"Slow week, what can I say? A lot of people took a licking with the Cowboys last weekend."

Joe nodded, folded up his puzzle, and put it in his raincoat.

"Remember to wait five minutes," he said.

"I always do," Bernie said.

"See you next week."

"Next week," Bernie said as Joe got up and headed for the

envelope full of cash in the men's room.

Joe told him there was nothing to worry about. Sure, making little bets on football wasn't exactly legal, but it wasn't something that would get a bunch of old men like them in trouble, as long as they were circumspect about it.

That's why Joe insisted there'd be no phone calls, nothing in writing, and the money would never exchange hands directly.

The condo gamblers who got in trouble were the ones who flaunted it, the ones who put up notices on cork boards, or played poker in the clubhouse, flinging green money on the table and making a lot of noise.

But Joe Loehmann had it right. You do it quietly, and nobody knows a thing. Bernie reached under his chair and felt for the envelope he knew would be there. He looked at his watch, figuring out how much longer he'd have to wait before he would take it.

Joe Loehmann, finished with his quick trip to the bathroom, walked out of the store, not even nodding in Bernie's direction. As the bookie stepped out onto the curb and paused to open his umbrella, a man in the back of a landscaping truck snapped his picture with a camera strapped to a weed whacker.

Bernie waited, unaware of the woman who was watching him as she stood partially hidden behind a rack of clothes in the back of the store.

It was still raining when Bernie walked out. He looked at his watch.

Before he had driven to the Shoppes of the Shady Palms, he had dropped Rose off at her quilt shop.

"Give me a half-hour," she had told him.

It was nearly time to go get her. But instead of going back to his car, he felt himself drawn, as usual, to the Winn-Dixie at the other end of the covered walkway.

He was thinking about the pregnant renter and what he would have to say. He'd have to be firm. Rules, after all, are rules.

Once inside the supermarket, he automatically wandered to the bread aisle. The shelf, as always, was a mess. Mechanically, he began stacking the loaves of Big Top bread, careful to put the fresher loaves in back and the ones with the more critical expiration dates up front.

He'd have to tell her that while pregnancy was a wonderful thing, it was something that couldn't be tolerated at Shady Palms. An adult community, he'd have to say, was for adults only. And then what? What if she said she didn't want to move?

He became aware that a woman with a toddler sitting in her cart had stopped behind him, waiting for him to take a loaf of bread and move on.

"Oh, I'm sorry," Bernie said. "I didn't see you there."

He stepped aside, and she reached for one of the nearly stale loaves Bernie had pushed to the front.

"No, wait. Take one of these," he said, reaching for one of the loaves in the back. "They're fresher."

The woman looked at him uncertainly.

"Really," he said. "See the date? It's coded on the side of the bag. You've got to know where to look."

Bernie spent a big hunk of his life looking. He worked for Big Top bread for 30 years back in Long Island, driving a delivery truck and hauling crates of bread to supermarkets five days a week. When he retired and moved to Florida with Rose, he thought he'd be glad to finally be finished with the bread business.

But he'd often find himself like he was on this day, drawn to the bread aisle to organize the shelves on somebody else's route. Sometimes, he'd run into the Big Top driver in one of the stores. Bernie would invariably try to start a conversation, talking about his years with the company, and get in a few war stories about the days before bar codes and computer inventory systems.

The drivers, who always seemed like kids to him, never were that interested. They were always in a hurry.

"I'd put out more," Bernie would occasionally say as they were preparing to leave the store. "You can't be afraid of taking out stale. In order to sell, you've got to have a lot of loaves out. People don't want to buy the last loaf of bread."

The drivers would ignore him, treat him like he was just another crazy old coot. There were times Bernie wanted to shake them by the shoulders and say, "Maybe you ought to call the Long Island bakery and ask in the executive office about Bernie Hamstein."

He was Big Top's top driver for 10 years in a row — and not because he was given a great route. It was a lousy route, but Bernie knew how to build it up, how to get the display and the selection just right. He wondered if his name was still on the wall at Big Top, or if time had already erased his achievements there.

He walked back to his car in the rain, telling himself to get used to it. Life goes on. He wasn't Bernie the Bread Man anymore. He was Bernie the Condo Commando, keeper of the rules, protector of the restrictive covenants and enforcer of all that is petty and vain.

It was time to deal with that pregnant renter and past time to get his wife, who would be waiting outside the quilt store, wondering why he was late.

6 The Hamsteins' dog day afternoon

The dog came trotting up to Rose Hamstein as she waited outside the quilt shop. He sniffed her feet, then looked up with rheumy eyes and the pleasant face of a mutt.

"Where are you supposed to be, boy?" Rose asked.

The dog wagged his tail and rubbed his matted, rain-soaked fur against her leg.

"I don't think so," Rose said, pulling back, which only caused the dog to adjust his legs and rub again.

She looked at her watch. Bernie was late. She said a half-hour, not 45 minutes. She moved away from the dog, walking down the covered awning a few steps. The dog moved, too, sitting down next to her, resting his head on outstretched paws and thumping his tail every time she glanced down.

"Go away," Rose said. "Go to your home."

The dog did have a collar. He must have belonged to someone. She bent down to look for a name on the collar, but he didn't have one. The dog sat up excitedly, licking her hand, her arm and then, finally, jerked his head up to get a quick slurp at the side of Rose's face.

"Ugh!" she said, wiping her cheek with the back of one hand. "You're a real lover."

Then she heard the toot of a car horn. Bernie was there at

While waiting for Bernie to pick her up at the quilt shop, Rose Hamstein attracts the attentions of a stray dog.

the curb, looking quizzically at his wife. She had gotten so wrapped up in the dog, she hadn't seen his car pull into the parking lot.

"Whose dog?" Bernie said after she got in.

"Beats me," Rose said, looking back at the dog, who had begun whimpering.

"Probably somebody who's shopping in one of these stores," Bernie said.

"Probably."

Bernie didn't look in his rear-view mirror as he pulled away. If he had, he would have seen the mutt trotting after the car.

"Gotta make a quick stop at the 7-Eleven," Bernie said, as

he paused at the end of the parking lot and looked for his chance to cut across Military Trail to the convenience store on the other side of the street.

Rose knew what that meant. Bernie was getting lottery tickets. She didn't keep track of the games well enough to know whether today would be one of his Cash Three, Play Four, Fantasy Five, scratch-off or Lotto days. She didn't care, as long as he didn't spend more than his weekly $20 gambling allowance.

It was all so foolish to Rose, spending money this way. He hardly ever won, and when he did, it was just a few dollars, not one of those big jackpots you read about in the paper. But that was his thing. She spent her $20 her way, and he spent his the way he wanted.

Rose, however, knew nothing about Joe Loehmann and the weekly bets. That was Bernie's little secret. Every year, he squirreled away a little pot of money to have for his football gambling. It wasn't hard, really, keeping a few bucks here and there. He kept it in a coffee can in the trunk of his car, tucked in the cubbyhole next to the jack. Out of sight, out of mind.

There was a brief pause in the traffic on the busy road. Bernie gunned the engine and crossed. It wasn't until he and Rose were parked in the 7-Eleven lot that they heard the first screech of tires.

It was a long screech, like the kind made by a car that suddenly went from 50 miles an hour to a full stop. Then there was a second screech, a third and then the awful sound of metal striking metal. One, two, three, four, five vehicles were stopped in the intersection now, all of them at crazy angles.

The drivers appeared to be all right. They each climbed out of their cars, inspecting the damage and talking to one another. Other cars continued driving through the intersection, rolling over crumbled headlight covers and twisted molding strips as if nothing happened.

"Everybody's in a hurry these days," Bernie announced.

"I'll bet somebody tried to run that light."

Bernie walked inside the 7-Eleven, heading for the Florida Lottery display. Rose waited outside next to their car to gawk.

She noticed the breathing first, more like heavy panting, coming up from behind her. She wheeled around, thinking Bernie might be having a heart attack. But it wasn't Bernie. It was that dog, the one from the quilt shop.

She looked at him, and his tail wagged.

"You again?"

The dog sat down next to her, leaning his body into her leg. Despite herself, she bent down and patted his head.

A shirtless man dressed in a ball cap, boots and a set of keys that flopped outside one of his pockets, walked from the accident scene to the 7-Eleven. He was rubbing his neck and cursing as he headed toward the pay phone near where Rose was standing.

A clerk walked out the front door, pulling out a cigarette from the pack he kept in the front pocket of his shirt, a shirt that identified him as "Ashneel."

"What happened?" he asked Rose.

"I don't know," she said. "We were in the lot when we heard the crash."

The clerk then noticed the dog at Rose's feet.

"That your dog?"

"No," she said.

"I called the pound about him three days ago. He's a problem. He hangs around here all day. Bothers the customers. Bad for business."

The shirtless man hung up the phone and started back to his car. He glanced at Rose and the clerk, spotting the dog.

"That your dog, lady?"

"No," Rose said, for the second time in 30 seconds.

"Well, I'd like to find out who owns it," said the shirtless man, who was now walking toward them. "Damn near got us all killed, the way it ran out across that intersection."

Rose started to piece things together now, how the dog must have come trotting after her.

"Very bad, very bad for business," Ashneel repeated. "I'm going to call the animal control again."

The dog leaned closer to Rose and averted his eyes from both men. She bent down and patted his head, instinctively putting herself between the dog and the shirtless guy. She was trying to imagine the scene: the dog running into the busy intersection, inches away from all that moving steel, rolling rubber and instant death, oblivious to anything but getting back to her.

The shirtless guy walked past her like she wasn't there and tried to give the dog a fierce kick. But the dog was smart enough to mark his approach and make a sudden leap at the right moment.

The shirtless man kicked nothing but air. The dog was up against Rose's leg again.

She stepped between the dog and the man, holding out her hand as he angled for another kick.

"That's enough!" she said. "Leave the poor beast alone."

"I ain't leaving him alone, no ma'am. Not after what he did to my pickup truck. I only made five payments on the thing, and look at it now," he said, motioning to the intersection.

The 7-Eleven clerk chimed in, speaking to the shirtless man.

"Maybe you take him to the pound," Ashneel said. "Get him out of here."

"Pound, nothin' " the shirtless man said. "I'll take him out to the woods and shoot him, is what I'll do. Dog's gotta pay."

Rose could feel the color rising in her cheeks, and without thinking, she had widened her legs to a fighter's stance.

"Get away from the dog!" she said in a voice that stopped the shirtless man and made Ashneel say, "Oh, my golly."

"I thought you said this wasn't your dog," the shirtless man said.

That's when she heard the whistling.

She turned around to see Bernie, walking from the convenience store with a fist full of tickets, and whistling *Luck Be a Lady*.

"Bernie, start the car," she commanded, barely looking back at him.

"Is this your dog, Bernie?" the shirtless man asked, saying the word "Bernie" in a derisive way that Bernie didn't like.

"No, it's not my dog," he said.

"Then tell your wife here to let go of it and get out of the way."

"Start the car, Bernie!" Rose said again.

Rose and the shirtless guy were in some sort of standoff. She held the dog by the collar with one hand and had her other hand out in warning.

"Oh, my golly," Ashneel said again.

"Rose, why are you …"

"Start the car, Bernie!"

"Tell your wife to let go of the dog, Bernie," the shirtless man said.

And then he pushed away Rose's arm and grabbed the dog by the collar. Rose hung on to one side of the collar as best as she could, but the younger, stronger man yanked it away.

The dog whimpered, looking at Rose, who was startled by what had happened.

Bernie, seeing his wife manhandled, charged the younger man like a bull, putting his head down and ramming him in the back.

The shirtless guy went down hard on the pavement, and as he fell, his legs got tangled with Bernie's, who flopped on top of him.

"Oh, my golly," Ashneel said. "I'll be calling the police now."

Bernie, still stunned by his own action, pushed himself off the young man, who had apparently cut his lip during the fall and was cursing loudly.

"Get in!" Bernie heard.

He turned around to see Rose behind the wheel of their Camry, prepared for their getaway with the passenger door opened.

Bernie hopped in, closed the door and Rose gunned the engine out of the parking lot.

Neither of them said anything for nearly a minute. Bernie thought it best to wait to see whether he was going to have a heart attack before quizzing his wife.

"You OK?" she asked.

"Rose, I just don't understand …"

"You really tackled that punk," she said, then smiled, putting a hand on his knee. "Thanks."

"But Rose, what were you …"

"Of course, if you just started the car like I said, we might have gotten out of there without …"

"Oh, my God!" Bernie shouted.

Rose thought her husband was finally having that heart attack he feared so much. She'd never forgive herself for this.

But Bernie's next words brought her great relief.

"My lottery tickets! They're gone! I must have dropped them back there."

Bernie figured that was the worst that could happen to him that day. But it was a sentiment that would last only a second. Because in the next instant, he became aware that they were not alone in the car.

A loud slurping noise was coming from the seat behind him.

"Rose! No. You didn't!"

The self-satisfied smile on her face told him that she did.

When Bernie turned around in his seat, the mutt was looking right at him. His tail thumped a few times, then he rolled on his back, inviting a belly rub.

7 Lois has her day in court

"Lois Rodgers?" the bailiff called.

Lois stood up in the courtroom, taking her time, letting the judge and the lawyers know she was in no hurry. Not for them, not for anybody. She straightened the hem of her dress and imagined how others might see her as she made her way from the back row of benches, up the middle aisle and into the jury box.

Not bad, Lois thought to herself. She was wearing her favorite dress, a floral print that made her feel younger than she often felt. Some people might think she was overdressed. There were some in her jury pool of 40 people who had come in blue jeans or work shirts. But Lois didn't feel overdressed in her pearls, heels and alligator bag.

The lawyers, the judge and even the murderer — one look at the young man at the defense table was all it took for Lois to make up her mind — were smiling at her.

Well, she would wipe those smiles off their faces soon enough.

When 12 members of the jury pool had been seated, the questions from the lawyers began. The idea, they explained, was to pick jurors who could be fair.

Lois had come there this afternoon with one mission in

mind. To get out of jury duty as quickly as possible. The supervisor downstairs had explained that once you were bumped off one panel, your service was through. So this was her chance.

"So, Ms. Rodgers," the female prosecuting attorney began, "have you had any experiences with the court system yourself?"

"Oh, yeah," Lois answered, deciding to let the woman draw her out.

The lawyer smiled.

"And what sort of experiences were they, Ms. Rodgers?"

"Liberating experiences," she said.

"Liberating?" the prosecutor said, perhaps thinking Lois had been a criminal defendant who had beaten the charges.

"I got divorced. Three times."

"And did those experiences give you any lingering animosity toward the court system?"

Lois thought maybe this was the point to say something rude and get herself thrown off the jury panel. Maybe something about how she thought she was treated unfairly by the judges, and how she has lost all faith in courtroom justice.

But instead, she just told the truth.

"No, the only lingering animosity I had was toward myself, to be foolish enough to marry again. I should have learned after the first divorce. I should have written off men right there. But no, I had to try again. And then again."

"Ms. Rodgers," the prosecutor said, trying to cut off Lois' narrative. But Lois didn't care to stop. Everybody had made her wait all afternoon in this courthouse, and now it was her turn to make everybody wait until she was finished talking.

"At least I killed the first two husbands. The third one, though, he almost did me in. Took a piece right out of me, but couldn't kill me. I hope he and that secretary of his end up in a dark alley one night coming face to face with a guy like that," she said, pointing to the defendant, who suddenly stopped smiling and began to look more like the baby-sitter killer he was supposed to be.

Lois' lengthy answers light a fire in the halls of justice.

By the time Lois took a breath for air, the judge was banging his gavel and looking as if he was ready to pass a kidney stone.

"Ms. Rodgers, please!" he said. "Please just answer the question as simply as possible and refrain from long narrative answers. Do you understand?"

"Well, sure I understand, but I thought …"

"Do you understand?" he asked again.

"Your honor, I …"

"Ms. Rodgers, this is a perfect opportunity for you to give a one-word answer," the judge said.

"Oh."

"That's not the word I had in mind," the judge said. "But at this point, I'll take it. Let's move on, madame prosecutor."

"So . . . you mentioned in your answer before that you killed your first two husbands. Can you elaborate, Ms. Rodgers?"

"Sure," she said.

She paused for a few seconds, then looked at the judge, who seemed to be waiting for her to say something else.

"I believe I just gave the required one-word answer," Lois said.

The prosecutor plowed ahead.

"Ms. Rodgers, now I'd like you to explain in as many words as you need, how you killed your first two husbands."

"Well, it's not like I shot them, or stabbed them — like our friend here in the rented suit," she said pointing to the defendant who was now scowling almost as much as his lawyer. "They died of natural causes after the divorces. But the first one blamed me for the heavy drinking that eventually killed him, and the second one said that one day I'd give him a heart attack. It turned out to be the day he wrote his final alimony check."

The defense lawyer was on his feet, clearly still upset from her quip about his client being a killer in a rented suit.

"Can I have a brief sidebar?" he asked the judge.

"No," the judge said. "Let's just move on here. You'll get your chance to ask questions and do what you need to do later."

The judge motioned for the prosecutor to proceed.

"You said your third husband, I believe your words were, 'took a piece right out of you,' " the prosecutor said.

"Left boob."

The court reporter, who sat at his little machine typing furiously to record all the words spoken in the courtroom, looked up and said in confusion, "Left what?"

"Boob," Lois said. "I wear a prosthesis, so you'd never know."

"And this was done by?" the prosecutor asked, who felt completely adrift by this older woman's baffling answers.

"Dr. Golden," Lois said. "You know a lot of these oncologists have a God complex, but Dr. Golden was ..."

"So you had a mastectomy," the prosecutor said, finding a toehold. "And you blame your husband for causing the breast cancer."

"You know what I really blame him for?" Lois said, surprising herself with the emotion that began to build despite herself. "Ah, never mind."

This was no fun anymore. It was time to go home.

"And this was how long ago?" the prosecutor asked.

"Three years," she said.

"And I take it you live alone now at ..." the prosecutor paused now to look down at the questionnaire each prospective juror filled out "... at Shady Palms."

"I have my friends," Lois said, perhaps a little too defensively, she thought.

"But you ..."

"Yes, yes. I live alone."

"And if you were picked to serve on this jury, it wouldn't be a hardship in any way, would it, Ms. Rodgers?"

"Yes, it would."

"In what way?"

"I'd miss my friends."

"But you wouldn't miss work."

"Work? Work's not important. Friends are."

"But it's not like you have a job you'd be missing."

"Well, I wouldn't say that. Gossiping is a full-time occupation at Shady Palms."

The prosecutor paused for a moment, checking over her notes, the questionnaire. She was only two years out of law school, and it didn't come close to preparing her for someone like Lois Rodgers.

Lois eyed the younger woman, taking in her no-nonsense business attire, her short hair and the lack of a wedding ring.

"Can I ask you a question now?" Lois said.

"Well, I ... I ..." the prosecutor stammered, looking toward the judge for help.

The judge was frowning again, about to instruct Lois not to ask questions, when Lois began asking her question anyway.

"An attractive woman like you must have had some experiences with men by now, don't you agree that …"

"Ms. Rodgers!" the judge boomed, banging his gavel, stopping her in mid-sentence.

The judge turned to his bailiff.

"Arthur, please escort the rest of the jury panel outside."

The bailiff strode down the center aisle, holding the back door of the courtroom open as the 39 other members of the jury pool filed out of the room.

"Folks, we'll have you back here in five minutes," the judge said.

His plastic smile disappeared the moment the last prospective juror left the room.

"How old are you, Ms. Rodgers?" he asked, scowling at her.

"That's not a polite …"

"You're old enough to know better, and not too old to be sent to jail for contempt of court. If you think you can come in here and …"

"I'll be 70 next month," Lois said.

"Don't interrupt me," the judge said.

The judge continued on his harangue, but Lois wasn't listening. She was thinking about what it would be like to be handcuffed and sent to jail. The thought of it almost made her giggle, imagining herself clutching her alligator bag while being led out of the courtroom in handcuffs and manacles.

"Judge Shorter," the defense lawyer said. "Let me just say for the record that Ms. Rodgers' unwarranted and unsolicited comments about my client have already prejudiced this jury, and I will be asking that you not only excuse her from the panel, but that we start from scratch with another 40 prospective jurors. We can't unring the bell that has already been …"

What did he say? Lois hadn't paid any attention to the judge's name until the lawyer called him "Judge Shorter." She searched for a nameplate and found one on the side of the judge's bench. "H.H. Shorter, Palm Beach County Circuit

Judge," it said.

The defense lawyer wrapped up his argument.

"I find your argument very persuasive, and I ..."

Lois was staring at the judge now, looking at him so hard that he stopped his ruling in mid-sentence and looked at her.

"Your name's not Harvey. Please. Tell me Harvey Shorter didn't become a judge."

He looked at her now, letting the anger become subservient to his own curiosity.

"C'mon," Lois said. "You don't remember me? Did you have that many clients who divorced their wives on their deathbeds in order to sleep with women young enough to be their children?"

"Lois Brockman," he said, probably not even realizing he was speaking aloud.

"I didn't die, Harvey," Lois said, "and I'm sorry to see that you didn't either."

"Lois," the judge said, trying his best to control his temper. "Throwing you in jail right now would be too easy. So I'm going to go back in my chambers, and five minutes later, I'm going to walk out here, and you will be gone."

"Does that mean I'm excused, your honor?" she said with as much mockery as she could muster.

But he was already off the bench. She watched him go, talking to his back as he retreated.

"I like the black dress, Harvey."

After he was gone, she turned around. The lawyers, the bailiff, the defendant and even the court reporter were looking at her.

"Harvey Shorter," Lois said. "What a piece of work."

8 Bernie loses his weigh

"Hand me the dog," Bernie said.

"What are you doing?"

"Just hand me the dog, Rose."

Bernie Hamstein was standing on the bathroom scale inside his condominium, looking down between his toes.

"Here, Lucky," Rose called out. "C'mere, boy."

The dog, which had already made himself at home by sprawling all over the Hamsteins' new living room couch, shook himself a couple of times and trotted, tail wagging, into the bathroom.

"Lucky?"

"Yes, I've decided we're naming him Lucky. The way he ran into that intersection to chase our car, it was a miracle he didn't get hit."

"Rose, you said ..."

"You saw those cars piled up. But somehow Lucky made it through there without a scratch. Just to be with us, Bernie."

"If one of those lottery tickets I lost back there protecting your foolishness turns out to be a winner, I'll never forgive ..."

"Oh, shush up, Bernie."

"Lucky," Bernie humphed. "Lucky, my eye. I thought you said we were just getting the dog off the street, and that you were going to make signs and post them around the …"

"I've changed my mind," she said.

On the way home, she had stopped at a pet store and bought a bottle of flea and tick shampoo, a rawhide bone and a small box of dog food.

"We're harboring a fugitive," Bernie had said. "This stupid mutt caused a big traffic accident, and we whisk him away as if he's our dog. We're going to end up getting sued by one of those people in the accident."

"Quit talking like a condo president and start talking like a human being," Rose said.

So they brought the dog home, with Bernie clinging onto hope that his wife's mothering instincts would last until she noticed the first hair shed on their new couch or the sound of a bark in their little unit.

It had been almost 20 years since they had their last dog, a beagle who got hit by a mail truck. The kids had cried for days about the loss of Spots, and Bernie himself never forgot what it was like to scoop the broken body off the street. At first, replacing Spots was as unthinkable as replacing Grandma. Then as the years went by, the kids got older, and Bernie and Rose got used to living without a dog. It became easier to think of dogs as something a young family should have but not a couple heading into their golden years.

Apparently, there was some new thinking going on by his wife. And Bernie knew it was dangerous. Once an idea took root in Rose's head, it was tough to dislodge. Soon it would be as impossible as convincing her that Gilda Troutman didn't cheat at cards. Bernie knew there was no way to undo that, and there'd be no way to undo her resolve that they should keep the mutt unless Bernie did some quick and persuasive lobbying against it.

Which was why he was standing on the scale now and asking for the dog. He wanted Rose to witness this.

"OK, look here, Rose. Without the dog, I'm 202. Now hand me the mutt."

Bernie recited the rule: 'Condo owners shall have no more than one dog or cat, and in either case, the animal shall weigh no more than 20 pounds.'

ACCU-SCALE©

"Bernie, you've added a few pounds," she said, ignoring his request. "You need to ..."

OK, if this was the way she was going to be, fine. Bernie, ignoring her lecture about his expanding weight, stepped off the scale and reached for the dog himself.

When he did, the dog rolled on his back so that his paws were suspended over his body. He looked at Bernie, expecting a belly rub. Bernie shook his head and scooped the animal up instead. The dog remained in his arms, stomach up, feet extended in the air, looking like something that just came from the taxidermist. Bernie stepped back on the scale.

"Now, look at the scale," he said to Rose. "What does it read?"

"Uh, 223."

"More like 224."

"So, what's your point, Bernie?"

"My point is that when you subtract my weight without Lucky …"

Why, he wondered, was he now also calling the dog Lucky.

"… from my weight with Lucky, you get Lucky's weight. So 224, take away 202, equals 22 pounds."

"OK, Lucky's 22 pounds," Rose said, taking the dog out of her husband's arms and giving him the belly rub he had been expecting. "So what?"

"So we can't keep him. Overweight dog."

Bernie recited the rule from memory: "Condo owners shall have no more than one dog or cat as a pet, and in either case, the animal shall weigh no more than 20 pounds."

He paused for dramatic effect.

"Rose, I helped write that rule three years ago. Don't you remember? It was right after the woman in F Building got that St. Bernard."

"Bernie, Lucky's just a little dog. Nobody's going to notice he's a pound overweight."

"Two pounds," Bernie said. "And you know as well as I that somebody, somewhere along the line, is going to complain — and probably to Herb Troutman — that the Hamsteins have a heavy dog."

Rose knew Bernie was right about that. But she didn't care.

"So what do we do?" she asked. "Take him to the pound and let them kill him in a few days? Or drop him back at the 7-Eleven, to dodge cars and angry clerks, and to sleep outside like a wild animal until he's shot or run over? "

Bernie shook his head and started to walk away. But as he did, Rose put the dog down and stopped him.

"Bernie," she said. "Listen to me. If you weren't late picking me up at the quilt shop, the dog would never have found me there. If you didn't stop to get lottery tickets at the 7-Eleven, the dog would have never followed us there. And if you didn't take on that young brute without the shirt, the dog wouldn't have been able to get free and follow me to our car.

"Lucky's here because of you, Bernie. You, not me, are the one who saved him. I just understand what's happened here before you did."

"Oh, Rose, please. Don't start with ..."

"Bernie, face it, this is meant to be," and then she smiled at him. "It's meant to be."

And suddenly, he wasn't standing in the bathroom with a small, gray-haired woman — a wife, a mother, a grandmother — he was looking at a teenager with long, dark hair, pale pink fingernails, and a man's shirt she had the habit of leaving untucked.

They were at Coney Island on a hot summer night, breathing in their forbidden romance.

"It's meant to be," she had told him that night, and they both believed it, believing that their love was stronger than the certain disapproval of their parents.

Saul Hamstein would sit shiva, the mourning ceremony for the dead, when he realized he lost his son to an Italian girl. And Gina Cangelosi would cry for a week, telling her headstrong daughter, Rose, that to marry a Jew would be the first step to a life of mortal sin.

Bernie's family had already assumed he would marry Susan Plock, a nice Jewish girl who had been paired with him since puberty. They had gone to the prom together and dated nobody else all through high school.

But secretly, it was always Rose, that little wiry daughter of Sicilian immigrants, who triggered his imagination. It wasn't until after high school, when Bernie was working in his father's tailor shop, that his unquenched fascination turned into something real. He put down a pair of pants he was mending, and before he had a chance to think about it anymore, he walked across the street and up to the lunch counter in the five-and-dime.

Rose was just finishing up making an egg-cream for

somebody, he remembered. When she got done, she turned around and looked at Bernie as if she had expected his arrival, and said, "What can I do for you, Bernie?"

"Go out with me," he said, his voice cracking, only able to look her in the eyes for a second before pretending to read the menu over her head.

The Hamsteins and the Cangelosis lived a block away from each other in their Brooklyn neighborhood. Their children went to school together, even played together. But the thought of them marrying each other was unthinkable. Bernie and Rose first thought about it on that night so long ago in Coney Island, about six months after he talked to her at the lunch counter.

He remembered holding onto her as they hurtled through space on the Cyclone, the two of them whipping through the night air, soaring above the boardwalk, above Brooklyn, and above life's limitations that had been spelled out to them by their families.

Everyone around them was screaming, Bernie remembered. But he and Rose just sat there, clutching each other, knowing somehow already that they had begun a ride that had many more dips and turns than the rickety roller coaster they were on.

"It's meant to be," she had told him as the roller coaster slowed down.

He kissed her, and told her, "Yes, it is."

And so here they were, five decades later, and that girl he married in disgrace was still there looking at him, reminding him to forget about the rules and to follow the uncontrollable path of the heart.

"It's meant to be, Bernie," Rose said again.

Lucky trotted off with one of Bernie's socks in his mouth.

9 A Samaritan who beeps

Lois Rodgers felt pretty good about herself as she left the courthouse and walked toward the city garage a couple of blocks away.

She had outdone herself, gotten out of jury duty with style. Even that baby-sitter killer seemed impressed, sitting there with his jaw agape as she did what even he wouldn't dare: tell off the judge.

Of course, that young punk, who probably already had some notions about the brutality of the justice system, didn't know the half of it when it came to Harvey Shorter.

In a way, Lois thought, it was too bad he didn't send her to jail. It might have given her the chance to stand up in open court before another judge and explain what a perfect monster Harvey had been as her husband's divorce lawyer. How he had shown up at her hospital bed in a white lab coat and stethoscope, asking her to sign some papers, which turned out to be a property settlement agreement.

Yeah, Lois thought, it was too bad that bottom-feeding scoundrel didn't try to throw her in jail. She'd show them contempt of court.

She was still thinking of Harvey Shorter when she crossed Olive Avenue and walked into the parking garage, waiting for the elevator to arrive at the ground floor.

When it did, Lois paused to let a woman on the elevator get out. The woman, almost certainly a street person, wore unlaced sneakers, long pants matted with dirt and two shirts. Despite the heat, she had a knit cap covering her hair.

The woman looked at Lois and made a motion as if she was leaving the elevator. Then she stopped, seeming to change her mind. She turned her eyes away and slunk back to the rear of the elevator. Lois was thinking too much about Harvey Shorter to give the woman anything but cursory attention. She got on the elevator and punched the button for the third floor.

Once the door closed, Lois could smell her. And even though it was a short ride, Lois nearly went running from the elevator, squeezing between the doors before they were fully opened.

Lois gulped the garage air, not bothering to look back. After a few steps, she slowed down, walking on the inclined, covered level, trying to remember where exactly she had parked.

She was halfway down the long row of cars when she was startled by a yank on her arm. She reached across her body, instinctively grabbing for her purse as her attacker pulled harder on the strap.

Even before Lois wheeled around, she knew who it was. She could smell her.

Lois was no match for the younger woman, who now had both hands on the purse and was trying to rip it out of Lois' grasp. The two women staggered, four hands on the purse, pulling, ripping and finally spewing the contents all over the pavement. The younger woman pushed Lois hard against the back of a parked minivan and then reached down for her wallet. Lois kicked it, sending the wallet skidding out of reach.

Rather than go after it, the woman turned back to Lois, and said, "Give me your gold. Now!"

And before Lois could get the word "No" out of her mouth, the younger woman was on her, tossing her to the ground, so that Lois was sprawled face down with this stinky street person sitting on her back and yanking on her fingers, hands and neck for jewelry.

Lois started to cry, not from the pain as much as the indignity of it all. The sound of her sobs and the blood rushing in her ears must have been why she didn't hear what happened next.

She just knew that suddenly the woman was off her back and running away, and an elfin, bronze-colored man with running shorts, an earring and a mane of white hair tied back in a ponytail was standing over her.

"Yes, I'm all right," Lois said, sitting up, rubbing her sore ring finger and feeling for her gold necklace, which had been snapped from her neck but left on the pavement next to her. "She didn't get anything — thanks to you."

She regarded the little man, who kept looking over her and then back down the length of the garage where the other woman had run.

"If you want, Ricardo can go chase her down," he said. "She get anything of yours, and Ricardo will bring it back."

"Ricardo?"

She rubbed the tears out of her eyes to get a better look at her Samaritan, who was now dripping sweat all over her, already beginning to annoy her.

"Who's Ricardo?" she asked.

"Ricardo," he said, "that is me. You sure she did not get anything of yours? Ricardo does not want to leave you like this, but if there is anything …"

"No. Just go," Lois said, trying to move herself out of the trajectory of the sweat that seemed to be popping from Ricardo's body.

She'd never seen such muscular legs on a man of Social Security age. And his legs were something she couldn't help noticing from her sitting position. They seemed to be made of strands of twisted rope, or more like cables, and the skin around them was pulled tight, straining to contain the bundle underneath. But what really struck Lois about his legs was that they were hairless. The old weirdo shaved his legs.

Lois groaned in disgust.

"Are you OK?" he said, thinking she was in pain. "Ricardo can call you an ambulance."

"No, I'm fine," she said. "Ricardo, do you always refer to yourself in the third person?"

She started to stand up and then cringed as he put one of his drippy, hot hands under her arm for support.

"There is a third person?" he asked.

That's when she first noticed he was beeping. Ricardo was ignoring it, but Lois kept hearing it, beep-beep-beep.

"You can go now, Ricardo. I'm fine. Thank you for helping me."

She started scooping up the scattered contents of her purse and wallet. He began helping her.

"No," she said curtly. "I can do this myself."

He began pacing around, as if he was trying to decide whether to run away or linger.

"Go," she said. "Really, I'm all right."

He looked at her, rubbing the earring in his left lobe, then exhaling deeply.

"No," he said, as if making a pronouncement. "Ricardo should make sure you get to your car. This place is not safe. Ricardo knows. He runs here all the time."

"And why," she asked, "does Ricardo — do you — run in a parking garage?"

"The inclines. Up, down, up, down. Ricardo needs to run hills. But there are no hills in South Florida, so Ricardo uses city parking garages for his hills."

The thought of this little man spending the hot part of the day running up and down a parking garage was too much for her.

She started walking faster to her car, trying to get away from him as quickly as possible. Ricardo quickened his pace to match hers. Maybe, she thought, he was just waiting for a show of gratitude.

That must be it. Why hadn't she thought of that in the first place?

She dug into her purse and pulled out a $10 bill, thrusting it at him.

"Here," she said. "For your services."

"Ricardo Vera does not rescue elegant ladies for money," he said, waving the bill away as if it were poison.

There was still a beeping sound coming from his body.

"Go answer your pager."

"Pager? Ricardo does not have a pager."

"Well, then perhaps you're about to blow up. Can't you hear that beeping?"

"Oh, that," Ricardo said. "That is a heart rate monitor. It is just telling Ricardo that he is below his target zone."

He thrust his arm under her face, showing her what she thought was a wristwatch, but instead displayed a number and a beating heart.

"See?" he said to her. "It is 95. Ricardo set his Polar Pacer to beep at him whenever his heart rate got below 110 during his training run."

He pulled up his sweaty running shirt to reveal a thick black rubber strap that encircled his chest.

"Do you see this?" he asked.

Lois didn't want to look. She wanted to get out of there as quickly as possible. They had reached her car. She fumbled with the keys as Ricardo explained the wireless technology of heart rate monitors.

When she started up the car and began to pull out of the spot, he was still standing there with his shirt pulled up to his nipples, revealing his leathery abdomen and that black strap.

"Well," she said, searching for a painless exit line. "Thank you, and ... I'm sorry I allowed you to get below your target zone."

He waved his hand, dismissing her apology as his monitor

continued to beep. He started to say something, but Lois closed the electric window on her car, shutting him and his sound out.

She nearly left rubber on the pavement as she drove away.

Ricardo was about to continue his climb to the roof of the garage when he noticed a speck of color on the pavement.

The gold credit card was where Lois' car had been parked. Ricardo bent down and picked it up. She must have dropped it while she was getting in the car.

Ricardo scooped up the card and raced down the zigzagging ramps of the garage, his heart monitor going silent as he felt the exhilaration of running hard.

She had a good head start, but she'd have to stop to pay on her way out. As Ricardo rounded the penultimate turn, he could see the red taillights of her car at the attendant's booth. He picked up his pace, convinced he would reach her before she drove out of the garage.

But when he was only 10 yards away, he could see her brake lights disappear as her car rolled under the upturned gate and into the street.

Ricardo followed, racing harder. Now, his heart rate monitor was beeping at him again, because he was exceeding the 150 beat-per-minute upper limit he had set for the day's run.

He was sprinting in the middle of Banyan Boulevard now, waving the VISA gold card in his left hand, racing toward Lois' car.

Lois slowed as she neared the Flagler Drive intersection. That's when she first glanced in her rear-view mirror and noticed Ricardo racing after her, flailing his arms like an idiot.

She quickly drove into the busy intersection without even checking to see if it was clear. She nearly hit two cars. They beeped their horns angrily at her. But she didn't care. She looked straight ahead, driving faster and faster, not bothering to look into her mirror again until she was miles away.

10 Jake's TV debut

Lucky barked at the answering machine, unnerved by the disembodied sound of a human voice. The dog stood near the end table in the Hamsteins' living room, looking around for Rose or Bernie to make some sense of this strange intruder.

"Mom? Dad? I guess you're not home," the Hamsteins' youngest child said, calling from a highway pay phone near New Orleans.

Sam Hamstein was actually relieved his parents weren't there. It'd be fewer questions he'd have to answer. Now, at least he'd have all night to think about how he was going to phrase this. And why, at age 28, he was driving across country. Alone.

"Be there around dinner time tomorrow," he said carefully. He knew his parents would take that to mean, "We'll be there around dinner time tomorrow." But he didn't want to explain that it was an "I," not a "We," who was taking this trip.

Lucky barked at Sam's voice until his message ended. The dog sniffed triumphantly and peed on the leg of the end table where the machine sat.

■ ■ ■

"I'm sure the dog will be fine," Bernie said as he pushed the overcooked vegetables around his plate.

Actually, Bernie was rooting that Lucky would be anything

but fine in their apartment. It was his idea to go out to Morrison's Cafeteria for dinner, claiming a sudden craving for the restaurant's fried fish and explaining that Rose didn't have time to shop and cook tonight because he had to go to the 7 p.m. show of *That's Entertainment* by the Shady Palms Players.

Bernie wanted Lucky to do something dreadful in their condo while they were gone, something that would persuade Rose to forget about destiny and start thinking about how impractical it was for them to keep the dog. A dog that violated the condo's weight limitations, to boot.

"It's just that I feel bad leaving him so soon," Rose said. "Lucky's just getting settled. And I don't want him to feel insecure in his new home."

"Home? Now, Rose, I told you, I'm going to post notices around that shopping center and …"

"Nobody will answer them, Bernie," she said. "I know it. You're wasting your time. Lucky is our dog."

"The dog," Bernie said, "belongs to somebody else, and I'll find who that is."

Rose smiled.

"You wanna know who, Bernie? Just look in the mirror."

"I'm posting those notices, Rose."

■ ■ ■

Jacqui Fisher puttered around her condo, pretending she wasn't anxious about anything.

"I could get you a lawyer," she said, unable to keep pretending, as her son, Jake, stood over the sink eating an orange.

"I don't need a lawyer, Mom," he said. "I can handle this by myself."

"But maybe a lawyer can find some loophole, and …"

"I don't care about a loophole, Mom. I propositioned a cute guy, who turned out to be an undercover cop. It's not the end of the world."

"Yes, but dear, maybe it was entrapment, or one of those

other kind of legal things."

"Mom, I'll be fine. I can handle it myself."

He gave her a kiss on the forehead and headed out the door. If he was concerned, Jacqui thought, he sure was doing a good job of hiding it from her.

"Where are you going?"

"Out," he said. "Just for a drive. I'll probably get some fast food for dinner, so just eat without me."

"But I was going to reheat the casserole from last night."

"Don't worry. I'll stay away from public restrooms, Mom. I promise."

Jacqui sat on her living room sofa, unable to do anything but imagine bad things happening to her only child. When it was time for the 6 o'clock news, she went to her bedroom.

It would be better to watch it here, she thought, on this small set in her sanctuary. It was somehow less public this way. She closed the door and turned the volume down so that it was barely audible.

For the first time, she found herself frowning at the Eyewitness News Team, the way the station made such a big deal about eavesdropping on the misfortunes of others. As if this was some noble calling.

"Topping the news tonight," the station's anchor said, almost breathless, "police arrest 23 men in an undercover sting in the men's room at a West Palm Beach park. Channel 5 was there, and we have exclusive video of …"

Jacqui gasped. There was Jacob on her television set, standing in a line of handcuffed men who were being herded into the back of a paddy wagon. Some of the men were trying to hide their faces behind the sleeves of their shirts, but Jacob was just standing there, as if he were waiting in line at McDonald's.

She cried softly to herself, barely able to watch the rest of the story, which focused on the arrest of the minister with the four children. Jacob was right about that. The TV news, in its hurly-burly way, seemed to have time only to dwell on the minister. The reporter, that perky little Suzie Ching, had gone to the minister's house, trying to elicit a comment from his wife, who slammed the door in Ching's face after a curt series of "no comments."

The station did manage to get an "I'm totally shocked" comment from the minister's neighbor. And then it showed video of the church, zeroing in for a close-up of the minister's name on the sign out front.

But nothing about Jacob and the other 21 men. They looked like such a pathetic lot to Jacqui. It was hard to imagine her son standing among them.

The news switched to some new bloodshed in the Middle East. Jacqui turned the set off.

The telephone rang. She thought about not picking it up. But maybe it was Jacob. Maybe he had been watching, too, and wanted to say something that would make her feel better.

"Yes?" she said, trying not to sound like a person who had been crying.

"So, then it was him. Oh, dear. Jacqui, honey. I can hear it in your voice. I'm so sorry. You OK?"

It was Maddy. Jacqui blew her nose and tried to sound chipper.

"I'm fine, Maddy. Thanks for asking."

"I was watching the news, and I couldn't help thinking that one of those fellas in line looked like your Jacob, and I ... Oh, I'm sorry, Jacqui. I didn't call you to be a gossip. I just want to make sure you're OK. I won't say a word of it to anybody. I'm just ..."

"I know, Maddy. You're very kind."

"Listen, you eat dinner yet?"

"I was just going to reheat some leftovers."

"Forget the leftovers, girl. Come up to my place. I've got plenty of ..."

"No, Maddy. Really. I think I'll pass."

"But we can ..."

"No, I think I just want to be alone."

"Nobody wants to be alone. Listen, if you won't come up here, I'll come down there. You got enough of those leftovers for me?"

Twenty minutes later, Maddy was in Jacqui's apartment, sharing her leftover Chicken-Rice Supreme and trying to cheer her up.

"So, listen," Maddy said. "Don't you want to hear about the pregnant woman in 26C? I went up there this afternoon. I met the boyfriend, too. There's something strange there. First, when I . . . Hey, girl, you're not even listening."

"I'm sorry, Maddy. It's just that I'm worried about Jacob." Maddy wiped her mouth.

"Listen, Jacqui, you never get anywhere worrying about anything. If something bothers you, then you just gotta do something about it."

"What can I do? I don't know anything about being … about being … gay."

"Jacqui, honey. Listen. This has nothing to do with being gay. Your boy's problem is loneliness. It's a people problem, not a straight or gay problem. Your boy just needs to meet somebody special. He does that, and he won't be looking in bathrooms anymore, I guarantee that."

"But what can I …"

"Jacob is smart. He's good-looking. Problem is he's just lacking some self-confidence, and he's stifled a little bit here, living with you. Have you ever told him he can bring somebody home with him?"

"You mean a man?"

"That's who he's interested in, Jacqui. If you're waiting for him to walk through the door with Cindy Crawford, it ain't gonna happen."

"I don't even think he has any … friends. You know, like that."

"Well, maybe you ought to find him one."

"What?"

"Find him a friend. A boyfriend. You did it when he was little, right?"

"We'd go to the park to play and meet …"

"See? Your boy's still going to the park to play. Except, today he tried to play with a cop. That's his problem. You got to find him a friend elsewhere now."

"But where? I don't know anything about that … that lifestyle."

"I'm sure there are other nice boys just like your Jacob out there. If he's too stifled to find them, then maybe you can help him."

"What do I do?"

"Girl, you've been leading a sheltered life. I can see you may need some help."

"Yes. Will you help me, Maddy?"

"If you want to do it, I will."

"Yes, I want to do something. I'm ready."

Jacqui was smiling now, clutching her friend's hand across the table.

"Please, help me," Jacqui said. "What do we have to do?"

"Have you ever been to a gay bar?"

Jacqui's smile disappeared.

11 Mort delivers the news

The Shady Palms Players' production of *That's Entertainment* was even worse than Bernie Hamstein had expected. Bernie started to doze by the third number, a medley of World War II favorites performed by three 80-year-old women who called themselves the Andrews Grandmothers. But he had too much on his mind to get a satisfying snooze. He shifted uneasily in his seat, his thought process refusing to shut down with his body.

Finding that puddle of dog pee on the rug when he got home from dinner wasn't as enjoyable as he had imagined. First of all, he had to clean it. And secondly, his wife blamed herself instead of blaming the dog, saying that if she had remembered to walk Lucky before they had left for dinner, it wouldn't have happened.

"Oh, you poor baby," Rose had said, bending down to accept the licks of that carpet whizzer, while Bernie was on his hands and knees trying to make the golden stain disappear.

"Blot, don't rub, dear," Rose was saying.

Then there was the phone message from Sam, his youngest son. The surprise visit meant he and Rose would spend all day tomorrow getting ready, cleaning out the extra bedroom for Sam and Jasmine. Going shopping for food. Dusting. He really hated dusting.

Sure, he would be happy to see his youngest son and his bride. But there was something in the brevity of the phone message that made Bernie think something was going on.

"Why would they just show up like this?" Bernie had asked Rose.

"Maybe they just want to surprise us," Rose had said.

Surprises. Bernie was getting tired of surprises. The pregnant renter. The dog. Now his son, the one who didn't listen to him and become a lawyer like his two older brothers did.

When was life supposed to get easier? He wished he was back on the bread truck again, working too hard and being too tired to give much of anything a second thought, except for the next day's stale returns.

He sat alone in the clubhouse auditorium, serving his prison sentence for accepting the ride from Johnny Fox on the previous afternoon. On the stage, about three dozen of his neighbors danced, sang and pretended that this was the Great White Way and they were still young enough to be undiscovered talent.

Intermission couldn't come soon enough. He raced to the lobby, trying to beat the rush to the coffee urn. The line, though, was already 15 deep when he got there.

"Some show, eh, Bernie?"

It was Johnny Fox.

"Some show, Johnny."

"Yeah, I'm proud of it," Fox said. "We really did it this time."

"You certainly did."

Fox walked away, trying to solicit rave reviews from other patrons. Bernie worked his way up to the front of the line, got his coffee and was about to find an empty stretch of wall to stand against when he felt a tap on his shoulder.

"Bernie."

"Mort."

SHADY PALMSGAZETTE

MORT GRANGER

Mort Granger found his niche at Shady Palms as the quarrelsome editor of *The Shady Palms Gazette*, a condo newspaper remarkable in its ability to consistently throw fresh gasoline on dying fires.

"C'mere, Bernie. We gotta talk."

Bernie followed Mort outside the clubhouse doors to the pool area. It was a sticky night, full of croaking frogs, distant sprinklers and omnipresent humidity. Now the night also included Mort Granger, the quarrelsome editor of *The Shady Palms Gazette*, a weekly condo newspaper that was remarkable in its ability to consistently throw fresh gasoline on dying fires.

Bernie knew Mort since grade school in Brooklyn. He was trouble back then, too.

"What's up, Mort?"

"Two things," he said. "*The Gazette*'s writing a story about the pregnant woman in your building. And I thought you …"

"Why you doing that, Mort? I mean, c'mon. Isn't there such a thing as privacy here?"

Bernie had been secretly hoping that Margo Zukowski wasn't pregnant after all. That it was all some vicious rumor. Bernie had imagined himself standing up to Herb Troutman and telling him that in the future, he hoped Troutman would keep his nose out of C Building's affairs … well, maybe "affairs" wasn't the right word to use.

But it didn't matter now. The renter was indeed pregnant, Rose had told him that afternoon. Her friend, Madeline, was even there to witness the woman telling her boyfriend the news. There was no use hoping for the impossible any more. The pregnant renter was going to be trouble.

Especially with Mort Granger getting in the middle of things.

"Bernie, this is a public issue. You know as well as I do that having a baby here would set a dangerous precedent that would …"

Bernie muttered something under his breath.

"What'd you say?"

"Nothing, Mort."

"Bernie, I'm telling you, this is a big story."

"Mort, let me talk to the woman and see if there's some way we can work it out."

"Work it out? Bernie, what the hell are you talking about? There's only one thing to do here, and that's get her out of here. Now. Before the baby is born."

"Please, Mort. Why don't you just leave this one alone for a while. Can't you write some more about the parking problem on weekends?"

"The people have a right to know, Bernie."

"The people already know. All you're doing is blowing things out of proportion."

Bernie sat down heavily in a lounge chair.

"Thanks, Mort, for brightening up an already rotten evening."

"Bernie, Bernie. C'mon. Don't take it personally. This is a great story. You just have the misfortune of being in the middle of it."

The lights on the patio flashed. The second act was about to begin. Bernie started heading inside when Mort stopped him.

"Wait, Bernie. Remember, I said I had two things to discuss."

"Look, Mort. I don't have the time or the head for …"

"No, Bernie. This isn't condo stuff," he said as he handed Bernie a soft-cover booklet he'd been holding.

"Where's this from?"

"Our old high school," Mort said. "It's the school's 100th anniversary or something, and somebody decided to make a directory of the school's graduates. You know, one of those 'Where are they now?' books. They sent me something in the mail about it six months ago, asking me for personal info on myself and any other graduates I knew. So I put you in there, too. I'd meant to tell you about it, but it slipped my mind."

Bernie started leafing through it, looking for the "H's."

"Show's starting," Mort said.

"Yeah, I'll be there in a minute."

Mort went inside the clubhouse, leaving Bernie by the pool, paging through his high school alumni directory until he got to his name. The lighting was bad, but he could still see that Mort was right.

"Bernard J. Hamstein, class of '43. Wife: Rose. Children: Steven, Simon, Samuel. Resides: 13989 Shady Palms Place No. 14C, Boynton Beach, Fla."

He paged through the book, looking through the thousands of names from all the graduating years, searching for someone else from the Class of '43. He found some, but the names were as foreign to him now as all the other names in the book.

The only name he still remembered from his old class was his high school sweetheart, Susan Plock. He had no idea what happened to Susan. Their young romance died with his infatuation with Rose.

He thought of her now, Susan Plock, the girl he was supposed to marry. Whatever happened to her? His fingers raced through the book, getting to the "P's."

He could hear from the muffled sounds coming from the wall that the second act of *That's Entertainment* had already begun. Good.

Pinter. Pirizzi. Plant. Plazure. Plistman.

He felt like a little boy leafing furtively through the pages of a dirty magazine.

Plock. There she was.

"Susan A. Plock (Rosen), class of '43. Husband: Dr. Jerome H. Rosen. Children: Sheila, David, Jerome, Sandra. Resides: 141 Willow Bend Court, Atlantis, Fla."

Bernie felt the blood rising in his face. His old girlfriend from 50 years ago was living a few miles away. Susan Plock. The mother of four children. She had been barely out of childhood herself when he had last seen her.

He read the booklet's summary of her life again, suddenly wishing to know more about the first girl he had ever kissed. What would she be like now, he wondered? Susan Plock. Whatever they had shared seemed like another lifetime. Ancient history.

Bernie married a Rose, she married a Rosen.

End of story. Or was it?

Bernie wondered if Susan Plock had leafed through the booklet just as he had. He wondered if she had searched for his name, surprised also to find him living only a few miles away. Was her face flushed by this, too?

Nah. That was silly. She married a doctor, for crying out loud. She lives in Atlantis. She wouldn't be caught dead in a dump like Shady Palms. And why would she give a second thought to a louse who dumped her, a louse who made a living selling bread off a truck.

Bernie imagined Susan's house now. He'd never been inside Atlantis. He'd just driven by the high walls, seeing the big tiled roofs. Big houses. Single family houses. No condo commandos there.

Susan Plock. It was something to think about.

Bernie thought about it through most of the second act and during the ride home.

When he walked in the door of the condo, Rose was already asleep. He got undressed quietly and slipped under the covers next to her.

He was almost asleep when he first noticed something strange was happening in their bed. Something was moving between him and Rose. Something hairy. Something that settled in the crook of his legs and began licking the soles of his feet.

12 Margo in Wonder-land

Margo Zukowski didn't get a very good night's sleep. She kept replaying Bill's visit from the previous afternoon.

"I don't believe you," he had said, pacing around the condo. "Getting yourself pregnant like this just screws up everything."

"I'm sorry, Bill. It's not like I planned it this way."

"We can't just go back to square one here, Margo. I was counting on you, and now you're …"

"I'm still there for you, Bill. Just because I'm pregnant doesn't change anything."

"It changes everything … I thought I could count on you."

"You can."

"So does that mean you're gonna get an abortion?"

"Is that what you want?"

"It would certainly make things simpler."

That's when Margo had started to cry. She just sat down on her couch and cried. It was so unprofessional. But she didn't care.

"Well, some things, Bill Johnson, aren't simple," she had managed to blurt out between sobs.

Bill had just stood there, pacing around, not even bothering to console her. What a jerk.

"How did this happen?"

"The way it always does," Margo had said, looking at him a little defiantly.

"I mean …"

"It was an accident, OK?"

"We can't afford accidents, Margo."

"Listen, Bill. Don't be so sanctimonious. If we want to get judgmental here, then you're partially to blame, too."

"Me? I don't see what I have to do with …"

Margo rolled over on the couch, clutching a pillow and curling into a fetal position.

"Listen," he had said. "I … I gotta go. I'll be in touch. Soon."

In a way, until Bill's visit, she hadn't thought much at all about her pregnancy. It had seemed remote in a way, unreal and unconnected to the business at hand.

But when she woke up this morning, she knew it was real. She felt sick to her stomach and, for the first time, afraid and unsure of the future for not only herself but the life germinating inside her.

She reached for the alarm clock on her nightstand to look at the time. It was 5:45 a.m., time to start getting ready for her rendezvous with the Wonder Walkers at the Boynton Beach Mall.

■ ■ ■

"What are you doing up so early?" Rose asked.

Bernie was sitting at the kitchen table, making rectangular cardboard signs.

"Worse night of sleep in my life," he muttered.

"Bernie, don't waste your time with that," Rose said, pointing to the signs.

He could hear Lucky, still in their bed, scratching himself.

"My shoulder's all stiff, Rose," he said. "That dog pushed me right to the edge. Did you see him when you woke up this morning? Sprawled out sideways on the bed."

"Cute, isn't he?"

"He's not spending another night in that bed."

Rose just shook her head and put the tea kettle on.

"I set up a little blanket and tried to get him to sleep on the floor in our room," Rose said. "But he kept crying and pawing at the mattress, begging to get in with me. When I put him in there, he snuggled up right away. I thought it was kind of nice."

"Nice? Maybe for you, but not for me. I want my bed back, I want my house back, and ..." as he was talking, Lucky bounded into the room with one of Bernie's socks in his mouth, "... and I want my clothes back."

"He just likes you, Bernie."

"Well, the feeling isn't mutual."

"Give it time."

"The only thing I'm giving it is away."

Bernie took out a black marker and began writing in big, block letters.

"Lucky needs to go outside, Bernie," Rose said. "Why don't you stop that nonsense and take him out."

Bernie was ready to say something flip, like, "Let the mutt wait." But then he remembered being on his hands and knees the previous evening, trying to make the carpet look white again.

"C'mon, you," he said to the dog, who wagged his tail and followed him to the front door. "Don't be so happy. Your days here are numbered."

■ ■ ■

Pacing up and down the empty corridors of the mall with the Wonder Walkers proved to be just what Margo needed to beat back her blues. The older women, much to her relief, seemed less interested in her than each other.

It felt good to Margo just to listen to other voices.

First, the one named Lois held everybody's attention with the tale of her brief but eventful jury duty service. When she got to the part about getting mugged in the parking garage, the

story was so good, the women abandoned trying to walk and listen at the same time.

They just all stood there in front of Victoria's Secret, circled around Lois as she told of being saved by somebody she
called "a Keebler elf in running shoes."

"He didn't tell you his name?"

"Rolando. Ricardo. Rodolfo. I can't remember. All I remember is that he was sweating all over me, and beeping … He had
some kind of rubber strap around his chest … He showed me.
Can you believe it? … The little weirdo …"

"He sounds sort of dashing," Jacqui said. "And you say he
was about your age?"

"He smelled like a paddock, which was only slightly better
than the homeless woman, who at least wasn't crazy enough to
go running in a parking garage during the hot part of the afternoon."

"He's an athlete," Rose said.

"At his age, if you do what he does, you're not an athlete,"
Lois said. "You're a nut."

"I'll bet you didn't even thank him," Maddy said. "Man
saved your life maybe, and you didn't even thank him. I'll bet. I
know you, girl."

"For your information, Ms. Jones, I even offered him 10
bucks."

"And he wouldn't take it?" Maddy asked.

"No."

"A gentleman."

"A nut," Lois said. "I'm telling you, he was just a nut. If I
would have hung around there any longer, he probably would
have . . . would have done something even worse to me than
that homeless woman was trying to do."

Then Rose unwound her tale of Lucky the dog. Margo kept
quiet, not feeling secure enough in the group to blurt out questions.

It wasn't until they had taken their seats in the food court and the first round of sticky buns was going down that the women's complete attention was focused on the newcomer.

If they had been measuring her before then, Margo never noticed. It was only now, as she sat there in her oversized Florida State University T-shirt and her shoulder-length brown hair pulled back into a ponytail, that she felt all of their gazes on her.

And after being lonely for so long, it felt good.

"So tell us a story, Margo," Maddy started. "How'd you meet your boyfriend?"

Margo flushed. This wasn't a good place to start. She really didn't have a good story to tell about Bill.

"I guess I met him when I first moved to Florida a couple of months ago," she said.

"Quick romance," Maddy said. "They're the best kind."

"Shut up, Maddy, and let the young lady speak," Lois said.

Margo fidgeted with her wristwatch.

"And so where did you meet?" Jacqui asked.

"Where he ... where he works."

That much was true.

"What kind of work does Bill do?"

"He's ... he's a tollbooth operator."

It just popped in her head. She was trying to construct some sort of scenario where a woman driving to Florida from North Dakota would meet somebody. She could have just said a bar. But that was too ... too ordinary. Especially after the stories she'd already heard this morning.

"Like on the Turnpike?" Jacqui asked.

"Yeah, the Turnpike. I had just driven into the state and was pulling off at the Lake Worth exit." Margo could almost see herself now, taking part in this little fiction.

The women pulled themselves closer to the table.

"I couldn't find my wallet. I misplaced it. It was somewhere in the car, but when I got to the tollbooth I couldn't find it ... and he said, 'That's OK. I'm going to trust you to pay me back.' And I said, 'When?' and he said, 'Over dinner tonight.' "

Margo looked at their faces. They were smiling at her. All except for Lois.

"And you trusted him? He could have been one of those weirdos, like that Keebler elf I ran into."

"But he wasn't," Maddy said.

"And now you're pregnant already, two months later?" Lois said.

Margo nodded.

"I know this is none of my business," Lois said. "But aren't you rushing things a bit?"

"I don't know."

"I just mention this," Lois said, "because after conducting much research in the field, I've concluded that men are pigs. Even the ones you know for 10 years, the ones you think are OK, they turn out to be pigs."

Jacqui waved her finger at Lois.

"You old dried-up prune," Jacqui said, and then she turned to Margo.

"Don't let Cruella De Vil ruin your happiness, dear."

"Is Bill happy about the baby?" Rose asked.

Margo swallowed and looked down, making tracks with her fingernails on the empty plastic plate in front of her. The sticky bun she had eaten was rising, not falling, in her throat now. And all the game-playing she had been doing suddenly felt less jolly.

She didn't look up to see the faces of the four women. It was easier telling the truth into the empty plate.

"I'm the only one who wants the baby," she said, so softly the women could barely hear her.

She really wasn't good at her job at all, she thought. She had come this morning to find out about them, and instead, she was the one laying her cards on the table.

Rose, who was sitting on her right, put a gentle hand on Margo's shoulder.

"Men are such pigs," Lois said.

"Did Bill … did he say you should get an … an abortion?" Rose asked.

Margo looked at her and nodded, her eyes quickly filling with tears.

"That's cold," Maddy said.

"Pigs," Lois said again.

The sticky bun felt like a fist now, working its way up Margo's throat.

"Oh my …" was all she was able to say before she erupted all over the table.

13 Ricardo finds a new sport

As the four older women drove back to Shady Palms, the plight of their new neighbor dominated the conversation.

"Here's what gets me," Rose said. "She's been here a month, and we don't even see this Bill character until yesterday."

"Yeah, and it's not like she's always running out, either," said Maddy.

"So when does this romance and pregnancy take place?" Rose asked.

"You only need about 15 minutes for the pregnancy," said Lois, whose turn it was to drive that day.

"Something doesn't add up here," Rose said.

"She's sweet, though, isn't she?" Jacqui added. "I hope the condo board doesn't overreact to her."

"You can count on that," Lois said. "If she thinks that boyfriend doesn't want the baby, wait till she hears the collective opinion of Shady Palms."

Margo had intrigued them in many ways. Her pregnancy had kicked off in each of them a maternal instinct that had been buried but not lost. She was needy, and in a way, so were they. If the pregnant renter had lived in another building, they might have joined the masses in wanting her out of Shady Palms.

But Margo Zukowski had become a real person to them

that morning. They had listened to her loneliness and watched her tears. They had felt an instinct that went deeper than the restrictive covenants of condominium law.

"Hey, Lo. Do me a favor," Rose said from the back seat. "Could you just make a quick stop here?"

Lois pulled into the shopping center parking lot.

"What store?"

"Not a store," Rose said. "I'm just looking for signs."

"You getting mystic on us, Rose?" Maddy said.

"No, not those kind of signs," Rose said. "Lost dog signs … There. Look."

On nearly every pole, she could see a cardboard sign. Bernie had really gone wild on this task.

Lois stopped in front of each pole, waiting as Rose hopped out, ripped the sign off and got back in the car. When they were done, Rose had a dozen signs in her lap.

Some of them said, "Lost Dog" with a brief description and her phone number. But the ones that irked Rose were the signs that began, "Free to a good home!"

"Bernie, you've gone too far," Rose muttered to herself.

When she got home 15 minutes later, Lucky rushed to the door to greet her. Bernie stayed on the couch, sitting hopefully next to a phone that wasn't going to ring.

■ ■ ■

Ricardo Vera, still dripping from a morning swim in his backyard lap pool, sat on his veranda, staring out at the Atlantic Ocean. His breakfast arrived on a platter.

Mushroom tea. Two pieces of whole wheat toast. And a side-order of blue-green algae.

"Gracias, Manuel," he said to his butler.

Ricardo, whose family made a fortune first in Cuba and then in the United States, had long ago stopped eating the sugar that made him rich.

His brother, Julio, was the sugar eater. Julio was 69, only a year older than Ricardo, and he was often mistaken by newcomers at Palm Beach social functions for Ricardo's father.

It didn't matter, because as the years went by, Ricardo went to fewer and fewer of those functions. That was Julio's passion, always overdoing it on destructive food, phony women and work.

Ricardo just had three passions these days. Swim. Bike. Run.

The brothers, who shared the oceanfront Palm Beach home, wouldn't be caught dead living each other's lives.

Ricardo couldn't imagine ever making the hourlong drive to their Belle Glade mill every morning to work when he really didn't have to.

And Julio couldn't imagine swimming 2.4 miles, then cycling 112 miles, and finally running 26.2 for the Ironman Triathlon in Hawaii — something nobody ever has to do.

As Ricardo sat staring contentedly at the ocean, he thought about the day before him. It would be like all the others, a training day. Today's schedule called for an afternoon cycling workout. He thought about beating his usual path up and down the beachfront A1A roadway.

Then he remembered the credit card sitting on the dining room table.

After he had gotten back from his run yesterday, he looked up the name in the phone book and wrote down the Boynton Beach address.

He'd just send it to her in the mail, he thought. But suppose it's the wrong Lois Rodgers. Maybe he should just call her, to make sure she was the one.

The more he thought about his brief, strange encounter with Lois, the more it intrigued him. Ricardo was so used to women who threw themselves all over him, it was refreshing to meet one who seemed so repulsed.

He could never tell whether the Palm Beach women loved him for his charm, or whether it was strictly his money.

For once, he'd like to rely on charm alone. Win a woman

the hard way, the right way.

Lois seemed like a challenge. Like the Queen K highway on the big island of Hawaii, where the crosswinds sometimes blow at 60 miles an hour, taking the heart of many cyclists.

Ricardo smiled to no one but himself, stood up and breathed a big gulp of the ocean breeze and raised his fists in the air to salute his new challenge.

He'd just cycle out to her place later that day. Deliver the card in person. He had nothing to lose. He'd still be getting a workout.

Manuel brought a road atlas out to the veranda, and Ricardo mapped his course to Shady Palms. He gulped down the rest of his algae and prepared his bike for the adventure.

■ ■ ■

Mort Granger spent the morning working the phones. Stacks of the latest edition of *The Shady Palms Gazette* would soon be delivered from the printer and left in piles all around his cramped clubhouse office.

It was going to be a great edition, Mort told himself, the kind of groundbreaking condo journalism that you don't see every day.

Which was why he was on the phone. Mort was making sure that all the local news organizations were paying attention to the story broken by his beloved little paper.

Mort knew tipping the press infuriated the board members of Shady Palms, which was another reason he liked doing it.

They told him he was giving Shady Palms a bad name to the rest of the community. He said Shady Palms already had a bad name, and he was just telling the truth. They had tried shutting him up by taking away his clubhouse office, cutting off support of the newspaper and firing him as editor and publisher.

But Mort had taken them to court and won. The paper had been part of the original vision of Shady Palms, and its existence and independence had been written in stone. Mort had the job as long as he wanted it.

Over the years, Mort had cultivated a file of media contacts, a bunch of young punks, actually, who showed little respect for Mort and usually cut him short when he tried to impress them with stories about "the golden years of journalism."

He'd get their attention this time.

"It's just a courtesy call," Mort was telling the guy from *The Sentinel*. "I've already called *The Post*, and I didn't want to play favorites here. I didn't want you to wake up and see the story on the front page of the other paper and wonder why I didn't call you ...No, I'm telling you. This is bigger than the story about the car in the clubhouse swimming pool."

It was like pulling teeth sometimes. He had wasted their time once or twice before, overpromoting a story that turned out to be slightly different from what he had advertised. And since then, these reporters had a wariness in dealing with him.

The only guy he could count on was a sociopathic former refrigerator salesman named Wally Lovell, who stormed out of the display room one day after losing a sale on a side-by-side, ice-maker-on-the-door Amana, and began a journey of self-discovery. The journey led to a small AM radio station in West Palm Beach, which didn't care what Wally said, as long as he sold advertising on his program.

Wally took the on-air name of Walter Wallbanger, and his brand of nuke-the-gay-whales commentary, peppered with conspiracy theory validations and the assumption that any majority opinion or elected official is wrong, fit in perfectly with the growing cynicism of the county populace.

Mort saved the call to Walter Wallbanger for last. As expected, Wally despised the majority opinion, which he sensed from Mort's description was that the condo residents didn't want the pregnant woman to stay.

"This is terrible," he told Mort.

"On the contrary," Mort said. "As my editorial pointed out, we have to be cognizant of precedent, and if we allow ..."

"Be quiet, Mort," Wallbanger said. "I'm thinking ...What about tomorrow's show? You could represent the view of the fascist condo majority, and then I need the woman. Can you get her on the air with me? It could just be a phoner from the condo."

"I don't know, Wally. I can try," Mort said.

"Don't try. Do it, my friend."

"It's just that I'm not sure if ..." Mort was saying.

But Walter Wallbanger wasn't listening. He was thinking about taking the story to the next level, about doing something that couldn't be ignored by the rest of the media in town. They always ignored him. They conspired against him. They knew he was the best, and they held him down by ignoring him, pretending that he wasn't telling the pure, unadulterated truth five mornings a week and three hours on Saturday mornings.

"Don't let me down, Mort," he said. "This is going to be big, bigger than the both of us."

"It is?"

Mort hung up the phone and wondered why he didn't feel better about what he had just done.

14 Señor Peppy: the reluctant bandito

Sam Hamstein stopped at a Cracker Barrel for lunch somewhere in North Florida.

"Just one," he told the hostess inside the restaurant, holding up a finger for emphasis.

He was going to have to explain this solo trip to his mom and dad. It'd be easier if he and Jasmine had a fight about something, if there was a specific event that defined their distance.

At least a guy who comes home unexpectedly and finds his wife in bed with somebody else has a defining moment.

Sam had nothing. His third wedding anniversary was in a couple of weeks, and he and Jasmine had not even a raised-voice spat to show for it.

His parents would never understand, Sam thought, as the hostess led him to a small table in the back.

Bernie and Rose had their share of loud fights. Sam remembered his father spending many a night on the living room couch, or his mother locking herself in the bathroom and crying until Bernie came with a screwdriver and removed the door.

Maybe that was the element missing in Sam's marriage. He couldn't imagine Jasmine locking herself in the bathroom

and crying, and he couldn't imagine himself ever trying to get
her out.

He had thought they had a higher form of love, something
more cerebral than the average couple you see fighting with
each other on that television show, *Cops*. But maybe he didn't
know anything at all.

Marriage might be as incomprehensible as those DNA
strands that captivated Jasmine's attention so completely. He had
read her dissertation, trying to make sense of the twisting
double-helixes and the coded messages they contained, but it
had all evaded him.

Just like she didn't understand him, sometimes. On the
rare occasions when she did come with him to a comedy club,
he'd see her looking up at him as he stood on the stage, and
unlike the strangers in the audience, her smile would be forced.

She could appreciate the intricacies of genetic engineering,
but she couldn't appreciate a good comedic premise. He knew,
even though she never told him, that she was always wondering
why other people found his humor so funny.

Sam did a whole segment on what it was like for a white
guy to be married to a black woman. It was his best material, but
he performed it only once in front of her. It wasn't that she was
angry afterward. She just said she didn't get the point.

"Everybody else did," he had said.

"But so much of it wasn't true," she said, not angrily, but
more with a sense of trying to decipher it.

"It's comedy," he had said. "It doesn't have to be true. It
just has to smack of truth to be funny."

"I guess I don't like when something just smacks of truth,"
she said. "I prefer the real thing."

He thought of explaining to Jasmine that if he had told the
real story about their marriage, about how the black woman he
had married was actually a DNA researcher who was much
smarter than anybody he had ever known, it wouldn't be funny.

It was funnier re-creating her to conform with the

audience's expectations, he would have said. But he didn't. The truth, he had figured, was that he had been foolish to perform the bit in front of her.

Sam sat in the restaurant, watching as a father at the next table slugged his son hard on the arm for sneaking french fries from his sister's plate. The boy, who couldn't have been more than 7, had a startled look at first, turning to gaze into his father's eyes — as if there might be some mistake as to where the blow came from — before allowing himself to cry from the physical pain of it.

"Chicken and dumplings," Sam told the waitress, handing her the menu.

There was nothing to do but tell his parents the truth. He had run away from home and from his wife. Why? He wasn't sure. For how long? Who knows?

Maybe, after a few days with Bernie and Rose, those veteran marital pugilists, he'd find what was missing in his own marriage.

The next time Sam looked at the people at the next table, the father was hugging his son, kissing him on the head and telling him he was sorry for losing his temper over the french fry. The boy caught Sam staring at him, and when the boy's eyes met his, the youngster made a little "o" with his mouth.

That's when Sam realized his own eyes were welling with tears. Before he could get the napkin up from his lap, one of them ran down his cheek and splashed in his dumplings.

■ ■ ■

Jake Fisher walked in the rear entrance of Kidz-a-Poppin' at 20 minutes past 2.

"You're late," said Cheryl, one of the party hostesses, as she breezed by him with empty soda pitchers in her hand. "Howard's been asking about you already."

"Howard today? Oh, no," Jake said. Howard was the day manager he liked the least.

"Hurry," Cheryl said. "We've got a big party going on. And

they're all asking about Señor Peppy."

"What age?" he asked.

"You don't want to know."

"Four?"

She nodded.

Jake walked back to the closet that served as his dressing room and quickly got into his Mexican bandit outfit, which did not pass the sniff test.

Jake Fisher was looking for an acting job, but the best he could find was playing Señor Peppy at Kidz-a-Poppin'.

"I thought this was getting laundered yesterday," he shouted to no one.

Out beyond the double doors, the din of kids' screams, video games and the constant loudspeaker announcements mixed with the smell of overused deep-fat fryer oil, spilled Pepsi and sweaty socks.

Jake put on the bandoleer, the sombrero and the fake mustache. He looked in the mirror one last time.

Now, this would have been a good picture to have in the newspaper that morning, instead of that minister cowering behind his wife outside the jail.

A picture of Señor Peppy the pervert would have brightened up many a day. He had watched the relief in his mother's eyes earlier that morning.

Jacqui had pretended to have only a cursory interest in the paper, as if this was just another day of glancing at the headlines before heading off to the mall to walk with her friends.

Jake sat on the couch, watching *Good Morning America* and observing her out of the corner of his eye. He saw her shoulders relax after she found the story about the police sting. There was no mention of him in the story. The minister, once again, had dominated the coverage.

Before she went on her walk that morning, Jacqui had come up to him and sat down next to him, showing him the story.

"No problem," she had told him.

"Viva Señor Peppy," he said, trying to sound carefree.

"Don't worry, Jacob," she had said, before leaving. "I'll take care of you."

He wondered what she had meant by that.

Señor Peppy walked out of the double doors, and as always, his appearance brought the din to a higher level. Jake took measure of the first wave of children heading for him. He drew out both of his six-shooters and fired off a couple of pop-pop rounds in their direction.

"Yee-hah!" he screamed. "Take that, Jankees."

A couple of kids clutched their hearts and dropped in playful death, another few burst into tears from the shock of it, and a few more did a 180, quickly running for the safety of their mothers' skirts.

But Jake wasn't looking for those kids. He was looking for the ones who would just keep charging. There were always a few of them in the group, the ones who were oblivious to his size, his menacing apparel and his cap guns.

These were the kids who made life difficult for Señor Peppy. He could see two of them now. He watched them, as they charged with mouths wide open and fists closed. He could hear parental admonitions in their wakes, but he knew from experience that the parents wouldn't be loud enough or quick enough to stop their children now.

Señor Peppy would have to fend for himself and do it in a way that didn't include laying a hand on any of these valuable paying customers.

Jake quickly holstered his pistols in time to fend off one of

his attackers with each hand, leaving them swinging wildly but
out of range with their short arms.

Just when he thought he had taken care of the first assault
of the day, he realized he had miscalculated. It hadn't been two
children charging him. There was another boy, running so close
behind one of the other two that Jake hadn't noticed him at first.

But as they had approached Señor Peppy, the third boy
broke to the middle, running between the other two.

Jake knew it was going to hurt. The boy was a redhead.

The boy's first windmill punch was a direct hit to the groin.
Jake dropped to both knees and used all the strength he had left
in his body not to strangle the little monster on the way down.

By the time Cheryl came to his aid, he had taken a karate
chop to the back of the neck and had one of his six-shooters
swiped from his holster.

"C'mon, Señor Peppy," Cheryl said, shooing the kids away
as she helped him to his feet. "We've got to get you to sing happy
birthday to Ricky."

She patted the head of Ricky, the redheaded kid who had
floored him. Ricky smiled a triumphant grin at Jake and shot
him with his own six-shooter.

Jake yanked the gun from the boy's hand and put it in his
holster.

He got to his feet and started walking slowly to the party
room. On the way, he noticed a man with a video camera, Ricky's
dad, taping it all.

His camera was following Señor Peppy's staggering trek to
the party room. Jake tried not to look at him, but he couldn't
help noticing that the man was laughing hysterically and
recounting to his wife how their darling son had bashed Señor
Peppy. Jake could make out the words America's Funniest
Videos coming from the man's mouth.

Funny for him, maybe.

"Hey, Señor Peppy," the man shouted as Jake got closer.
"You got anything to say to the camera about the pounding you

just took from my kid?"

"Now that you mention it," Jake said, stopping a foot from the man's face. "I do have something to say."

Cheryl, the hostess, knew it was trouble. Because Señor Peppy wasn't using his fake Mexican voice, and Señor Peppy always used his fake Mexican voice when he was in front of customers.

She squeezed Jake's arm and tried to get him to keep walking. But Jake wasn't budging.

Thinking back on it later, Jake couldn't remember the exact words he had spoken. But he remembered that he had suggested what the man could do with his camera, and in that single sentence reply, Jake had used the most forbidden word in the English language as a noun, a verb and twice as an adjective.

He had delivered his line dramatically, Jake remembered, and Howard, the day manager, had walked up just in time to catch his performance.

Howard got between the two men and faced Jake. Howard's line was easier to remember. It was delivered to Jake and contained only a single word.

"Adios."

15 Lois: A new pig in the pen

Margo turned down the television's volume with the remote control and picked up the phone on the second ring.

It was Bill.

She figured he was calling to apologize for the way he had behaved yesterday in her apartment, and she would be professional, but not too quick to forgive, either. But Bill began talking as if nothing had been said between them.

"Listen, things are starting to happen on this end," he said. "And I need you to keep an eye on somebody over there. I know this is risky. You're just getting settled there."

"No, that's fine. Who?"

"A guy named Hamstein. Bernie Hamstein."

There was a silence.

"Margo?"

"Yeah, I got it."

"What's the matter?"

After a pause, she said, "Nothing."

"Do you know him?"

"I'm eating dinner with him and his wife tonight."

"Great."

No it's not, Margo thought.

■ ■ ■

Lois Rodgers wasn't expecting an afternoon visitor, but it wasn't unusual for one of her friends to stop by for a cup of coffee. She was wondering if she had enough pound cake in the cupboard when she answered the knock on her door.

To her heart-clutching surprise, she saw a short man in black spandex shorts, a skin-tight shirt with a zipper down the middle, and a pair of goggle-like sunglasses resting on top of a mane of sweaty, gray hair.

Lois immediately slammed the door and fastened the chain.

"Go away!" she shouted. "I'll call the security guard."

"You mean Hector?" Ricardo said. "He is a nice guy."

Hector had been more than helpful to Ricardo. Maybe it was their common Cuban heritage. Or maybe that crisp $50 bill he put in the pudgy guard's shirt pocket.

Either way, after Ricardo pedaled up to the gate at Shady Palms, Hector told him all he needed to know. Lois Rodgers was a classy broad all right. And yes, she was divorced and lived alone. But she was one tough cookie.

"You know, I flirt around with a lot of the ladies," Hector had told him. "There's plenty of loneliness inside these gates. At first, like you, I noticed this Rodgers woman. Nicest-looking woman in this whole place. So naturally, I tried a little extra hard with her, you know. Trying to be charming and all. But it just makes things worse. She's something else, man. One cold broad. Muchacha fria."

Ricardo had laughed at that.

"You're crazy to make a play for that one," Hector said.

"The heart is crazy, my friend," Ricardo said.

"What's that beeping sound?" Hector asked.

"That is Ricardo's heart."

"Is it going crazy?"

"No, Ricardo is below his target heart rate now," he said, holding up his shirt to show the black strap around his chest.

Ricardo was still beeping as he stood outside Lois' door, listening to her fingers fumbling with the chain.

"Come, Lois. Ricardo is not here to hurt you. Ricardo, once again, has come to save you."

"How do you know my name?" she asked, her voice muffled by the door that separated them.

"It is on your credit card, the one you dropped in the parking garage yesterday. After you pulled away, Ricardo found it and ran after you down the street, trying to give it back to you. But you did not see Ricardo."

He slid the VISA card under the door.

She picked it up. It was hers, all right. So that explained him chasing her down the street. But it didn't explain why he was here now.

"You could have just sent this in the mail," she said.

"But how would Ricardo know it was the right Lois Rodgers?" he said.

She quickly popped open the door so that it strained against the chain, which was still in place.

"Listen up, Ricardo. If you're going to continue to speak to me, you're going to have to stop referring to yourself in the third person. You should say, 'How would I know if it was the right Lois Rodgers?' Not, 'How would Ricardo know?' Got that?"

He smiled.

"Ricardo will ... I will try."

"And furthermore, you're beeping again. Maybe it doesn't bother you, but ..."

He switched off his heart rate monitor and smiled.

"No problem, Lois."

"So why didn't you call? I'm in the book. I assume that's how you found the address."

"Yes, but the telephone is so impersonal," Ricardo said. "And besides, Ricardo would still ... I would still ... have to get you the card somehow."

"And this outfit you're wearing?"

"Cycling," Ricardo said.

"Ugh. What, are you in some senior citizen's branch of the Hell's Angels?"

"No, not motorcycle. Bicycle."

"You rode a bicycle here?"

"See?" he said, fetching his bike from its resting place against a wall in the corridor.

"Where do you live?"

"West Palm," he lied.

If he told her Palm Beach, she'd begin wondering whether he was rich, and then he'd never know how he was really doing with her. But West Palm Beach was a different story.

"And you rode your bicycle from West Palm to west Boynton?"

He nodded and said, "Twenty-five miles."

She shook her head.

"Well, thank you for returning the credit card," she said. "I have a busy afternoon planned so …"

"You are lucky Ricardo found it," he said. "Somebody else might have grabbed it, and you would not find out until you had thousands of dollars charged against it."

"Yes," she said. "Well I …"

"So, once again, you were fortunate to have met somebody like Ricardo … I mean, me."

"Yes, yes," she said. "Wait here a second."

She left the door cracked but with the chain still attached. A moment later she came back with the same $10 bill she had offered him the previous day. She thrust it through the door at him.

"Take it this time," she said. "You deserve it for all the trouble you've been through."

"Trouble? No trouble," he said. "I do not want your money, but I would like a refill of my water bottle."

He pulled an empty drink bottle from his bicycle and waved it in front of her.

"You need a lot of water on a hot day like today," he said.

She extended her hand past the door, and he passed her the empty bottle. She left him there again to refill it.

He could hear the rumble of thunder outside. An afternoon storm was approaching. Lois returned with the full bottle and handed it to him.

"A storm," Ricardo said.

"You'd better hurry," she said, "or you'll get wet."

"No," Ricardo said. "It is better waiting for it to pass."

"Suit yourself," Lois said. "I've got to go now, Ricardo."

"You know what Ricardo would really like, is if you would let him … I mean, me … take you to dinner. That would be …"

"Impossible," she said. "I'm married."

"No, you are not," he said. "Divorced three times. Hector told Ricardo."

She made a mental note to say something nasty to Hector.

"Listen, Ricardo. I don't know any other way to tell you this, but I'm not interested."

"You just have not given it a chance," he said. "Men have treated you badly. You just need to meet a good one, and lucky you, you just did."

A little man with an earring, who still rides a bicycle and runs in parking garages? She didn't think so.

"Goodbye, Ricardo," she said, and then she closed the door and locked it.

She could hear him sigh, and then the clickety-clack of his bicycle as he walked it down the hallway of the condo. By then, the leading edge of the storm was quickly approaching. A few big drops pelted her windows, and the winds picked up, making the palm trees rustle and sway.

Lois walked to her window, sneaking a peak through half-opened blinds at the front entrance of C Building. She watched as Ricardo wheeled his bike out the door and paused, looking up at the sky.

He wasn't really that short, she thought. Probably an inch or so above her 5-foot-5.

Ricardo sat under the awning on the AstroTurf rug, fiddling with the chain on his bicycle.

What a strange man, she thought. Lois was used to men chasing her all her life, and even her cancer hadn't changed that. Doctors, lawyers, businessmen. She had her share of suitors. But never anything like this one. She looked at Ricardo, playing with his bicycle like a little kid, and for a second, thought about asking him up for a cup of coffee.

But it was only for a second.

Then she said aloud: "Get a grip, Lois. Men are pigs."

An hour later, the storm had passed. Lois took another look at the front entrance. There was a part of her, she realized, that was hoping Ricardo would still be there.

But he was gone.

■ ■ ■

Jacqui answered the phone.

"OK, girl, you ready to go tonight?"

It was Maddy.

"Go where?"

"You know, like we talked about," Maddy said.

"Maddy, I don't know if I … well … if I can …"

"What, is Jacob there?"

"No, he went to work this afternoon. He won't be back until later tonight."

"That'll work out great," Maddy said. "Leave him a note. Tell him you and I went out to dinner and a movie."

"Maddy?"

"Yes."

"Have you ever done this before?"

"Done what?"

"Go to a gay bar?"

"No."

"Then how can you be so calm about it? I mean how can you just, you know …"

"Gay. Straight. Hey, it's all the same. People out trying to meet other people. We'll just see if there's anybody there who might be nice for your boy, Jacob."

"And if we find somebody, then what?"

"Don't worry, girl. You'll know what to do."

There was a pause.

"Maddy?"

"Yes."

"I have a question. How do you find a gay bar?"

"Oh, that's simple. You look for those flags."

"Flags?"

"Yeah, I'm sure you've seen them. They're these flags with horizontal stripes in the colors of the rainbow."

"Those flags?"

"Yeah, those are the ones. I've seen a couple of bars on Dixie Highway with them flying out front."

"You mean, that rainbow flag, that means gay?"

"Yes, it does."

"How did you know that?"

"I thought everybody knew that."

"I didn't know that."

"I guess not."

"You know what I thought those rainbow flags were for?"

"What?"

"Greenpeace."

16 Lucky break for Ricardo

Bernie Hamstein was disappointed that no one had called about the dog. He'd waited by the phone all morning and half the afternoon, but not a single caller had responded to his signs.

The rain was ending, and the Hamstein condo was the kind of clean it reached only on those rare occasions when important company was imminent. Rose was just finishing up the guest bathroom.

"Lucky probably needs to potty," she called out.

Bernie looked over at the mutt. He jumped off the couch, tail wagging.

"And then I need you to go to Publix," Rose said. "We need to get some coffee. Sam and Jasmine don't drink decaf."

Sam and Jasmine were due in a couple of hours. Rose had made a big lasagna after she got back from her mall walk. That's when she told Bernie about inviting Margo over for dinner, too.

"You should have seen her, Bernie," Rose had said. "I felt so bad for her, being alone at a time like this, with her boyfriend talking about abortion. It's terrible."

"Rose," Bernie had said. "It's wonderful to befriend someone in need, but you know the situation with this woman as well as I do. There's going to be an uproar about her living at Shady Palms, and we can't ..."

"I don't want to hear it, Bernie," she had said, cutting him off. "Take out the dog."

That's the other thing Bernie didn't like about having a dog. Why was he the one who had to walk the dog and pick up after him? But that was the way it was shaping up. He would start airing some grievance with Rose, and she'd tell him to take out the dog. Or like this afternoon, she'd be in the other room doing work with the sense that he was idle, so she'd tell him to take out the dog.

Bernie grumbled something under his breath, not loud enough for Rose to hear him, and then headed for the hallway door, Lucky happily in his wake.

Rose had bought a leash for the dog that day, a sure sign she had already considered Lucky a permanent resident. But Bernie wasn't ready to acknowledge that yet. He left the leash on the dining room table, choosing to take only the item next to it, a plastic Publix bag, which he would use to clean up after Lucky.

Bernie had walked the dog this way earlier in the day. He half expected him to bolt when he got outside, but Lucky seemed to know where he belonged already. The dog had allowed himself to get only a few yards away from Bernie before trotting back.

Lucky wasn't about to run away, Bernie realized, dashing a secret hope. That would have been best, Bernie thought. To be able to tell Rose that the dog was a free spirit, that after a day with them, he yearned to be free, to be out on his own again.

If only it were true. If only he weren't licking Bernie's shins as he led him outside for the second time that day. The dog sat next to him on the elevator and waited for him to open the front door leading out to a short covered walkway and finally the C Building parking lot.

The grassy strips between the rows of cars were all Lucky had as far as nearby green space. Bernie led the dog to the nearest strip, and Lucky began sniffing for the right place. But something was different this time. The dog's head jerked up

suddenly, his nose twitching, his ears now swiveling to a position
Bernie had not seen before.

Bernie followed Lucky's stare to a stray cat silently making
her way toward the C Building dumpster corral across the
parking lot. The cat was pretending not to notice Lucky, who was
now emitting a low growl from somewhere deep in his chest.

Bernie waited to see what would happen next. He didn't
have to wait long. Lucky took off, faster than Bernie ever
imagined the dog could run, but not faster than the cat.

The cat looped around behind where Bernie was standing
and then headed up the road leading to the clubhouse.

"Lucky, come back here," Bernie said once. But he didn't
have his heart in it.

He thought about just walking inside and telling Rose that
the dog had run away. But he knew he first needed to show
some effort, to at least come in panting from a brief chase.

So Bernie started lumbering up the drive, feeling his heart
beating far too fast. He was shuffling in his white patent leather
shoes, his lime green socks starting to droop now, bunching up
around his ankles.

He would give up the chase in just a few more steps. He
had done enough. By the time he walked back inside, he knew
his polyester sports shirt would have dark patches of sweat, and
Rose could never accuse him of not trying to get Lucky back.

Then Bernie's heart really got a jolt. He was startled to
hear a voice right next to him.

"That your dog?" the man said to Bernie.

"No ... well, yes. I guess it is," Bernie said, regaining his
composure. "Sorry, you scared ... me."

Bernie turned to see a man about his age sitting on a
souped-up bicycle with long, low handlebars, bladed spoke
wheels and thin racing tires. But he didn't spend too long
looking at the bike, because the man sitting on it was even more
exotic looking to Bernie, and that's without noticing the earring
yet.

The chase had now left the road, and Lucky was chasing

Ricardo Vera takes matters into his own hands at Shady Palms.

the cat on the lawns between the condo buildings.

"Do not worry," the man told Bernie, stepping off the bicycle and motioning for Bernie to hold it there. "Ricardo will catch your dog."

"Who's Ricardo?" Bernie said.

Bernie got his answer when the man popped off his cleated cycling shoes and took off running in his socks after the dog.

Bernie picked up the cycling shoes and wheeled the man's bicycle back to the entrance of C Building, resting the bike against an awning pole.

After 10 minutes, he began to worry. Maybe the guy had a heart attack running as fast as he was going. Bernie thought he should probably get in his car and start looking for the guy. But he didn't want to leave the bicycle unattended, so he called Rose on the lobby phone and explained everything.

Two minutes later, she came downstairs. Bernie left her there with the bicycle while he got in his car and began driving around Shady Palms, looking for a little man in cycling shorts chasing after a dog he wished he never saw again.

No luck. After five minutes, Bernie circled back to C Building, and there was that Ricardo fellow standing next to his bike and talking to Rose, who was holding Lucky in her arms now.

By the time Bernie got out of the car and began walking

across the lot, Ricardo had mounted his bicycle and was beginning to pedal away.

"Hey, thanks a lot," Bernie shouted, waving his hand.

"Thank you," Ricardo said, waving back before he dropped his hands down on the black aero bars that extended over his front wheel. Then he pedaled away at an impressive speed.

"Look at him go," Bernie said as he approached Rose.

"You missed it," she said.

"Missed what?"

"Seeing him catch Lucky. He dove, right over there by that berm. Just left his feet, stretched out like Superman, arms way out in front of him, fingers reaching the back end of Lucky before he hit the ground."

"And he hung on?"

"Sure did," Rose said.

"What a strange guy," Bernie said. "We should have at least offered him a drink."

"I did," she said. "And he wouldn't take it. He wanted something else instead."

"Something else? What do you mean?"

"I don't have time to explain now, Bernie. I need you to add a few things to your list at Publix."

She told him what she needed. Bernie turned to head back to his car. But she stopped him with a question to his back.

"Now, why did you take Lucky outside without a leash? You're not trying to lose him are you, Bernie?"

"Lose him? Rose, what a thing to say. I just … just forgot the leash. That's all."

As he drove toward the supermarket, his mind kept going back to the little man on the bicycle, in particular, the last thing he had said to Bernie.

Bernie could swear the man said, "Thank you."

"Why in the world would he be thanking me?" Bernie asked himself in the empty car. "What did I ever do for him?"

Bernie had the unsettling feeling he would soon find out.

17 Sam and Margo compare notes

"Thanks," Sam Hamstein said to Margo after she joined him on the screened patio overlooking the C Building parking lot.

"For what?" Margo asked.

"For giving me some breathing room with them," Sam said, motioning with his head beyond the sliding glass doors.

Inside, Bernie and Rose were cleaning up the dinner mess, taking plates from the dining room to the kitchen, loading the dishwasher and wrapping up the leftovers.

Bernie had insisted he and Rose could handle the cleanup faster without the help of their guests and suggested they relax on the "veranda," as he called it. The night was still sticky, but it felt good to be out in real, rather than conditioned, air.

Lucky joined them, stretching out on the AstroTurf carpet, resting his head on his paws and narrowing his eyes to a squint.

"I didn't know you needed breathing room," Margo said.

Sam laughed.

"Yeah, well … these past four days as I was driving cross country, I kept thinking about this first meal and what it would be like. I imagined a lot of awkward silences and hard questions to answer. I had come to dread it. But 15 minutes after I arrive, there's a knock on the door and there you are."

Sam looked at her now, trying to remember what it was first like seeing her at the door, holding out a box of cherry cordials to his mother.

"If I'd known their son was coming from out of town, I would have …" Margo started to say.

"No," Sam interrupted. "It was perfect. I'm thanking you. You see, my parents never had a daughter. I'm the youngest of three boys. They tried once more after me, and my mom had a miscarriage. So they gave up. 'It wasn't meant to be,' was how my mom put it.

"When they opened the door to you, and the way they welcomed you into their condo, it was as if I was seeing a sister walk in. The way my mother was fussing over you was quite touching."

"Yes, I feel bad about the …"

"No, Margo. Don't feel bad. It was great. How did you know about the cherry cordials?"

"I asked one of your mom's friends for advice on what I could bring them," Margo said.

"You know, if I was 15 minutes later, we might have both bumped into each other on the elevator, both of us standing there holding boxes of cherry cordials."

Margo laughed.

"You mean, you also …"

"Stopped at the mall to pick them up on the way."

There was an awkward silence. Sam was looking out in the parking lot, thinking of something. Margo looked at him closely now, trying to figure out if he could somehow end up looking like Bernie when he got older.

"You know what I can't figure out," Sam said, "is why they were making such a big fuss over you. Don't take it the wrong way. At first I thought it was because you were young and …"

He almost said "pretty" because he thought Margo was pretty. But he didn't want to say it to her, not now. He wasn't in the habit of telling women he hardly knew that he found them attractive.

"… that a young woman in Shady Palms is a novelty. But that wasn't it. Then I thought maybe my arrival had triggered off some latent chemistry. That seeing you and me sitting across the table from them made you seem more like a daughter, the daughter they never had. But I have the nagging sense that wasn't it, either."

"You ought to be a detective," Margo said.

"You don't have cancer, or anything, do you?"

"No, I don't have cancer."

"But you have something?"

"I'm pregnant."

"Pregnant," Sam said, feeling disappointed despite himself. "Congratulations."

He had noticed an empty ring finger on her left hand, but it was her empty smile now that told him more.

"Sorry," he said. "I'm not usually so nosy. Maybe it's this place. Two hours at Shady Palms and you just can't help wanting to know everybody else's business."

"I guess they didn't tell you," she said.

"No," he said. "Unfortunately, we didn't stray far from the subject of me during the 15 minutes I've been alone with them."

"I made a scene in front of your mother and her friends this morning during their mall walk," she said.

"Some people will do anything to get some of my mother's lasagna."

"I guess I was acting pretty pathetic."

"Pregnant in Shady Palms," Sam said. "It sounds like a supermarket tabloid headline. Woman expected to give birth to 80-year-old man complaining of bursitis."

Margo wasn't laughing this time.

"Hey, I'm sorry. I think I had too much wine at dinner," Sam said.

He wanted to ask her why she was here. Why a woman her age would move to a place like this. But he didn't know how to phrase the question.

"I wish nobody knew," she said.

The day Margo suspected she might be pregnant, she made a trip to the nearby Eckerd Drugs and bought one of those home pregnancy kits. After the water turned purple, she took a walk outside to let the news settle in.

She found herself crying in the clubhouse restroom. She thought she was alone, until a woman in tennis whites walked out of a stall.

"I'm fine," Margo had told her.

"If you're sick, I can call 911," the woman had said.

"No, it's nothing," Margo had said. "I'm just ... pregnant. That's all."

She remembered the way her voice sounded in that bathroom, the way the word "pregnant" bounced off those tiled walls. She said it just to hear herself say the word out loud, to hear what it would sound like.

She didn't tell anyone else, not even Bill, until her pregnancy had become common knowledge in Shady Palms.

Margo had no way of knowing that the woman in the bathroom was Jane Kravitz from F Building. Kravitz was in the bathroom dealing with pre-match jitters. Minutes later, she would walk onto the nearby courts to join her doubles partner, Gilda Troutman, the same Gilda Troutman who was married to Herb Troutman, chairman of the governing board of building presidents. So it didn't take long for Margo's condition to spread to the far reaches of all 12 buildings of Shady Palms.

"You don't seem too happy about being pregnant," Sam said.

Margo shrugged.

"There are complications," she said, letting it drop at that.

"I hope you work them out."

"Yes. Well ... and what about your complications? You said you needed breathing room from your parents."

"You know what's funny?" Sam said. "All during dinner, we talked continuously, yet we didn't talk about the two most important things in our lives. You being pregnant, and me ..."

He saw her looking intently at him now, as if she was really interested in his life. It made him feel good.

"Take a guess, Margo. Guess correctly, and you move on to the lightning round, where the questions get harder but the points are doubled."

"You've got cancer?"

"Hey, that square's already been used up this game. What's the matter? Are you afraid of guessing?"

He held up his left hand and pointed to his wedding band.

"She still love you, Sam?"

"I don't know."

"And you? Do you still love her?"

Bernie walked past the sliding glass doors and on to the porch, sitting down in an empty chair between them. Margo was still looking at Sam, waiting for his answer. But Sam was happy for a diversion.

"Dad," he said, slapping Bernie's knee. "Tell us a good horror story about the joys of condominium living."

Sam and Margo never did get to finish their conversation that night. Bernie talked for a while, then Rose joined them. They chatted about current events, friends' vacations, the weather and other people's problems. But they never talked about Sam's marriage or Margo's pregnancy.

Then one of his mother's friends arrived for dessert.

Sam wondered why his mom had invited Lois over. Lois seemed to wonder, too.

"It's not like I've never had the Key lime pie from Publix before," she said, as they were getting ready to sit down.

Things went along pretty smoothly until there was another knock on the door and in walked a little man with his gray hair pulled back in a mini-ponytail, a gold hoop earring in one ear and a bouquet of flowers in his arms.

"Ricardo hopes he is not late," the man said as he walked into the room.

Lois spewed Key lime pie halfway across the table, ran to the bathroom and locked herself inside for the next half-hour.

18 Cruising with Jacqui and Maddy

It took some time for everybody in the Hamstein condo to realize this was no ordinary trip to the bathroom for Lois Rodgers. They had just assumed that Ricardo Vera's surprise arrival had triggered a slight choking episode with the piece of Key lime pie. And that rather than go into a coughing fit there at the table, Lois had quickly retreated to the hallway bathroom, where she would soon regain her composure.

But after five minutes, there was still no sign of Lois. Oh, well, perhaps she was reapplying her makeup.

After 10 minutes, Rose shot a worried look at Bernie, who was too wrapped up listening to Ricardo talk about his training schedule to pay much attention.

After Lois had been in the bathroom for 15 minutes, Rose found some excuse to leave the table. Before she returned, she stopped by the bathroom door, noticing it was locked.

She knocked softly and whispered.

"Lois, you OK?"

"Go away!" Lois said.

"Lois, do you need ..."

"Go away!"

After she had been gone for 20 minutes, Sam looked around the table and, noticing for the first time, said, "Hey, what happened to Lois?"

"Bathroom," Rose said.

Five minutes later, Rose huddled with Bernie in the kitchen, whispering by the refrigerator.

"I don't think she plans to come out," Rose said.

Bernie was wondering if all women were like this, if there was something in the genes that caused them to lock themselves in the bathroom when things got tough.

"I can get a screwdriver and get her out. I think I still remember how to do it," he said, smiling like an impudent child.

"No," Rose said. "Just give me some room. Have everyone sit out on the porch. I'll talk to her through the door."

And so that's what happened. After five minutes of low-volume pleading, Lois unlocked the bathroom door, and Rose walked in.

"Are you going to tell me why you're acting this way?" Rose asked.

"You set me up, Rose."

"I didn't set you up."

"Yes, this is all some big joke to you."

"Lois, listen. This afternoon Lucky got loose and Ricardo happened to be going by on his bicycle ..."

"Man his age riding a bicycle!" Lois interjected.

"... and he ran after Lucky and brought him back. We started talking, and he told me why he was here. And ..."

"He looks like a Keebler elf," Lois said.

"No, he doesn't. He's kind of dashing in a swashbuckler kind of way."

"Spare me the commentary," Lois said.

"And so I offered him a drink. But all he wanted was to somehow get you to give him a chance."

"And so you set up this little ambush."

"I told him I would invite you over for dessert tonight, and that he could just pop by. I thought it would be a nice surprise."

"Nice surprise? You know what it's like to have a piece of

pie crust lodged in your nasal cavity?"

Rose was laughing now. She hugged her friend, who didn't return the hug but didn't reject Rose, either. Rose knew it would be all right then.

"C'mon, Lo. Go out there and be your charming self."

"Men are pigs, Rose," she said. "Don't think you can play games with me."

"I'm not playing games. I just like you, and he seems like a nice guy and I thought ..."

"Well, don't think," Lois said. "That's what gets you in trouble. Why would you assume that I would be happier if I had a man again? Is there something in writing that says a person can't be happy while being alone?"

"No, there's nothing in writing, but ..."

"But nothing. I don't need a mate, Rose. I've had more than my share."

"Are you coming out?" Rose said.

"Is he beeping tonight?"

"Who?"

"Ricardo."

"No, I didn't hear any beeps."

"Give me a minute," Lois said.

After Rose left, Lois looked at herself in the mirror, brushing her hair with her fingers. She discovered she was disappointed she wasn't wearing her red dress.

"Don't get any ideas, you old cow," she told herself in the mirror.

■ ■ ■

Maddy said she would drive, and at the appointed hour, she and Jacqui eased over the final speed bump of Shady Palms and began their adventure.

The radio was playing Gershwin's *Someone to Watch Over Me*, and Jacqui found herself singing the lyrics.

Twenty minutes later, Maddy pulled into a parking lot that was pocked like the surface of the moon.

"The Manhole, where there's never a cover," Jacqui said, reading the sign painted on the side of the shoebox-shaped building.

Maddy bounced into one of the few remaining parking spaces.

"Crowded tonight," she told her friend.

"Are you sure about this place?"

"You saw the rainbow flag out front, didn't you?"

The two women held each other's arms as they walked to the front door. They paused for a second inside the doorway, momentarily stunned by the loud music, cigarette smoke and the sight of a man wearing what appeared to be leather underwear and nothing else.

"Good evening, folks," he said to them. "Would you like a table, or would you rather sit at the bar?"

Jacqui tugged harder on her friend's arm, pulling her back toward the door. Maddy ignored her.

"I think we'll sit at the bar," Maddy said.

As they made their way to two empty seats at the bar, Jacqui noticed the dance floor, which was full of men. But what really struck her was that nearly all the men were dressed in leather.

Jacqui spotted a few other women in the room, but on second glance, she reconsidered. They were just dressed as women.

The bartender, a huge man with tattoos on both arms, walked over and took a swipe with his rag on the bar. But Jacqui hardly noticed him. She was reading the chalkboard, which said in big letters: "Leathermen 2-for-1 drink nite."

"What'll it be, ladies?"

"I'll have a vodka and tonic. Jacqui? … Jacqui?"

"Oh, sorry. Tom Collins, please."

The bartender craned his head over the bar, pretending to inspect them.

"You ladies forgot your leather tonight."

"Aw shucks," Maddy said.

"Can't give you the drink special."

"That's OK," Maddy said. "We're just here to mingle."

"Isn't everybody?" the bartender said, giving them a wink and turning away to make their drinks.

"See?" Maddy said. "He's a nice guy. I'll bet you there are lots of nice guys here. So many people get caught up in the wrapping of the package that they never consider what's inside. It's something you'd … Jacqui? …You're not even listening."

Jacqui was looking over Maddy's shoulder.

"Maddy," Jacqui whispered. "There's a man over there wearing a bullwhip."

A half-hour later, both women were sitting in the car.

"You didn't give it a chance," Maddy said, putting the keys in the ignition but not starting the car just yet.

"Let's just go," Jacqui said. "Maybe this wasn't a good idea."

"That one guy we were talking to was kind of nice. Craig was his name," Maddy said.

"Maddy, I didn't come here to find my boy a person who goes out in public wearing a gold lamé Speedo with chaps."

"Craig is a paramedic."

"Craig is an exhibitionist."

A car pulled into the parking lot, which was full now. The driver waited to see if the women would pull out and give him the spot.

"It's my fault," Jacqui said. "I should have known this wouldn't work."

"We could try more places," Maddy said. "Places where they don't wear leather, if that's what's bothering you."

"No," Jacqui said. "It's not just the leather. It's everything. It's the hugging. The slow dancing …"

"Girl, I think I know your problem. You still want Jake to walk in the door with the girl of your dreams."

Jacqui didn't answer. She just stared out the window,

glassy-eyed now.

"It ain't gonna happen, Jacqui."

Maddy started her car and backed out. The other car was still waiting. After she pulled clear, the other car passed in front of her and took her space.

"Place is just jumpin' tonight," Maddy said.

As she pulled onto the roadway, the driver who pulled into her parking spot turned off the ignition, stepped out and stretched.

Jake Fisher, like his mother, was going to the Manhole for the first time.

He had driven around most of the afternoon and evening, trying to figure out what was next. Getting fired from Kidz-a-Poppin' wasn't the worst thing in the world for him. But the job, as bad as it sometimes had been, was probably the only productive element in his life.

Maybe it was time to go back to California and write off Florida as one miserable year. After a solitary walk on the beach, a grouper-fingers dinner at Howley's, and three beers on Clematis Street, he thought he was done for the night.

But there was no need to rush back to Shady Palms, where his mother would undoubtedly be crushed by the news of Señor Peppy's profane outburst. She'd "poor Jacob" him to death. And he couldn't handle that.

He walked into the Manhole and had a seat at the bar.

He was halfway through his beer when the guy sitting next to him said, "Bad day?"

Jake looked over at him.

"Is it that obvious?"

The man was smiling now, a nice pleasant face.

"You want to tell me about it?"

And so Jake did. It took him two more beers because he ended up giving the long version. He wasn't planning to, but something in his listener's tone and questions made him want to go on.

"I'm sorry for boring you with all this," Jake said when he was finally done.

"Boring? I wasn't bored at all," the man said. "Listen pal, you're quite an improvement on the evening for me. Before you got here, I was locked in endless chitchat with a couple of granny lesbians."

"So, tell me something about yourself," Jake said.

"Sure," the man said, "But first, let's dance. I love this song."

Jake got up and followed him to the dance floor. The beers made Jake feel giddy, and he suddenly felt grateful for this moment, this music and this dance.

"My name's Jake," he shouted in the man's ear as they neared the dance floor.

The man whirled around and took Jake's hand.

"I'm Craig."

19 The get-acquainted tango

Ricardo Vera walked a step behind her, not because he wanted to but because every time he got shoulder to shoulder with Lois, she pulled ahead. So Ricardo resigned himself to trailing her down the corridor, into the elevator and out at Lois' floor.

It made him feel like a runner, staying close on the heels of the leader, waiting patiently to make his move.

"You really don't have to do this," Lois had said when Ricardo followed her out of the Hamsteins' condo.

"Yes, yes," Ricardo said. "But it is no trouble."

Lois had managed to have a good time at the Hamsteins' despite herself. After she emerged from her bathroom hideaway, she simply took her place in an empty chair, acting as if it was perfectly reasonable for a person to bolt from the others for 30 minutes without explanation.

As she sat there in the circle of friends, she was able to observe this newcomer to her life, this Ricardo, who for some reason kept finding ways to be with her. Everyone else seemed to be endlessly fascinated with his racing stories.

What Lois found most intriguing, though, was the way he would constantly refer to himself as "Ricardo" and then correct himself by saying "I" in mid-sentence. A couple of times he would shoot a look at her, as if to remind her he was trying to please her.

It was touching the way he did it, Lois thought.

Not that Lois was getting swept off her feet. He still looked like a Keebler elf to her, and the way he sat there with his heartbeat for all the world to see — 62, 63, 64, 60 constantly changing on his wrist — was like sitting next to a human stock market ticker.

Yes, he had saved her from a mugger and returned a lost credit card, but that still was no reason to make room in her life for him. Yet, she didn't stop him when he insisted on leaving the Hamsteins' with her.

When she got to her door, she fished for the key. In one quick motion, she opened the door, stepped through and wheeled around, facing Ricardo while blocking his way from following her.

Lois was looking eye to eye with him. The door was only opened a few inches beyond her head.

"Safe and sound," she said.

"Ricardo has … I have enjoyed seeing you again," he said.

"Yes, well it's late, and I'm sure you've got a long way to pedal. So good night."

"Pedal? No. Ricardo has a car."

And not just any car. Ricardo had parked his brand new Viper sports coupe in the lot for B Building, because he didn't want Lois to think he had $75,000 to throw away on what was actually his third car.

"I just assumed you rode your bike everywhere," she said.

"See, you think you know Ricardo, but you do not."

"Listen, Ricardo. I appreciate your gallantry, but you are wasting your time with me."

"You are a beautiful woman, Lois."

"It's not going to work, Ricardo. I didn't let you in this afternoon, and I'm not going to let you in now."

"Just to talk to you through the door is enough," Ricardo said.

"Goodnight," she said.

But she didn't close the door. She stood there waiting. For what, she wondered?

"Ricardo is ... I am going to be riding my bike a lot this week, and I might be in the neighborhood. Maybe I will stop by ... you know, just to get the water bottle filled."

"I'm out a lot during the day."

"Then perhaps Ricardo will die of thirst," he said, winking at her.

Before she could react, Ricardo darted like a cat, sliding quickly to cover the space between them, rested his hands lightly on her shoulders and gave her a feathery kiss on the cheek.

"Well," she said, flustered.

By then, Ricardo had already retreated back to the hallway.

"Goodnight, Lois," he said.

Lois put the chain on the door and bolted it. She put her back to it, listening to his footsteps recede down the hallway.

When it was quiet again, she walked to her window and peered through the blinds, waiting to see him walk out.

But when she saw him, he wasn't walking, he was running, running past the rows of parked cars in the C Building lot and into the night.

At first she thought he was chasing something or someone again, but when he got halfway across the lot, he spun around and waved in the direction of her window.

She quickly moved away from the blinds, hoping he didn't see her there.

Ricardo ran all the way to his car. His heart monitor was flashing 115 when he stopped. Ricardo stood there, watching with pride as the most prized muscle of his body went to work, quickly circulating blood through his legs. And now, as he caught his breath, he watched the numbers begin to tumble. An untrained heart would still be beating wildly, but Ricardo's heart was no ordinary heart.

He opened the door and got behind the wheel of the Viper. Yes. His heart was back to the low 60s. That was good, he thought.

And Lois was back in her condo wondering if this Ricardo knew more about hearts than she had ever imagined. This was not so good, she thought.

■ ■ ■

Sam Hamstein wished he had the nerve to walk Margo to her door. He had wanted to talk more to her. In the brief time they had spent chatting on the patio while his parents cleaned up the dinner mess, Sam got a sense they were connected souls somehow.

But for the rest of the evening, the conversation stayed light, bouncing from Bernie to Rose to Lois to Ricardo, with Sam and Margo doing a lot of the listening. He would shoot glances at Margo, looking at her like an unsolved crossword puzzle. And he thought he saw her looking at him, too.

Maybe it was his imagination. Maybe it was the long trip, or the longing for the kind of companionship he and Jasmine had shared in the beginning but then seemed to forget.

"Nice meeting you, Sam," Margo had said, shaking his hand before leaving. "You going to be visiting for long?"

"Yeah, well … who knows? I'll see you around. I'll probably hang out at the pool a lot," Sam said. "Maybe …"

But he never got to finish his sentence because Bernie was suddenly there, barging in with a plate of leftovers for Margo to take home. And then she left. Sam wasn't even looking up to see her go. He was on the floor, petting Lucky.

It wasn't long after Margo was gone that Rose sat on the couch near his spot on the floor.

"You've got a nice dog, Mom," Sam said.

Lucky, by then, was trying to get Sam to chase him.

"Sammy, what happened?" Rose said, ignoring his attempt to avoid the big subject.

Sam told her as best he could why he had decided to put some space between him and Jasmine. As he talked, Bernie moved closer, standing behind his wife and putting both his hands on Rose's shoulders.

"I'm hoping the separation will make us take stock in our relationship. It's time we stop taking it for granted," Sam said.

In all their years of marriage, Bernie and Rose had slept under separate roofs for three nights — the nights after their children were born. Neither could imagine what Sam was doing now.

"Why don't you go call her, tell her you're OK," Rose said.

Sam walked back into the extra bedroom, the room that would now be his for who knows how long. He looked at the pictures first. He and his two older brothers, Steven and Simon, at the park when they were just kids. His high school graduation photo. The photos of Steven's children. He and Jasmine on their honeymoon.

He picked up the telephone on the nightstand and dialed the number. She picked up on the fourth ring.

"I was hoping it was you," Jasmine said. "Where are you?"

"At my mom's and dad's."

"In Florida? I thought you were on the road this week."

She didn't even remember. He had told her he didn't have another comedy gig for the next two months.

"Listen, Jasmine …"

She cut him off.

"I've been turning the apartment upside down looking for the box of computer diskettes," she said. "You had them last. Remember? You were putting some jokes on them the other day and …"

"Forget about the diskettes, Jasmine."

"No, I need them. I have a presentation to make, and some

of my notes are on them."

"They're in the Bass shoebox in the walk-in closet. But that's not as important as …"

"The shoebox? Why do you put computer diskettes in the shoebox?" she asked in a voice with more amusement in it than anything else.

"I always have. Listen, Jasmine …"

"Hang on," she said, putting the phone down.

He could hear her walking across their apartment. A minute later, she was back.

"Yep," she said. "Here they are in the shoebox. I never would have looked there. I'm glad you called."

"About the call, Jasmine. There's something we need to …"

The phone beeped a few times.

"Hang on," she said. "I've got a call on the other line. I think it's Roger. We're doing this presentation tomorrow … Oh, just hang on a second."

She put him on hold. Sam sat there, listening to the dead line, connected across the continent, but silent.

He walked around the bedroom, now finding the wedding picture of Bernie and Rose. They never had a big wedding. They ran away and got married by a justice of the peace in Fort Lee, New Jersey. The photo, the only one they have of that day, was snapped by a passerby as they stood on the courthouse steps after a brief ceremony.

Rose had a bouquet in her hand. Bernie had the marriage license rolled in one of his. They clutched each other with their free arms. They both were wearing overcoats. Behind them, the scene looked gray and bleak. You could even see the pigeon droppings streaking the courthouse wall behind them. The wind was whipping the lapels of their coats, and some of Rose's hair had blown across her mouth.

But none of that was as striking as the look on their faces.

It was the look of triumph and of knowing that nothing was missing. That all that was necessary for a long and happy life was what they had there that day between them. And nothing could sully that.

Sam stared at the picture for the next 10 minutes, uninterrupted by the silence on the phone line.

He hung up and went to bed.

20 A Rosen by any other name

As Margo put the key in her door, she heard the phone ringing.

Nobody ever called her, especially at this hour. But since only one person knew her number, she didn't have to wonder who it was.

Bill sounded like he was calling from a bar or a bowling alley.

"How'd it go, Margo?"

She almost said "How did what go?" Because there were times this night when she completely forgot that she was working. That this wasn't real life. That she wasn't really the girl next door.

She had felt for most of the night that she was the person the Hamsteins and that lonely-eyed son of theirs thought she was.

"OK, I guess," she said.

"What'd you find out?"

Now that was a question. What did she find out? That she wished she had a mother like Rose. That she was looking forward to finding Sam sitting by the pool. That Bernie seemed so harmless. How could Bernie be somebody Bill wanted?

"I didn't find out much," she said. "They have a son who's

visiting with them."

"Is he connected?"

She laughed.

"No," she said. "He's … he's lost."

"Lost?"

"Yeah, just kind of lost."

"You sound a little lost yourself," Bill said. "Listen, I was thinking about your problem."

"It's not a problem, Bill. It's a baby."

"What I'm saying is that if you think you can't handle things there, we can …"

"No, I can handle things," she said. "Bernie's wife is taking me to a gynecologist tomorrow."

"What for?" he asked.

"To make sure everything is all right."

"Oh."

She could hear the disappointment in his voice.

"Bill, this is my baby. It has nothing to do with you."

"I was thinking back to that night, the night before you moved to Shady Palms. That was it, wasn't it?"

"Let's not talk about it."

"That was it? That's when it happened, right?"

"Listen, Bill. What happened, happened. I …"

"I plan on talking to the others about it."

"Don't you dare."

"They were wrong. I was wrong."

"Let's move on."

"I could take you to that gynecologist tomorrow."

"No you can't," she said.

■ ■ ■

Bernie was brushing his teeth, watching his wife, who was sitting in bed paging through a magazine. The lump under the comforter shifted, and Bernie knew if he didn't hurry, Lucky would take up most of his half of the bed.

He rinsed his mouth and sat next to Rose, nudging the dog

with his arm.

"Worried about Sam?" he asked.

"Aren't you?"

"Yeah, but at least he came to us," Bernie said. "That's something."

"He and Margo got along pretty well," Rose said, closing the magazine and putting it on the night stand.

"Another stray," Bernie said. "Sam, this dog and now the pregnant renter. What makes you think we can help any of them?"

"What makes you think we can't?" Rose said. "You're not turning into an old fool on me now, are you, Bernie?"

"Rose, I've been an old fool for years, you just haven't noticed."

He set the alarm clock.

"I'm going to need the car at 11 tomorrow morning," she said. "Is that going to be a problem?"

"No, I don't think so. Where are you going?" he asked, turning out the light and lying next to Rose. Lucky moved so that he was touching both of them.

"I'm taking Margo to see a gynecologist. She hasn't even seen a doctor yet, so I offered to take her to see my guy, Jerry Rosen."

"That's nice," Bernie said, already starting to slip into the beginning of sleep, a sleep aided by the three glasses of wine.

But something lodged in his brain, rolling around in there like a lost connection.

Jerry Rosen. Jerry Rosen.

"What's your gynecologist's name?" he asked, his tongue already thick.

"Jerry Rosen."

It's funny, he thought. His wife had been going to a gynecologist for years, and until now, he didn't even know the guy's name.

Jerry Rosen. Dr. Jerry Rosen. Dr. Jerome Rosen.

Dr. Jerome Rosen? Wait a minute.

"Where's he at?" Bernie said, suddenly less sleepy.

"By the hospital. JFK. You know, the one off Congress near Atlantis."

Dr. Jerome Rosen. Atlantis.

"What's he look like?" Bernie asked.

Rose laughed and rolled toward him.

"What? You jealous? He's just another old fool like you. It's the son you ought to worry about. He's the cute one."

Bernie waited for her to go to sleep. When her breathing had become long and raspy, he slipped his arm from around her and walked to the bathroom, flipping on the light.

Then he dug into his sock drawer and found the high school directory that Mort Granger had given him. Turning the pages to face the light, he flipped to the one he had dog-eared. Dr. Jerome H. Rosen.

Susan Plock's husband had been peeking between his wife's legs for years. Imagine that.

Bernie turned off the light and got back in bed. Lucky had already flopped into his half of the bed, so he had to move him.

"What's a matter, can't sleep?" Rose said, as Bernie got under the sheet.

"I just had to go to the bathroom."

He flopped on his back, staring at the ceiling for a while.

"Rose?"

"Mmmm."

"I can give you a ride to the doctor's office tomorrow."

"It's not necessary."

"I know, but I'd …I'd like to have the car. Maybe run an errand while you're in there."

"Suit yourself," she said, and then she was asleep again.

Lucky crawled from under the sheet, and Bernie could feel the dog looking at him in the dark, sensing that he was awake.

"What?" Bernie said to the dog. "You don't trust me?"

Lucky sniffed twice, then retreated under the covers again.

Jacqui glanced at the clock. Nearly 1 a.m., and still no Jake.

■ ■ ■

Jacqui was surprised to find that her son wasn't home. She had fully expected to see him there when she returned from her ill-fated trip to the Manhole. But when she got in, he wasn't there watching television or reading in his room. The kitchen had been untouched since she left.

It was nearly 11 p.m. He was always home by this time. She checked her messages. There were none.

Jacqui got into her night clothes and sat on the living room couch.

She woke up about an hour later, startled by a loud commercial from a credit card company.

"It's everywhere you want to be," the voice on the television said.

She clicked it off with the remote. This isn't where she wanted to be. She glanced at the clock. Nearly 1 a.m., and still no Jake.

She walked in the dark to her bedroom. There was nothing

to do but wait. And worry.

She dozed off again, for how long she wasn't sure. The next thing she remembered was hearing the front door open. Jacob was home.

Where had he been? Why hadn't he called? Had he been in some sort of trouble again?

She sat up in bed and was about to call out his name when something stopped her cold.

It was a voice. A man's voice, but definitely not the man's voice belonging to her son. She started to reach for the princess phone, her first thought being that a burglar was in her condo. She needed to dial 911. But before she could do that, she heard another voice, and this one was Jacob's.

It was close to her room.

"Don't worry," he was saying. "She's gotta be asleep by now."

And then he giggled like a little kid. Or someone who had too much to drink.

Jacqui kept perfectly still and strained to hear the conversation just outside her closed door.

But she couldn't make out much. There was too much rustling going on.

"C'mon," she finally heard Jacob say. "Let me show you my room."

Jacqui gasped. Her son had never done this before, taken somebody to her home like this. And not just into the home. But into his room. In the middle of the night.

But what really took Jacqui's breath away was that as the two men walked down the hall, she heard an unmistakable sound.

Even after Jake's door was closed and locked, Jacqui thought she could still hear it.

The sound of creaking leather.

21 Margo's wake-up call

Sam Hamstein woke up, surprised to find himself in his parents' condo and wondering why he had come here. He put on his jeans and found his father carving a cantaloupe in the kitchen.

"Morning."

"Morning. Where's Mom?"

"She's out walking at the mall with her friends."

Lucky, who had been sitting patiently at Bernie's feet, got up and sniffed Sam's leg.

"You hungry?" Bernie asked. "I'll make some eggs."

"Sure. I'll help."

"Tell you what. Walk the dog, and I'll make breakfast," Bernie said. "The mutt hasn't been out yet."

Bernie didn't think to mention the leash, and Sam didn't think to ask.

And Lucky didn't think to check his primal urge when the stray cat wandered into the C Building parking lot again.

Sam watched helplessly as dog and cat disappeared. He stood there for a while, hoping Lucky would come back. But there was no sign of the dog. He went inside to ask Bernie what to do.

"For cryin' out loud," Bernie said, as he scrambled eggs in

a bowl. "I'm tired of chasing that dog."

"But we can't just let him run around, can we?" Sam asked.

"Why not?"

"He might get lost or hit by a car," Sam said.

"Let's sit and eat," Bernie said. "After breakfast, we'll go look for the mutt."

"No," Sam said. "I've got to find Lucky first. I couldn't stand it if Mom came home and found out I lost her dog."

Bernie saw there was no point arguing. He put down the bowl, turned off the stove and wiped his hands on a towel.

"C'mon," he said. "With two of us looking, we'll have a better chance."

Sam headed on foot toward B Building. Bernie got in the car and started in the opposite direction.

A few minutes later, Bernie spotted the dog at the tennis courts. Bernie was happy to see Lucky wasn't chasing the cat anymore. He wasn't happy to see that, instead, the dog was now chasing tennis balls.

Bernie quickly got out of his car and hustled over to the courts, where Lucky was pacing around proudly with a bright yellow ball clamped tightly in his jaw.

He ran over to Bernie, dropping the now-slimy ball at Bernie's feet.

"Lucky," Bernie said. "I ought to ..."

Then he heard a familiar voice, which was slightly out of breath from running and sounding even more venomous than usual.

"That's my ball, Bernie."

Herb Troutman, chairman of the Shady Palms Council of Building Presidents, was thumping his oversized Prince racket on the palm of his left hand.

Bernie picked up the soggy ball, nearly dropping it in revulsion, and extended it toward Troutman.

"That your dog?" Troutman asked.

"Not really," Bernie said.

Troutman didn't take the ball, so Bernie let his hand drop. Sam came running up.

"Great. You found him," Sam said to his father.

"Herb, this is my son, Sam. He's visiting from California."

Troutman looked at him and nodded.

"This your dog?" Troutman asked Sam.

"I wish," Sam said. "No, Lucky's my parents' dog."

Bernie smiled weakly and gave a feeble explanation.

"Rose … she found him the other day … A stray."

"Surely, Bernie, I don't have to remind you about the leash law here," Troutman said. "You do have a leash for your dog, don't you?"

The way he said "your dog," leaning on those words for emphasis, made Bernie want to stuff that drippy tennis ball right in Herb's mouth.

"That was my fault," Sam piped up. "I forgot to put the leash on Lucky when I took him out for a walk."

Sam bent down and picked up Lucky, groaning a little as he straightened.

"Heavy?" Herb said.

Sam shrugged. Bernie tried to give a meaningful glance to his son. A glance that conveyed the message, "Shut up and watch your step here." The message obviously didn't get through.

"About 25 pounds, I'd say," Sam said.

"Less than that," Bernie quickly added. "Much less."

"Looks like a heavy dog to me," Herb said.

"Well, he's not," Bernie said. "I weighed him myself the other day, and he was not even 19 pounds."

Bernie wasn't quite sure why he was lying about Lucky being under the 20-pound limit. It was probably just Herb's tyranny that sent Bernie over the edge.

"It's a bad example if we people who make the laws here don't follow them ourselves," Troutman said.

Bernie had the urge to tell Herb to mind his own business.

But instead, he said to his son, "C'mon, Sam. Breakfast is waiting."

He dropped the tennis ball on the ground at Herb's feet and turned to walk away.

"Bernie, there's something else," Troutman said. "Stuart Fine is coming this afternoon to discuss a few board matters, and I think it would be a good idea if we discuss that problem in C Building."

Bernie bristled. He had told Herb he would handle the matter of the pregnant renter, and two days later, Troutman was already calling in the condo's lawyer.

"I don't think that's necessary at this point," Bernie said.

"I already got a call from a radio talk-show host this morning, Bernie. We've got to deal with this now. Two o'clock in the board's office. If you're not there, that's OK. We'll just proceed without you," Troutman said.

Bernie shrugged his shoulders.

"I'll see if I can make it," he said.

On the way back to the condo, Sam asked, "What was that all about?"

"Trouble," Bernie said. "Just more trouble."

■ ■ ■

Jacqui usually takes a shower and makes herself a cup of coffee before leaving the condo to pace the mall corridors with the Wonder Walkers. But this morning, her quest was to get out of her condo as quickly and as quietly as possible.

She got dressed and brushed her teeth with only a trickle. She was at Maddy's door 15 minutes early, but she didn't care.

"You in a hurry this morning?" Madeline Jones said, still rubbing the sleep out of her eyes.

"Maddy, there's somebody in my condo!"

Jacqui told her friend the story.

"Isn't that something," Maddy said. "We go out to find your boy a guy, and he ends up bringing one home. What does he look like?"

"I don't know. I told you, I didn't see him. I just … heard him."

That morning, Jacqui wasn't the only one subdued during their exercise and chit-chat session. Even though the Wonder Walkers had a lot to talk about, they were uncharacteristically unwilling or unable to get things rolling.

Rose was probably the most talkative of the bunch. She did go on a bit about the dinner with Margo.

"What's wrong with the rest of you?" Rose finally said as they sat in the mall's food court.

Maddy would have talked about her outing with Jacqui to the Manhole, but her friend had sworn her to secrecy. So Maddy just sat there quietly.

Rose tried to get Lois to chime in when she told the story about Ricardo running after Lucky and then coming for dessert to see Lois. But Lois wasn't saying much.

"He even walked Lois to her door," Rose said.

The others looked at Lois.

"And?" Maddy said.

"And that's the end of the story," Lois said, balling up her napkin and crossing her arms.

"You people are no fun at all this morning," Rose said.

■ ■ ■

The ringing sound woke up Margo. She reached over and slapped at her alarm clock. But that didn't stop the ringing. It was her phone.

It was just after 9 a.m. The sun was pouring in the windows, and as Margo stumbled out of bed, she wondered why Bill was calling again so soon.

But it wasn't Bill.

Margo didn't recognize the woman's voice on the other end of the phone.

"Margo Zukowski?"

"Yes."

"In Shady Palms?"

'Right now, right here on Walter Wallbanger's *Search for Truth* we have Margo Zukowski herself …

"Yes."

"Hold please for Walter Wallbanger."

"Walter who?" Margo said.

But there was a click on the line as she was transferred to another line, which already had a conversation in progress on it.

"Hello?" Margo said.

But the voices apparently didn't hear her. There was a woman saying something about how "it wasn't right" and that she hoped "people would be outraged and they would …"

She was cut off by a male voice.

"Hold on there, caller. Because right now, right here on Walter Wallbanger's Search for Truth we have Margo Zukowski herself …

"Welcome to AM-1570, Margo. You're on the air with Walter Wallbanger, the bravest, boldest, smartest defender of personal liberties in this county, and I am here to help you."

"What?" Margo said.

"This is the Margo Zukowski who is pregnant in Shady Palms?"

Wallbanger's voice was deep, affected and loud. Margo hadn't been awake long enough to digest all that was happening, but she was alert enough to realize she was on a radio show.

Walter Wallbanger? Like most people in the county, she never heard of his show, which had a small but rabid audience that barely registered a blip in the Arbitron ratings.

"Do I know you?" Margo asked.

"You will, honey," he said. "When they try to kick you out of your rightful place at Shady Palms, it will be I, Walter Wallbanger, who will lead the fight to restore your freedom."

"Somebody's kicking me out?" Margo said.

"Margo, my little lamb, haven't you read the latest edition of your own condo's newspaper, *The Shady Palms Gazette*?"

Margo had seen those papers, stacked by the clubhouse, but she had never read one.

"Listen," she said. "I've got to go."

"I realize this is upsetting you," he said. "I would be upset too if a condo board tried to do this to me. One question I have, and frankly, it's been bothering me. I wonder if you could answer just this one question?"

He paused. Margo debated hanging up the phone right then. But she had a curiosity to find out what burning question this cretin could possibly have.

"My question is," Wallbanger said, "I've got a hunch that the father of your child is actually one of the senior citizens who lives in Shady Palms, and probably one of the same people who want to kick you out. Am I right about that, Mar ..."

22 Jacqui falls for Jake's new boyfriend

"So, what if he's still there?" Jacqui asked her friend as they drove back to Shady Palms after their morning mall outing.

"Just walk in and introduce yourself," Maddy said. "There's nothing to it."

"If there's nothing to it, then why don't you come with me?"

"He's your son," Maddy said. "I don't need to meet his new lover, you do."

"You don't know that."

"Don't know what?"

"That business about Jacob having a new lover."

"You're the one who told me they spent the night together in his room …"

Jacqui just frowned and gave her friend her best you're-no-help look.

They rode in silence for another minute before Maddy relented.

"All right. You win. I'll come in with you. But I still don't see what good it will do."

When Jacqui reached her condo door, she and Maddy pressed their ears close to listen. It was quiet inside.

Jacqui crossed her fingers and hoped with all her might

that her son's visitor would be long gone. She put the key in and opened the door.

What she saw almost made her yelp. The floor of her living room was strewn with a trail of discarded clothing that led to her son's bedroom.

Two T-shirts, two wet towels and two pairs of bathing trunks — both pairs she bought her son for Christmas — were lying here or there.

They must have gone to the pool together for a morning swim and now they were here again, perhaps right in the middle of ...

"Jake, that you?" came the voice.

It wasn't Maddy's or Jacqui's voice. It was a man's voice, and as Jacqui heard the footsteps approaching from down the hall, she imagined the worst. That a nude stranger would suddenly be standing in front of her in her own condo.

Instinctively, she grabbed Maddy and pulled her into the nearby coat closet, barely getting the door shut before Craig Shelbourne rounded the corner, wearing only his gold lamé Speedo.

"What's that, Craig?" came Jake's voice from the kitchen.

"Nothing," said Craig, who walked just beyond the closet and stopped. "I thought I heard somebody at the door."

There really wasn't enough room in the closet for both Maddy and Jacqui. It dawned on them as they stood facing each other with a row of windbreakers and jackets poking at them in uncomfortable places. Not only was it dark and tight in there, but the floor was also littered with so many discarded pairs of shoes that both women couldn't avoid being precariously perched on the shifting mound of footwear.

They held onto each other's shoulders and barely breathed, for the words they heard surely must have been spoken right on the other side of the door that concealed them.

"My mom should be back pretty soon," Jake said. "You'd better get dressed. I'll pick up these clothes out here."

"You don't think she'll go for the gold lamé?" Craig said.

"I think the paramedic look will work better," Jake said.

"You sure it's OK?"

"What's OK?"

"Me sticking around. You know. My feelings won't be hurt if you'd prefer me to go. I'll understand."

"No, Craig. I'd like you to meet her. Really."

"That's nice."

"Come here," Jake said.

And then there were some sounds that made Jacqui feel grateful she was standing in the dark, so her friend wouldn't have to see the expression on her face.

Jake and Craig had stopped talking, but they were still outside the door. The changing rhythms of their breathing unsettled Jacqui.

A slight twitch in her right leg caused her foot to slip off the edge of a forgotten Aigner pump, pitching her foot sideways, destroying her balance. In a last-ditch effort to keep from going down, she pulled hard on her friend's shoulders, which did nothing but send Maddy tipping in her direction.

Jake and Craig were startled by the sudden rumble and then the pitching of the two older women from the hall closet. Jacqui popped out first, stumbling backward and ending up in a sitting position between Craig's and Jake's legs. By the time Maddy broke free of her friend's grasp, it was too late. She was going over like a felled tree, landing on top of Jacqui as she sat on the carpet.

Jake recovered quickly.

"Craig, I'd like you to meet my mom," he said. "She's the white one."

"I thought we were the ones who were supposed to come out of the closet," Craig said.

Jacqui and Maddy sat up, dazed and embarrassed. Jacqui was trying to think of something to say when she found herself staring at that gold lamé Speedo. Then she looked up at the face above it. She recognized him, even without the chaps.

Craig was looking down at her and Maddy, and Jacqui was horrified to see that he too had the look of recognition on his face.

Craig slapped Jake on the shoulder and laughed.

"Jake," he said, "you never told me your mother's a dyke."

■ ■ ■

The Hamsteins were on their way to the doctor's office with Margo sitting in the back seat.

"You don't have to thank us," Rose was saying. "We don't mind, right Bernie?"

Bernie, lost in his own thoughts about his childhood romance with Susan Plock, just managed a grunt as he drove.

"It's just that I don't want to be a burden to you," Margo said.

"Burden? What's the burden? Listen, a woman in your condition should have a support system. It's important."

Margo leaned forward and placed a hand on Rose's shoulder.

"Thanks," Margo said.

Rose patted her hand.

"And don't you listen to some of the nonsense that's going around Shady Palms," the older woman said to her, giving Bernie a meaningful glance.

The whole condo was buzzing, thanks to Mort Granger's yeomanlike effort in *The Gazette* to make Margo's pregnancy seem like one of the cataclysmic events in the history of Palm Beach County.

"It's not only Shady Palms," Margo said sheepishly. "This morning, a phone call woke me up and it was a talk-radio show, and they were talking about me being pregnant. I couldn't believe that ..."

"What?" Bernie said, suddenly transported back to the present. "A radio show was talking about it?"

"Yeah."

"What show?"

"I don't remember exactly. The guy kept telling me that he would help me. He had a funny name."

"Walter Wallbanger?" Bernie said.

"That's it. Do you know him?"

By then Bernie had flipped on the car's radio and was spinning the dial to get to the nether reaches of the AM band, where Walter Wallbanger's *Search for Truth* is buried.

"He's the dregs," Bernie said, then looking at his wife, he added, "This has got to be the work of Mort."

The car was now filled with Walter Wallbanger's voice. He was still talking about Margo, fanning the flames of outrage among his small band of listeners who had too much time and not enough smarts to be doing anything else with their mornings.

"You heard from Mr. Troutmouth! The rules are the rules," Wallbanger was saying. "Well, I say it's time that we Americans show the Troutmouths of the world what freedom is all about, and that we won't stand for the tyranny of condo commandos like him. It's time we …"

Bernie did like hearing Herb Troutman being called Troutmouth. But the idea that Walter Wallbanger had found Margo's pregnancy fodder for his program worried him.

Like most people at Shady Palms, Bernie had tuned in to Wallbanger in the past and soon became repulsed. Wallbanger's politics were too far to the right for the average Shady Palms resident, and his conspiracy blabber and constant railings against mainstream society were too cartoonish for all but the feeble-minded.

Bernie clicked off the radio.

"I wouldn't let that nonsense bother you."

Rose turned the radio back on.

"Don't you want to hear what people are saying?" she asked.

"I don't see any reason to," Bernie said.

A caller was on the air. He and Wallbanger were sharing a laugh about something. Then the caller said, "Hey, but seriously, Walter, I know the real reason why babies aren't allowed to live next to all those fossils in Shady Palms."

"What reason is that, my friend?" Wallbanger said.

"Shady Palms has got a rule about it ..."

"The fascists in charge there have a rule about everything," Wallbanger said.

"And they've got a specific one about this," the caller said. "It says that Shady Palms residents are only allowed to spend their second childhoods there, not their first."

The radio filled with the sound of laughter.

"Maybe you're right," Rose said to Bernie.

She reached forward and turned off the radio.

23 Bernie goes uptown

Bernie pulled into the parking lot of the doctor's office. He'd passed by this place hundreds, maybe thousands, of times and never gave it a second thought.

Now, he paid attention to everything. The sign near the street said "Rosen, Rosen, Shiner and Brindle — The Women's Care Center." The building was painted an ugly brownish gold, and it had no windows. But people didn't come here for the architecture. The lot was nearly full, and Bernie wondered if one of the cars there belonged to Susan Plock, who was still learning to drive when he last saw her.

"You're not parking?" Rose asked.

"No, I'll be back in about 20 minutes," he said. "I'm just going to take a peek in that bookstore down the road."

She and Margo got out of the car and went into the building. Bernie drove back on the busy street but rode past the bookstore. He pulled a slip of paper out of his pants pocket. On it, he had scribbled the address he got from the alumni directory: 141 Willow Bend Court.

Two minutes later, he was in Atlantis.

It was easier getting into Atlantis than it was getting into Shady Palms, which struck Bernie as funny. At Shady Palms, Hector gave visitors the third-degree before hitting the button

that opened the electric gate. In Atlantis, Bernie was waved in
after saying he was going to the golf course, and left free to
cruise among homes he knew he could never afford.

Rather than ask for directions, Bernie decided to find the
house by chance. Atlantis was small enough so that his wander-
ings would eventually bring him to Willow Bend Court.

After a few turns, he was there. It was a sprawling ranch
house with powder blue stuccoed walls and a white barrel-tiled
roof. There was a three-car garage, and on the paving stone driveway, a lemon yellow Cadillac with a "Jeb!" bumper sticker.

"Figures," Bernie said, driving on.

He circled around the block one more time. For a moment,
he was tempted to pull in the driveway and ring the doorbell. But
on second thought, what would he say? "Hi, Susan, this is
Bernie. Remember me? I'm now an old schlemiel living in Shady
Palms."

No, he just wanted to observe what had become of Susan
Plock. She was tall, almost his height, when they had dated in
high school. She was angular, with long arms, legs and fingers.
She had strawberry blond hair that she wore long and parted
down the middle, and she often took off her tortoise shell glasses, chewing the ear pieces as she sat in the school lunchroom.

She was everything that the slight, wiry Rose Cangelosi
wasn't. And although Bernie had long ago become captivated
with Rose, he was now interested in seeing what had become of
Susan.

He wanted to see the woman that had grown from the girl
that made his pulse quicken when he was 15, when he was still
dangerous.

He had thought about telling Rose this morning. But she
probably wouldn't understand. It might even hurt her feelings.
No, it was better this way, Bernie thought.

So he studied the house, picking up a few more details on
the second pass — the golf cart parked on the side, the stork
painted on the mailbox, a pair of muddy shoes, maybe her gar-

dening shoes, by the front doorstep.

No, he couldn't imagine knocking on the door. Not now. It would be better meeting her by chance. Like at her husband's office. Bernie would be there with his wife, and she might be visiting her husband. They'd both look up at each other and she'd say, "Bernie?" and he'd say, "Susan?"

That would be the way to meet again. Not this way. Not by circling around her house like a vulture and then popping in unannounced.

Bernie drove back to the doctor's office, where he expected to surreptitiously observe more footprints left by his old high school girlfriend.

■ ■ ■

Jacqui, still sitting on the floor of her condo and looking at the stranger in the gold lamé Speedo, might have corrected his assumption that she was a lesbian. But there was something else that commanded even more attention than that.

Her right ankle.

As she was flopping out of the closet with Maddy, her right foot turned in, and in her final attempt to keep from falling, she shifted just enough of her weight to the leg to make the ankle collapse. For a couple of seconds, the indelicacy of the situation overrode her central nervous system, subjugating the pain in her ankle to the feeling of panicked embarrassment.

But suddenly she was in too much pain, and all she could focus on was her right ankle.

"Look," she finally said to the others. "It's enormous."

Then they saw, too.

"Oh, ma'am, that looks like one nasty sprain," Craig said. "You just stay right where you are."

Then he took charge of the situation, getting her ice, elevating the foot and eventually deciding they should take Jacqui to the hospital emergency room for X-rays.

"Mom, what were you doing at the Manhole last night?" Jake asked her while they waited for Craig to get dressed.

"He's not going to wear the chaps to the hospital, is he?" Jacqui said, ignoring her son's question.

"Mom, be nice," Jake said.

Craig didn't wear the chaps. He had on jeans and one of Jake's T-shirts. And he fussed over Jacqui all the way to the hospital.

A couple of the emergency room nurses at Bethesda Memorial knew him, and Jacqui got the red carpet treatment as she was whisked in a wheelchair past a long line of waiting patients.

"So how did this happen?" the doctor asked her as he poked at her puffy ankle.

"I fell."

"How did you fall?"

"Tumbled."

"Were you out walking?"

"No, I was inside my condo, but I don't see what that has to do with …"

"We fell out of a coat closet together," Maddy said.

The doctor, a young guy probably right out of medical school, just kept poking and said, "I see," as if falling out of a closet with a friend is one of the common ways for women her age to get hurt.

Then they wheeled Jacqui to another room for X-rays, and then back to the first room, where she, Maddy, Jake and Craig waited for the results.

"I can't tell you how sorry I am that this happened," Craig said.

"It's not your fault," Maddy said.

"I'll go see what's holding up those X-rays," Craig said.

After he was out of the room, Jacqui turned to Maddy.

"It's your fault," Jacqui said to Maddy. "If you didn't grab me when I started to go down, I might not have gotten this foot pinned under me."

"My fault?" Maddy said. "It was you who pulled me into the

closet in the first place."

The women weren't really arguing, Jake noticed. They were doing something far more complex. They were sparring with each other for sport, as a way to pass the time.

"You know, neither of you has explained yet what you were doing at the Manhole last night," Jake said.

"I don't think this is the time or the place to discuss it," Jacqui said.

"Your mother was worried about you, that's all," Maddy told Jake.

"Maddy, I don't need you to tell my son about how I feel."

"Maybe you do," Maddy said.

"I'm perfectly capable of telling my son how I feel on my own."

"Well, then do it," Maddy said.

"Jacob, I was … oh, never mind," Jacqui said. "Not here."

Jake bent down and kissed his mother on the head.

"Jacob, aren't you going to be late for work?"

"I got fired yesterday, Mom."

"Oh, Jacob."

"No, Mom, don't be sad. It's the greatest thing that has happened to me. It was a rotten job. I can do better. If I didn't get fired, I would have never ended up at the Manhole last night, and if I wasn't …"

Jake's voice tailed off as Craig walked back into the room with a big smile on his face.

"Great news, Mrs. Fisher," he said. "Nothing is broken. It's just a sprain. It'll hurt, and you're not going to be able to do much walking for a while, but in a couple of months, that ankle will be as good as new."

"Let's get you home and comfortable," Jacob said.

On the car ride back to the condo, Jake asked Craig if he'd like to spend the day there. Craig said he would, only if they let him make supper that night for the four of them.

"I never turn down a free meal," Maddy said.

"Sounds good to me," Jake said.

"You don't have to fuss," Jacqui said.

"When it comes to cooking, Mrs. Fisher," Craig said, " 'Fuss' is my middle name."

Jacqui put her head back against the headrest in the back seat, watching as her son, who was sitting in front of her, slowly edged his hand near Craig's right hand until their two hands lightly touched.

She should be happy, she told herself. Jacob had found a decent friend. That was something in life, to find a good friend. She looked at the bemused black lady sharing the back seat with her. Maddy had a little crooked smile on her face and was eyeing Jacqui, perhaps reading her mind.

Jacqui raised her eyebrows as she spoke:

"What are you looking at, you old dyke?"

24 In the doctor's office

By the time Bernie got back to the doctor's office, Rose and Margo were no longer in the waiting room. The collection of other women there looked up at him briefly and then went back to reading their magazines or staring into space. Bernie took a seat next to an enormously pregnant woman who was watching her 2-year-old son amuse himself with trucks on the floor.

After a couple of minutes, a nurse opened a door leading to the rest of the office, sticking her head in the waiting room to summon the pregnant woman, who had a tough time convincing her son he had nothing to worry about by following her inside.

Bernie winked at the boy. Bernie didn't like doctors' offices, either.

"Good luck," he told the woman, who only managed a polite smile in return.

Bernie wondered how Margo would make it. She was obviously alone. Whoever the father of her child was, he wasn't taking much responsibility. As Bernie sat there, he began wondering if this office visit was just the beginning, the first step he and Rose were taking in being Margo's primary support system.

Rose seemed so ready for it, the way she immediately began fussing over the woman, volunteering her doctor and not giving Bernie a choice in the matter. Just like she was with that dog. Rose had made room in her life for the two strays, and now it was up to Bernie to get with the program or risk a serious marital spat.

The truth was, Bernie would enjoy having a baby around the building. But there was no reason to tell that to Rose, who was carrying on as if she were the child's grandmother.

Bernie got up and walked to the small window opening, where two women in crisp white uniforms worked, one of them filing paperwork and the other one typing intently on a computer.

He scanned the office, wondering if Susan Plock had ever worked here, perhaps helping out her husband when an employee called in sick. He tried to imagine the girl he knew sitting here, scanning calendars for future appointments and telling patients how to fill out their checks.

"Can I help you?" the woman at the computer said to him, not even bothering to take her eyes off the screen.

"Yeah, I was just wondering about the two doctors with the names of Rosen. Are they father and son?"

"Yes, they are."

"Oh, that's nice that a father gets to work with his son," Bernie said. "It's a real family affair."

The nurse didn't say anything to that.

"How about the son's mother?" Bernie said. "Does she work here, too?"

"The son's mother?"

"Yeah, Mrs. Rosen. The older one. "

The nurse looked up at him now.

"You want to know about Mrs. Rosen?"

Bernie sensed that he had crossed the line of acceptable questioning. He quickly tried to repair the damage.

"No, it's not like I wanted to know about Mrs. Rosen," he said. "It's just that I was thinking that probably I am Dr. Rosen's age, and if I were a doctor I might have my wife working in the office — just to keep her out of the stores and spending all my money."

He laughed, perhaps a little too hard.

The woman put her eyes back on her computer screen.

"No," she said. "Mrs. Rosen doesn't work here."

Bernie was glad that a patient walked up to make an appointment. He slid aside and rather than going back to his seat, he walked down the hallway, peeking in open doors and listening for the voices of Margo or his wife.

He was just about to give up and head back to the waiting room, when he heard his wife's laugh coming from the last doorway down the hall. When Bernie got to the room, he saw from the rich, dark paneling and the expensive furniture that this was the doctor's inner sanctum.

A short, extremely tanned man with hair that appeared to be kept black through coloring sat behind the huge desk, regaling Margo and Rose about his recent trip to Italy. He looked up and stopped when he saw Bernie standing in the doorway. Rose turned around in her chair.

"Bernie, what are you doing here?"

"I got tired of waiting in the reception room," Bernie said. "Those magazines you've got out there, doc, are mostly from the Reagan administration — the first one."

Which wasn't true. But Bernie suddenly felt like getting a little macho with this guy who has had intimate access to his wife's body during her Florida years.

"Dr. Rosen, this is my husband, Bernie," Rose said.

"Jerry Rosen," the doctor said, standing up to shake Bernie's hand.

"Don't mind me," Bernie said. "I didn't mean to interrupt."

Rosen went on talking and Bernie stood there, letting his eyes roam around the office. The diploma on the wall was from Cornell University.

Bernie seemed to remember that after he broke up with Susan, she went off to college some place. Cornell, wasn't that in upstate New York? Maybe that's where she had landed this doctor.

Jerry Rosen looked at least five years younger than Bernie. But that just could be because he was so well preserved. Even with a white lab coat on, he appeared to be trim and fit, probably by playing squash or something like that at a private club.

He never hauled boxes of bread into supermarkets at 5 in the morning for most of his life, that's for sure. He wouldn't be looking so good if that's how he made a living, Bernie thought. Jerry Rosen would have a bad back, like most of the Big Top delivery men, and his squash game would be hampered by a degenerating disk.

While Rose seemed to listen rapturously to the doctor's description of Florentine architecture, Bernie wondered what Susan Plock's view on overweight dogs and pregnant women at Shady Palms would be.

Bernie used the doctor's storytelling interlude to scan the office for family pictures. He spied them on the desk, but unlike some doctors, who have their family portraits facing out, as if to show off their family to their patients, Rosen's framed photos were all facing toward him.

So all Bernie saw was the back of a bunch of frames. He started walking around the room, pretending to get a better look at a piece of art on the wall nearly behind the desk. But he was actually trying to get into a position to study the doctor's wife, who undoubtedly would be in at least one of the desk photos.

Bernie had slowly worked himself into position, when his own wife's voice stopped him.

"Bernie, what are you doing?"

He turned around to face three sets of eyes. On the edge of his vision, he saw the photos on the desk, in particular a 5-by-7 that appeared to be a recent studio portrait of the doctor and his wife. But Bernie couldn't look at the photo of Susan Plock. Not now. Not with all those eyes on him.

He just caught a glimpse of his former girlfriend, but not enough to recognize any of her features. Later on, he would try

Bernie used the doctor's storytelling interlude to scan the office for photos.

to remember as much about that glimpse as possible. But it was so short, the only thing that stuck in his head was her hair, which appeared to be puffy and no longer parted down the middle. It seemed darker than he remembered, too. But as for describing the rest of her face, he just couldn't say.

"I'm just looking at this painting here," Bernie said. "Interesting piece of art."

Rose thought about telling him that it was a pencil drawing, not a painting, and that in all their years together she could never remember him ever being interested in art before. But instead, she said, "Sit down, Bernie, and listen to this. Maybe one day you'll take me to Italy."

Sheepishly, Bernie circled back to an empty seat on the other side of the room. He never had the chance to look at the photo again.

After the doctor got through with his tour of Florence, he finally got to the subject of Margo's pregnancy.

"Everything's fine," he said. "You're in good health, and I don't see why you shouldn't have an uneventful pregnancy."

Too late for that, Bernie thought. It's already eventful.

"Do you have a good support system, Margo?" the doctor asked.

Margo hesitated.

"I don't mean to pry," the doctor said, "but it's important, especially with the first one, to have plenty of emotional support."

"I'm … There won't be any support from the father," she said.

Bernie had to stop from piping up, "Or from the condo board."

"She's got plenty of support," Rose said, patting Margo's hand. "We'll take good care of her. Right, Bernie?"

Before Bernie could answer, a younger man popped his head in the door.

"Mom, on line four," he said.

"What's she want?" Dr. Rosen asked.

The son shook his head and walked out.

"Now you've seen Jerome, my son," the doctor said to Margo. "As I started to tell you earlier, he'll probably be the one who ends up delivering your baby. He handles most of the obstetrics part of the practice, so his poor old father can get a good night's sleep."

Poor, my eye, Bernie thought. "I've seen your house," he felt like telling the doctor, "and while you might be old, you certainly aren't poor."

But of course, Bernie said nothing. Instead, he began considering how the younger Rosen didn't look much like his father at all. What was it about him that looked so different? It was the eyes. The father had small, beady eyes. The son had those almond-shaped ones — just like his mother.

"You'll excuse me," the father said, as he punched a button on his phone console and picked up the receiver.

"Yes, dear," he said.

Bernie could hear the faint staccato of a voice on the other end of the line.

"No, tonight would be fine," the doctor said, then pausing before saying, "About six o'clock … Yes, I'll get it on my way home … I'd love to, but I've got patients in the office right now."

Bernie felt like shouting out, "And also Bernie Hamstein, the boy who held your hand through *Gone With the Wind*, and taught you how to French kiss. He sends his regards."

But instead, he sat there speculating whether Susan Plock had ever wondered what became of him.

25 Ricardo and the art of bicycle maintenance

Rose suggested they stop for lunch on the way home from the doctor's office. Bernie pulled into a Denny's.

"This OK?" he asked.

"Sure," said Margo from the back seat.

It was the same Denny's she had come to the day before she moved into Shady Palms. The waitress guided Bernie, Rose and her to the same table where she had sat with Bill when he gave her the North Dakota license plate and spelled out her assignment at the condo.

She felt dirty.

She sat across the table from the Hamsteins, watching how they shared each other's food and talked in the tender shorthand longtime couples sometimes achieve. She saw them now for what they were. Decent people. People who didn't deserve getting screwed.

Especially by a woman whom they were treating like a daughter.

"Margo, you haven't touched your soup," Rose said.

Margo shrugged.

"I guess I'm not as hungry as I thought I was."

It's was true — in more ways than one. At one time, she was hungry for this assignment. She considered it a kind of vacation, a relief from the troubled world she was leaving behind. But instead, she had found this wasn't as easy as it had seemed.

Margo had experienced regret many times in her professional life and certainly much more acute than the regret she was feeling now. But still it wasn't easy sitting across the table, watching Bernie and Rose feeding each other a piece of coconut creme pie, oblivious to what was about to happen to them.

On the way back to Shady Palms, Margo said little. She would go back to her condo, she told herself, and go to sleep. Maybe when she woke up, she'd get her professionalism back.

As Bernie rounded the corner to Shady Palms, he whistled at the sight. Parked outside the main entrance were two television news trucks with their tall transmitter poles telescoping above them.

"I wonder what happened," Rose said.

"The person in our back seat is what happened," Bernie said.

Mort's overblown coverage in *The Gazette*, combined with hours of radio rantings by Walter Wallbanger, awakened the local media to the story of Margo's pregnancy, which suddenly had become irresistible.

Bernie knew he was right after taking one look at Hector, standing outside his guard shack, surrounded by a circle of television, radio and newspaper reporters. Bernie could see he wasn't letting them inside the gate, which wasn't making them happy.

And when Hector saw Bernie's Camry approach, his eyes seemed to grow wide, and Bernie sensed the guard's alarm.

"Margo!" Bernie said with an urgency that made Rose pop up in her seat. "Lay down! Quick, Margo! We're going to sneak by them."

Hector's face relaxed. He opened the gate, and the Camry went by. A couple of the reporters turned to look at the occupants of the car, but when they didn't see a young woman, they went back to complaining to Hector.

"Ladies and gentlemen," Hector said. "You're wasting your time. She's not here."

"Then where is she?" one of them shouted.

"Who knows?" Hector said. "Do you think I know everybody's business around here?"

He could barely keep a straight face.

■ ■ ■

Ricardo Vera didn't get the flat-tire idea until he had pedaled his road bike nearly 60 miles, taking A1A south through Palm Beach County, into Broward County and then back north again. He was planning to ride 100 miles this day, which meant when he reached Ocean Ridge on his northern leg, he would head west, winding his way over I-95, past the mall and into suburbia and the sprawling Shady Palms complex.

That would put him somewhere around 75 miles. With any bit of luck, Lois would be there, and he'd chat with her a while. Maybe she'd even let him in her condo — although that was probably still days away.

After visiting Lois, he'd saddle up again and do the 25 or so miles from Shady Palms to his oceanfront Palm Beach home. At least, that was the original plan.

But the flat-tire idea, which at first sounded too risky to contemplate, finally grew into something he just couldn't resist trying. Oh, it was rushing things, to be sure. He had no real expectation that it would work. Not so soon. Not when he could tell she didn't know what to make of him. To rely on her so soon would be folly, he told himself.

Yet it was the potential folly of it that made the flat-tire idea such an attractive one. And so at a busy intersection near the 70-mile mark, Ricardo slowed his bike and pulled into a gas station at the corner of a busy intersection.

He climbed off his bike and did what he had never done before. He had gotten plenty of flats in his cycling days, one of them even knocked him out of a triathlon. But he had never intentionally given his bike a flat.

   He reached into one of the three pockets on his cycling jersey and took out his bike tool, which included a mini-screwdriver. His front tire was getting a little worn, anyway. He was due for a new one soon.

   Once the job was done, he wheeled the bike to the bank of pay phones in the corner of the lot, fished change from his jersey and looked up the number in the hanging phone book.

   "Lois? … Hi. Ricardo here … Ricardo Vera … Yes, hello. How are you today? …Good. That was a nice time last night …Yes, enjoyable. Yes … Busy, yes, I understand, but the reason for the call is not just to talk. Ricardo has … Yes, sorry. I have had a small problem. I was riding my bicycle just now and I got a flat tire. I ran over a nail and … No, I do not carry an extra tire. I carry an extra tube. But this nail, it went right through the tire, too. Ricardo needs a tire and …Excuse me? Why is Ricardo calling you? Ricardo, sorry I, yes, I need a ride. There is a bike shop not too far from here …Boynton Beach. Yes, Boynton Beach. Ricardo could walk to this shop, buy the tire and tube, bring it back and put it on. But the bicycle would not be safe left alone …No, there is nobody else, and being that it is only a few miles from your condo, Ricardo thought that … About five miles … Congress and Boynton Beach Boulevard … At the gas station … Oh, you are too busy … Yes, Ricardo understands …Yes, not to worry, Lois. When you are busy, you are busy … Ricar … I understand. Yes. Goodbye."

   He hung up the phone and looked at his slashed front tire.

   "Idiot!" he said, kicking his bike.

   Ricardo, so full of self-confidence, hadn't thought to call first, then slash the tire only if she said she was coming to help him. Now, he had a woman he couldn't see and a bike he couldn't ride.

   "Idiot!"

   The thought of walking the bike along the side of the road

for a couple miles to a bike shop didn't appeal to him. He'd just call back to Palm Beach and summon one of the household staff.

Ricardo called the mansion. Manuel, the butler, answered. In rapid Spanish, Ricardo gave him the particulars.

Manuel said he personally would be there to get Ricardo, as soon as he cleaned out the trunk of the Bentley so there would be enough room for the bike.

For the next 20 minutes, Ricardo sat on the curb, watching passing traffic and wondering how much longer he would pursue this condo woman. Sure, she was pretty. But not prettier than some of the women who had been chasing him in Palm Beach.

Ricardo got a sense that underneath all that bluster, there was a real woman in Lois, somebody genuine and kind. It was hard to see, but he sensed it was there. It wasn't something he could explain.

Maybe she just didn't like him. Thought he was ugly. Too foreign. Too exotic for her tastes.

And she was now affecting his training schedule, he told himself. He was supposed to do 100 miles today, and he only got in 70. That wasn't good. He wasn't going to finish the Ironman competition in Hawaii next month if he shorted his training schedule. He would have to control his wild impulses.

He sat there, tossing little pebbles in the street and wondering if he had overestimated himself.

Finally, he heard a car rolling up slowly behind him and coming to a stop. He stood up and turned around.

But it wasn't the Bentley, and it wasn't Manuel who walked out of the driver's side door, closed it and took a few steps toward him.

"Lois," Ricardo said.

His heart monitor started beeping.

26 Turning up the heat on Margo

The reporters camping outside Shady Palms had put Herb Troutman in a foul mood. No, he wouldn't comment, the condo president told them, and no, they couldn't come in and interview other residents.

By the time Bernie walked into the meeting with Herb and the condo lawyer, Stuart Fine, Troutman was pacing around the clubhouse office like a caged beast.

"Hamstein," he said, pointing his finger at Bernie, "you've got to make this thing go away."

Stuart Fine, who reminded Bernie of what a rat would look like if it got to be the size of a bear, rubbed the maroon circles under his glasses, and said, "Have a seat, Mr. Hamstein."

Fine spoke slowly, perhaps because at $225 an hour, there was little motivation to speed things up.

"You've met with Ms. Zukowski, isn't that a fact, Mr. Hamstein?" Fine said.

"Yes," Bernie said, feeling like he was on the witness stand.

"I realize she's claimed to be pregnant," Fine said, "but other than that, is there anything else that would lead you to believe that she actually is pregnant?"

Bernie looked at Fine and laughed, then he turned to Troutman.

"What's this guy talking about, Herb?"

"Bernie, just answer the questions," Troutman said.

"Yes, of course, she's pregnant," Bernie said. "We just got back from taking her to an obstetrician. She's definitely pregnant."

"Bernie, are you getting friendly with this woman?" Troutman asked.

"Just, you know. Rose, she thought Margo didn't have anybody ..."

"Margo?" Troutman said, raising his eyebrows. "You calling her Margo now?"

"I don't see any harm in being friendly. Why do we have to ..."

Fine cut him off this time.

"And this doctor said she was indeed pregnant?" he asked Bernie.

"Yes. She's pregnant. Everything normal," Bernie said. "What's this about?"

Fine ignored the question and addressed his next comment to Troutman.

"OK, that answers that question," Fine said. "Now we just proceed knowing that the pregnancy isn't a ruse."

"A ruse? What are you talking about, Stu?" Hamstein asked.

Once again, the lawyer ignored his question.

"Mr. Hamstein, how do you think she'd react to a small cash settlement — say two months rent — in exchange for her moving out?"

Bernie sat for a second, thinking about this.

"Why does she have to move out now?" he asked. "It's not like she's got a baby right now. She's got another seven months to go in her pregnancy. Maybe by then ..."

"Mr. Hamstein," Fine said. "I'm afraid the longer we don't act here, the more troublesome this could become for Shady Palms."

Troutman, who had been pacing behind Bernie, bellowed.

"Bernie, women make nests, Bernie! C'mon. Women make nests."

Fine rubbed his eyes again, extracting something out of the corner of one of them.

"I think what Mr. Troutman is trying to say is that once it starts getting close to the baby's birth, she's going to be getting the condo ready. Painting, maybe. Buying furniture. Things like that. Then afterward, with a new infant and apparently no father around, she's not going to be predisposed to move."

Troutman added, "Not when she's already got her nest!"

Fine continued, "And unfortunately for us, the baby will be nearly 4 months old by the time Ms. Zukowski's yearlong lease expires."

Troutman exploded again.

"Precedent, Bernie! Precedent! We let her stay, we open the door. Next thing you know, there'll be tricycles on the green areas, and nobody will go in the pool because of all the you-know-what going on in it."

Bernie laughed.

"Herb, if you're worried about pee in the pool, we don't have any kids here now, and I still won't go in for that reason."

Fine plowed on in his droll monotone.

"The point, Mr. Hamstein, is that now is the best time for parting company with Ms. Zukowski."

Troutman again: "We've become the laughingstock of the county. I could just wring Mort's neck for what he did to us this time. I'm sure it was Mort who got that jerk, Wallbanger, all wound up. Did you hear any of that radio show?"

"Just a little," Bernie said. "I make it a point not to listen to him. He's worth avoiding."

"He was saying how he was going to stand up for her and picket here if he had to," Troutman said. "Maybe you can ignore him. But it's Wallbanger's antics that got all the rest of those jackals camping out at the front gate now."

"So, Mr. Hamstein," Fine said, "While we may be at a public relations disadvantage by removing Ms. Zukowski right now, it is still the best time to do it, legally."

"So what do you want from me?" Bernie asked.

"You've apparently talked to her more than we have," Fine said, "and we thought you would be the best point of contact in relaying our offers to her — at least until we get into a legal situation."

"A legal situation?" Bernie said. "Margo, she's a nice girl. You guys aren't planning to be jerks with her, I hope."

"As long as she moves out promptly, we will be exceedingly nice," Fine said. "As I said, we would even be willing — if your first attempt fails — to offer her a couple of months rent."

Bernie sat back in his chair.

"So let me get this straight," he said. "I tell her, 'Sorry Margo, now that you're pregnant, you've got to get out of here immediately.' "

"She took this unit in bad faith," Troutman said. "It says right in the documents that all residents here shall have no children residing with them. She was pregnant when she signed it."

"How do you know she didn't become pregnant after she signed it?" Bernie said.

Fine scratched his chin.

"For lawsuit purposes, our position would be that she was pregnant before. It may not be true. But it'd be enough to let her think we're going to drag her through the courts over it. Mr. Troutman did mention that she wasn't even fully employed."

Bernie nodded. "She's got a part-time job."

"So how can she afford to live here?" Fine asked.

Bernie shrugged.

"She said she's looking for full-time work," he said. "Maybe she's got some money saved up. From North Dakota."

"That's another thing, Mr. Hamstein," Fine said, taking off his glasses, folding his hands and leaning forward in his chair for emphasis. "The reason we questioned her pregnancy with you before was that we must be careful before relying on Ms. Zukowski's word."

"C'mon," Bernie said, growing irritated with the both of them. "Margo's a nice girl. You act like she's on the FBI's most wanted list."

Fine smiled, waiting for Bernie to finish, before saying his next words.

"Mr. Hamstein, you just mentioned that perhaps she had saved money up from her time in North Dakota."

"Yeah, so what?"

"Bernie, she's making a fool of you!" Troutman said, pacing again.

"Mr. Hamstein, we did some preliminary checking on Ms. Zukowski. That license plate she has from North Dakota is a phony. There's no employment, driving or birth records for a Margo Zukowski in North Dakota. However — and I find this very interesting — there is a Margo Zukowski who has a Florida driver license. She's had her Florida license for eight years. And she has a West Palm Beach address."

Fine sat back in his chair.

"So?" Bernie said. "Maybe it's another Margo Zukowski."

"Extremely unlikely," Fine said. "The date of birth on the driver license and the renter application matches."

"So what are you saying?" Bernie asked.

"The girl's a fraud, Bernie!" Troutman bellowed. "And we're getting rid of her, either the nice way or the nasty way."

Bernie tried to digest all this.

"A scam artist, Bernie!" Troutman was saying. "That's my guess. Getting pregnant may be part of her plan. Who knows? She could be cooking up some plot. Some lawsuit against Shady Palms."

"Margo?" Bernie said. "Nah."

"Mr. Hamstein," Fine said. "It could blossom into something where it might be advisable to notify the local police."

"No," Bernie said. "Don't do that. I'll talk to her."

"Good," Fine said. "I think that would be best for all the parties involved."

Then he shuffled his papers.

"I believe there was one other matter here that needed your attention," Fine said. "Ah, here it is."

He handed Bernie the notice. Anonymous complaint. Just as Bernie had suspected.

"Ridiculous," Bernie said, folding the notice and sticking it in his pocket. "That dog is not over the weight limit."

27 Margo and Sam: poolside strays

Lois Rodgers looked at the front tire of Ricardo's bike. Yes, it really was flat.

"Hello, Ricardo," she said, standing in the gas station parking lot. "You're beeping again."

"Thank you for coming," he said. "It is a nice surprise."

After Lois had hung up from his phone call, she had gone back to watching her soap opera.

"Imagine that," she had told the television. "He thinks I've got nothing better to do than to pick him and his bicycle up on the side of the road."

But then, inexplicably, she reached for the remote control two minutes later, clicked off the set, changed clothes, reapplied her makeup and was on her way.

"I guess it's a repayment for the time you helped me in that parking garage," Lois told him.

It had nothing to do with the feathery kiss he gave her the night before, she kept telling herself.

"And Ricardo really appreciates it," he said.

She popped the trunk of her car, and he put the bike inside.

"What do you think you're doing?" Lois said.

"I will just ride in the trunk," he said. "Ricardo is all

sweaty."

"Ricardo," she said. "Get out! Now! I'm not riding with a person in the trunk."

Ricardo shrugged as best he could for a man curled into a ball.

"I've got a beach towel in the back seat. You can use that," she said.

She spread the towel out on the front passenger seat, and Ricardo was just about to climb in when a car horn sounded.

It was the Bentley.

Manuel climbed out of the luxury car and approached his boss.

Ricardo walked toward the butler.

He put his arm around Manuel, turned him around and walked back to the Bentley speaking in soft, rapid Spanish. Thirty seconds later, Manuel got back in the Bentley and waved goodbye.

"What was that about?" Lois asked Ricardo, after he got into her car.

"That is Manuel," he said. "He is a butler for some rich people in Palm Beach."

"Was he coming to pick you up?" Lois said.

"Yes."

"And here I thought if I didn't come and get you, nobody would," Lois said.

"Sorry. I called you first. Ricardo … I did not know if I could get in touch with my friend, Manuel. I did not even know if he was working today. In desperation, I called him after you said you were busy."

She looked at him.

"His boss is going to be mad he made the trip here for nothing," she said.

"I do not think so. I met his boss. He is a nice guy. You ever meet any of those Palm Beach people?"

"Not me," Lois said. "I hear they're a bunch of phonies,

anyway."

"Yes, but it would be great to have their money, no? To be rich?" Ricardo said.

He studied her face hard now and hung onto her next words as if they would be the key to determining whether she was truly a woman worth chasing.

"I don't know," she said. "You know, I used to think that money was everything. My second husband made a lot. We had a boat, a cabin in Vail. Vacations around the world. But you know what? It still wasn't worth living with the louse."

"So if money does not make the world go around, what does?"

"Ricardo," she said, taking her eyes off the road to look at him, "Don't play stupid with me. You know."

Yes, he did know. And now he knew that she knew, too.

■ ■ ■

Margo wasn't in her condo for five minutes before the first news reporter called. She told him she was busy. She told the same thing to the second one a couple of minutes later. When the third reporter called, she just hung up without saying a word.

She might have spent the rest of the afternoon sitting on the couch and staring into space if it hadn't been for the knock on the door. It turned out to be Sam Hamstein in a bathing suit with a beach towel rolled around his neck.

"I was heading to the pool," he said, "and I thought you might want to go, too."

"I don't think so," Margo said. "I'm not feeling so hot."

"Sick?"

"No, not sick."

"Just got the blues?"

"Yeah, I guess."

"C'mon," Sam said. "Get your suit on. I'll wait for you."

The phone rang again. She looked back and considered answering it. Then changed her mind and looked at Sam.

"OK," she said. "Give me two minutes."

On their walk to the pool, Sam asked her, "So, do you always ignore ringing phones?"

"Today I do."

She was glad he didn't ask any more questions. And she was glad three hours later that Sam, this intriguing variation of Bernie and Rose, had dragged her away from her condo and out into the sunshine to swim lazily and lounge on a clubhouse chaise.

"Sam?" she said, after waking up from a brief snooze.

"Yeah?"

"Can we do this every day?"

"Absolutely not," he said.

"Why not?"

"It's too much fun," he said. "My mom tells me they never let fun go unpunished here at Shady Palms."

When the sun started slanting over the clubhouse roof, they slowly made their way back to C Building. As they did, they passed several older couples. Many of them stared at Sam and Margo, not even bothering to smile or politely avoid eye contact as they crossed paths.

She grew quiet as they approached the building, and then she said, "Sam, do you get along with your father?"

"Bernie?" Sam said. "Who can't get along with Bernie?"

Then he told her his favorite story about his father.

"I remember calling from college and saying, 'Mom, this girlfriend I'm bringing with me, I just want you to know, she's black.' Then there was a pause on the phone, and she said, 'I'll tell your father. He'll be thrilled.' I tried to prepare Jasmine, telling her she probably wasn't going to get the warmest reception from my parents.

"But when we got here, the opposite was true. They were both great, especially my father, who went out and bought a bunch of soul music. I remember walking in and seeing my dad in his Bermuda shorts and white patent leather shoes, sashaying across the carpet to *She's a Brick House*, by the Commodores.

"It was embarrassing at first. I remember the next morning I went with him to get bagels, and I told him he didn't have to play soul music for Jasmine, who actually preferred Italian operas to Marvin Gaye. But my father explained he was just trying to make her feel comfortable. Then he told me that, yes, at first he was surprised and disappointed I was dating a black girl, but the more he thought about it, the more he realized he wasn't going to get in the way of me following my heart.

"Then he told me about how his own father had refused to speak to him again after he married my mom. I never knew that. It was the only time I had ever seen my father cry. We were standing there in the middle of this bagel shop, and the guy behind the counter was asking, 'Did you say you wanted the chive cheese or the lox spread?' and Bernie's there bawling into a paper napkin.

"So to answer your question, 'Yeah, I get along with my father just fine.' "

They had reached her door now, and Sam could see that she was sniffling.

"Hey, I didn't mean to make you all weepy," he said.

She surprised him by burying her head in his chest and hugging him, while saying, "Oh, Sam. What am I going to do?"

He put his arms around her, and despite himself, felt a tingle of electricity as her smooth lotioned flesh met his. He was too stunned from the nearness of her to digest what she said next. It wouldn't be until later that her words would ring in his ears.

She went inside her condo, where her phone was ringing again. Sam went back to his parents' condo. Lucky was asleep on the living room couch. The note in the kitchen from his mother said they were at the grocery store.

Sam found some of his father's soul CDs buried in the back of the music cabinet. He put on Harold Melvin and the Blue Notes, then called Jasmine for the third time that day. Like the other times, he left a message after the beep. When he walked out of the bedroom, the Blue Notes were singing, *The Love I Lost.*

He opened a beer and sat out on the patio, wondering, like Margo, what he was going to do now.

Then her words came back to him. When she had hugged him at the door and said, "Oh, Sam. What am I going to do now?" he had assumed she was talking about herself and her pregnancy.

But the next thing she said didn't make any sense.

"Sam," she said. "Look out for your father. Please."

Now why would she say something like that?

Bernie and Rose came home with the shopping. On his way to the patio, Bernie flipped off the stereo.

"Oy," he said, taking a seat next to his son. "That music gives me a headache."

■ ■ ■

Jacqui sat at her dining room table with her swollen right ankle propped on an empty chair. She could sense the throbbing, but it was numbed right now with a pain killer, three glasses of wine and one of the best dinners she had eaten in years.

As she took the last bite of dolphin with macadamia nut crust, she looked across the candlelit table and complimented the chef.

"Craig, you must be a very popular guy at the firehouse."

"I hope you've saved a little room for dessert, Mrs. Fisher," Craig said.

"Craig made crème brûlé, Mom," Jake said.

Maddy said, "And to think, I was going to eat one of those Stouffer's frozen dinners tonight."

28 Wallbanger's cavalry storms Shady Palms

The next morning, this story appeared on Page 2B of *The Palm Beach Post* under the heading titled Metro Report:

Pregnant woman causes stir in Shady Palms condo

BOYNTON BEACH — The pregnancy of an unmarried renter in the Shady Palms condominium has raised concerns among its elderly residents that their way of life could be jeopardized.

Margo Zukowski, who moved into the complex two months ago, will not be allowed to stay for the duration of her one-year lease, said the condominium's attorney, Stuart R. Fine.

"This is an adults-only condominium," Fine said. "Ms. Zukowski is free to have as many children as she pleases, as long as she doesn't have them here."

In a strongly worded editorial, the community's newspaper, The Shady Palms Gazette, wrote that Zukowski was about as welcome there as "the Hong Kong flu."

She is, however, getting support from an unlikely source. Radio talk-show host Walter Wallbanger said he plans to broadcast from outside the front gate of Shady Palms today.

"It's time those condo commandos wake up and smell the

Metamucil," Wallbanger told his audience. "Margo, sit tight, honey. The cavalry is coming!"

Zukowski could not be reached for comment.

■ ■ ■

The cavalry consisted of Wallbanger's five chronic listeners and acolytes. They were: a local gun collector who was trying to start his own militia; a woman who believed the stop signs in her neighborhood were encoded with secret United Nations attack instructions; a disgruntled former postal worker who was weighing whether to begin shooting abortion doctors; a neo-Nazi who kept trying to get Wallbanger to consider doing a show titled "The Holocaust Hoax," and a childless born-again Christian who wanted to be on the school board in order to force other people's children to pray.

They began gathering outside the Boynton Beach Boulevard entrance to Shady Palms about 8 a.m. Wallbanger's staff provided the doughnuts for sustenance and the signs for waving to passing traffic.

The born-again Christian exchanged the "Hell no, she won't go!" sign for the "Way to go, Mar-go!" sign. The United Nations conspiracy theory buff chose the "Commandos must go! Save our Margo!" And the disgruntled former postal worker said he was fundamentally opposed to carrying anything.

Wallbanger set up on the side of the road, next to a mobile van with the call letters of his station displayed in big red letters, and a huge banner saying Walter Wallbanger's Search for Truth draped over the windshield.

Hector, the gate guard, made the short walk from his shack to the grassy strip where the talk-show invaders were setting up.

"Excuse me," Hector said. "But what do you think you are doing here?"

Wallbanger, not missing a chance for confrontation, stepped up and stood a few inches from Hector, while speaking in a voice loud enough for his group to hear.

"We are exercising our First Amendment rights to assembly," he said. "That's what we're doing."

"You want to exercise, go to a gym," Hector said. "You got a permit for all of this?"

Wallbanger, detecting the guard's foreign ancestry, smiled.

"My good man, in America we have a thing that's called freedom," he said. "People from your country might not be aware of it."

Wallbanger got some snickers from his group, which had circled behind him now.

"But in America," Wallbanger continued. "There's such a thing as people having the right to air grievances."

Hector didn't like getting a lecture from this big mouth. It was times like this when he wished he was a real cop. He'd have this radio guy on the ground already with one of those big flashlights poking in his back.

"There's also such a thing as having permits," Hector said.

"Señor," Wallbanger said, his voice dripping with sarcasm, "we are not on Shady Palms property. You are out of your jurisdiction. We are on the public right-of-way. And we are the public. And as the public, we have the right to rise up in opposition to the Draconian elements of our society, wherever we see them."

The others murmured their approval. Hector got a good look at the rest of them now and decided it best to retreat.

"We'll see about that," he said, as he walked back to the guard shack, trying to block out their jeers.

If only he were a real cop, Hector told himself again.

When he got back to the guard shack, he reported the gathering to Herb Troutman.

"I don't know, Mr. Troutman," Hector said into the phone. "Something about Dracula in our society."

■ ■ ■

Bernie had put off his discussion with Margo as long as he could. The story was in the real newspapers now, and he knew if he didn't talk to Margo soon, Troutman or that lawyer Fine would.

After the morning mall walk, Rose announced she was taking Lucky to the dog groomer for a clip.

"It's so hot, Bernie," Rose said. "Think how much better Lucky will feel with a shampoo and clip."

Bernie shook his head.

"This dog is already more trouble than he's worth," Bernie said.

Lucky looked at him and wagged his tail. Rose reacted less favorably to the remark.

"Bernard Hamstein," she said. "I'll be back in an hour. I'll expect by then you will have had an attitude adjustment about our beloved new pet."

Bernie just grumbled and walked away.

Now was the time, he thought. He needed to talk to Margo now. But instead, he just sat there, still trying to figure out why she had lied to them about being from North Dakota.

What was she hiding? Bernie wasn't sure he wanted to find out.

He watched his son, Sam, lace up his running shoes and stretch in preparation for a jog.

He waited for Sam to leave. And then Bernie just sat there for another 20 minutes, listening to the ticking of the living room clock.

"Ah, just get it over with," he finally said to himself.

Bernie walked out of his condo, took the elevator and knocked on the door of 26C.

"Margo," he said. "We need to talk."

She looked like she had just rolled out of bed, even though she'd been up for hours. The blinds in the living room were drawn. On the coffee table, a copy of *The Palm Beach Post* was opened to the Local News section. And the small condo was filled with the voice of Walter Wallbanger.

"This isn't the first time the rotten among us have told a pregnant woman that there's no room at the inn," Wallbanger was saying.

She looked toward the radio on the kitchen counter.

"He's been carrying on like that all morning," she said.

"With friends like that, you don't need enemies," Bernie said.

She nodded.

"I've had to take the phone off the hook. He keeps calling."

"I see you've seen the paper, too," Bernie said.

"Yeah, Maddy brought it over to me," Margo said.

Bernie took a seat.

"Are you OK, Bernie?"

"Yeah, fine."

"You look ... I don't know, pale or something."

"I'm just worried," Bernie said. "You can't stay here, Margo."

"Excuse me?"

"I said ... you can't stay here at Shady Palms. You have to go."

She paused for a second.

"So you're here now to tell me I have to leave? Is that it?"

"It's not my idea," he said.

"And if I don't want to?"

"Listen, Margo. They told me to tell you that they'll give you a couple of months rent. But I'll bet you can get more from them. I'll just tell Troutman that you'll only leave if they pay you four months rent."

Margo looked up at Bernie.

"What happens if I don't go?" she asked.

"They'll sue you. Force you to go. It'll be ugly. You don't want to put yourself though that."

Margo asked, "Sue me for what?"

"I don't know. I'm no lawyer ... Listen, Margo. There were things you've said that just aren't true."

"What do you mean, Bernie?"

"You're not really from North Dakota, are you?"

She didn't answer.

"I don't even know why you'd want to live here, Margo. We're not your people. You should be around people your own age."

"But I'm happy here," she said.

Wallbanger, unable to draw many people from the condo to participate in his show, had to fill up a lot of air time with his own ranting.

"So if you happen to be in the area of the Shady Palms asylum, stop by and join the crowd who is out here protesting for the rights of one of our citizens," Wallbanger was saying. "You don't see the so-called mainstream media out here today because, ladies and gentlemen, they don't care about your rights. It is only I, Walter Wallbanger, who has the guts to stand up to tyranny wherever it may be."

"I like you, Margo," Bernie said. "And I don't want to see you getting hurt."

Margo nodded.

"Does Rose know you're here?"

"No. Rose would kill me if she knew I was asking you to leave."

"I won't tell her," Margo said.

"Good."

"But I'm not leaving, Bernie," she said. "I can't."

"Why not?"

Margo shook her head. She was about to say something, but suddenly Wallbanger's voice had changed.

"When condominiums act like outlaw nations," he was saying in his usual overbearing way, "it becomes incumbent on the people to … OH MY GOD! NO! …"

There was a loud commotion, the sound of wood shattering, metal on metal contact. Then Wallbanger said a bunch of words that might have cost the station its FCC license had they been said in less stressful circumstances.

Mixed in all these calamitous sounds, Bernie thought he

recognized something familiar. It wasn't a human sound. And it wasn't a crashing sound, either.

It was more like a dog sound. And the dog sounded just like Lucky.

Then the station went off the air, and all over Shady Palms, the residents got up from their chairs and adjusted their radio dials, eventually realizing there was nothing left of Walter Wallbanger's Search for Truth but the sound of static.

29 The dogged 'Search for Truth'

The poor driving habits of the residents of Shady Palms are legendary. Not many months go by before someone ends up depositing an automobile where it doesn't belong. In the condominium's short history, cars have ended up in the bottom of the clubhouse swimming pool, in the bedrooms of first floor residents and in the thick mud of the adjoining canal bank on the east end of the property.

Casual inspection of the palm trees and shrubs reveal the wayward path vehicles have taken in sudden off-road routes to their destinations.

Hector, the gate guard, puts in regular orders for the orange-and-white-striped wooden gates, which are routinely shattered by cars with drivers who either are too impatient to wait for the mechanical arm to rise or just plain forget that it's there.

The citizenry outside the gates of the condo complex have reacted to the mayhem caused by Shady Palms drivers with sentiments that range from fear to amusement.

"Pray for me — I drive by Shady Palms every day" is a big-selling bumper sticker in a nearby novelty shop.

Nearly all of the Shady Palms automobile misadventures can be traced to operator error, and nearly all the initial operator error is made worse by a common problem: The driver, when trying to slam on the brakes, somehow manages to miss the brake pedal by a few inches, flooring the gas pedal instead.

And that's what happened to Rose Hamstein this morning — although it could hardly be said her actions started the chain of events.

These events began when she was returning home with a freshly clipped Lucky sitting on the front seat next to her. The dog was hanging his head out the window, gulping down the wind and trying to focus on the rapidly changing scenery zipping by.

When Rose approached the Shady Palms entrance, she slowed her car and noticed the Walter Wallbanger entourage standing on the swale, only a few inches from the pavement of the turning lane.

The group had been on the side of the road nearly three hours by then, and except for that brief, satisfying flap with Hector, they had been largely ignored.

They had expected mobs of old people to stream out of the gates of Shady Palms, demanding that they leave. They had expected police officers being dispatched to maintain an uneasy calm. They had expected Wallbanger, their standard bearer, to lead a spirited radio debate with people inside Shady Palms.

They didn't expect that they'd be ignored. But that's what was happening. The gun collector, U.N. conspiracy theorist, disgruntled postal worker, neo-Nazi and born-again Christian school board hopeful just stood there baking in the sun, waving their signs to an indifferent public.

Not even the woman they were saving, Margo what's-her-name, was willing to talk to them. They knew that because they kept hearing Wallbanger's show producer saying, "Wally, I've tried a dozen times already. I think she's taken her phone off the hook."

The neo-Nazi kicked a discarded soda can and told his fellow protesters: "This just won't do."

"Yeah," piped up the disgruntled postal worker. "We need some action."

It was the militia-loving gun collector who fired the first shot. He didn't have a gun with him. But he had a Boston creme doughnut, and he was about to put it in his mouth when he saw Rose's car slow down and move into the turning lane.

"There's one of those old tyrants," he said, halting the progress of the doughnut toward his mouth.

The neo-Nazi took a step into the road and held up his sign, "Stay, Margo! Don't be a Geezer Pleaser!"

When Rose saw the man step into the roadway about 50 yards ahead, she gave what she thought was a polite tap on the Camry's horn.

Lucky, startled by the sound, barked. The gun collector smiled. This was all the provocation he needed. He stopped the sticky doughnut a few inches from his lips and brought back his arm all the way down to his camouflaged pants. He paused for a second, then hurled the doughnut, coming over the shoulder with his throwing motion, releasing the brown-and-tan orb like a fastball.

The doughnut struck the windshield of the approaching car with an impressive splatter, imprinting a Rorschach pattern of custardy creme and chocolate icing on the outside of the glass.

For Lucky, it was a sight too delectable to pass up. The dog lunged toward the dashboard, expecting to gulp down the creamy treat, but instead banged his skull on the inside of the windshield and toppled, momentarily stunned, into Rose's lap.

Lucky's fall caught Rose's right arm, which caused her to jerk the wheel, making the car leave the pavement. Lucky lunged again for the doughnut and again came flopping back toward Rose, who now had a dog in her face blocking her view. She could tell from the sound of the tires that at least half her car was off the road.

She tried to jerk the wheel to the left, but Lucky was now

sitting on her left arm. So she did the only other thing that might be wise under these circumstances.

She reached with her right foot, and with all her might, tried to stomp on the brake.

But in the grand tradition of Shady Palms residents before her, Rose Hamstein didn't move her right foot far enough. And so instead of stepping on the brake, she floored the accelerator, kicking up clumps of sod as her Camry, pedal to the metal, roared straight for the group of protesters.

They all, perhaps out of political instinct, dove to the right, bumping into each other as they narrowly avoided becoming hood ornaments. It wasn't until they did that Walter Wallbanger, who was sitting at a wooden table behind them, got a good look at the reason for their sudden evasive action — an out-of-control car with a barking dog and senior citizen driver heading his way.

Wallbanger had been in the middle of an aimless diatribe when he looked up and saw that his three hours of boredom was about to end.

"OH MY GOD! NO! ..." he said, certain they would be his last words on this planet.

But moments before, Lucky had finally decided it was time to get off Rose's lap, and when the dog jumped back into his seat, Rose saw with clarity that she had to act fast to avoid disaster.

She found the brake pedal and pushed it hard. With her arms free, she gently eased the wheel to the left, so that the car was now slowing and sideswiping the radio van.

With grass flying, the Camry demolished the wooden table Wallbanger had been sitting at, then the car bounced into the radio van, creasing the fenders on both vehicles before Rose's car came to a stop.

Her deft maneuvering in the final seconds had averted a true disaster. The material damage was minimal. Most of the radio equipment had been spared. Both vehicles were drivable, and Wallbanger and Rose were shaken but not seriously hurt.

As soon as the Camry came to a stop, Lucky hopped out
the window and jumped on the hood of the car to make short
work of the doughnut's remains, still smeared on the windshield.

Rose sat behind the wheel, dazed for a moment. The next
thing she remembered was the ring of angry faces standing by
her door and screaming at her.

"She tried to kill us! She tried to kill us!" the U.N.
conspiracy buff shouted.

"Murderer!" the disgruntled postal worker said.

"You'll burn in hell," the born-again school board hopeful
chimed in.

They parted when Wallbanger walked up. His clothes were
dirty, because at the last moment before the crash, he dropped
to the ground. His broadcast had been involuntarily terminated a
few seconds later, but not before he spit out a string of expletives
while buried under the splintered remains of his wooden table.
In a rage, he flung the wood off and stormed toward Rose's car.

"You," he said, poking his finger hard against Rose's
shoulder, "are going to pay for this."

"Ouch," Rose said. "Get your hands off me."

Then she looked at the others.

"Which one of you threw that doughnut at the car?"

"What doughnut?" the U.N. conspiracy buff said.

"Yeah, I don't see no doughnut," the neo-Nazi said.

"Get out of the car," Wallbanger told Rose.

"What?" she asked.

"You heard me," he said, then he grabbed her under the
arm and pulled her out.

"Ouch!" she said again. "For the last time, get your hands
off me!"

A quarter-mile away, Hector had just finished placing the
911 call. He hung up the phone, grabbed his heavy flashlight and
started running to the accident scene.

Even from his distance, he could see that the protesters
were giving poor Mrs. Hamstein a bad time. Now, it didn't

matter if he was a real cop or not, Hector thought. He was just
going to do what needed to be done.

But Hector would never get the chance to act out his
fantasy that day.

Because when Wallbanger pulled Rose out of the car,
Lucky's post-doughnut bliss evaporated. The hair on the back of
his neck stood up as the dog watched the radio bully manhandle
Rose.

Wallbanger, too in love with the sound of his own voice, did
not appreciate the sound of the low growl coming from the dog
standing on the hood of the woman's car.

"You, lady," Wallbanger said, poking her again, "are going
to spend the rest of your life living in a hovel when my lawyers
get through with you."

He was going to say more, but by then Lucky had jumped
from the hood, knocking Wallbanger to the ground. When the
talk show host got to his knees, preparing to run away, Lucky
took aim at his substantial rear end and sunk his teeth in the
meaty flesh.

Wallbanger howled, staggering to his feet.

Lucky stood next to Rose and faced the others with a look
that said, "Who's next?"

The disgruntled postal worker, who was already plagued
by a recurring nightmare about dogs, was the first to walk away.

**Lucky gets
acquainted
with Walter
Wallbanger.**

30 Bernie and Rose on a steak-out

The next morning, the following story appeared on Page 1B of *The Palm Beach Post*:

Talk-show host hospitalized after Shady Palms dog bite

By T.S. Kleinfeld
Palm Beach Post Staff Writer

BOYNTON BEACH — Radio talk-show host Walter Wallbanger was hospitalized yesterday after being bitten in the left buttock by a dog during his show.

Wallbanger, who was broadcasting from outside the gates of the Shady Palms condominium, had his show knocked off the air when a resident lost control of her car and plowed into Wallbanger's mobile broadcast equipment.

The resident, Rose Hamstein, 72, was returning home with her dog, Lucky, when she drove her car off the roadway, causing the accident.

Lucky attacked Wallbanger shortly after the crash, police said.

Wallbanger had been broadcasting outside Shady Palms in support of Margo Zukowski, a renter who is living in the adults-only complex despite being pregnant.

Police say they don't believe Hamstein intentionally tried to injure Wallbanger with her car. This is the 15th time this year Shady Palms drivers have lost control of their vehicles on or around the complex, a Palm Beach County Sheriff's Office spokesman said.

Wallbanger, however, said he believes the incident was orchestrated by the condominium board of Shady Palms.

"They tried to silence me," Wallbanger said. "I was exposing their injustice, so they sent one of their storm troopers and her mongrel dog to rub me out. Well, it didn't work, and I won't be silenced."

Wallbanger said he intends to broadcast his show today from his bed at Bethesda Memorial Hospital.

■ ■ ■

"Turn it off," Rose said.

Bernie reached over to the car radio, and in an instant, the sound of Wallbanger's voice was gone.

"He wasn't even hurt," Rose said. "He's just in the hospital to make a stink."

Bernie was only half listening. He was distracted with thoughts about the Camry and whether it was driving a little funny since Rose's off-road mishap. He was also trying to make sense of Rose's cryptic explanation of the accident.

"So, the guy stands out in front of your car, you beep the horn, and then the wheels leave the roadway," he had said to her that morning. "That I understand. But what I don't understand is what prevented you from turning the wheel to the left and getting back on the road when the right tires went in the grass?"

Rose had left out the part about the doughnut, because a discussion of the doughnut would lead to a discussion about Lucky's attempts at getting the doughnut. And that, of course, would lead to a discussion on how the dog had caused her arms to be pinned and her vision blocked.

Rose didn't want Bernie to think the dog had anything to do with the accident. Lucky was already on probation with

Bernie. The poor beast didn't need another mark on his record — especially after the way he protected her from those radio savages.

They drove north on Interstate 95 in silence.

Bernie followed the directions he had gotten from the recorded message, exiting on Belvedere Road and driving west, past the airport. After a few more miles, he was sure he had gone too far. But then he saw the building up ahead on the left.

The Palm Beach County Animal Care and Control office was bigger and newer than he had imagined. He parked in the lot, following Rose inside.

"I'm here to see an inmate," Rose told the woman at the information desk. "His name is Lucky Hamstein."

This was new to him, his wife giving the dog his last name. Lucky Hamstein? Oh, his father would be spinning in his grave over this one.

The young woman behind the counter clicked her computer keyboard for about 30 seconds and then looked up at Rose.

"I'm sorry," she said. "My computer is showing that your dog was brought here on a bite case."

"Lucky was just protecting me from a pack of lunatics," Rose said.

"Dogs in bite cases are quarantined here for 10 days," the younger woman said.

"Quarantined?" Rose said. "The guy who came in the truck yesterday just said something about how they had to check the dog to make sure it wasn't rabid."

"Yes," the woman said, "and then there has to be a determination made as to whether it's a dangerous dog."

"Lucky? A dangerous dog?"

She looked at Bernie for support.

"Pain in the neck, maybe," Bernie said. "But dangerous?"

Rose scowled at him. So OK, then. Let her handle this on her own, he thought. Bernie stepped away from the counter and took an empty chair, sitting three seats away from a woman who was holding a pit bulldog on a short chain.

"Now this looks like a dangerous dog," he told the dog's owner.

The woman just glared at him. Apparently a dangerous owner, too. Bernie moved over one more seat.

Back at the counter, Rose was just getting warmed up.

"So, you mean I can't see my dog?" she said, trying to sound incredulous.

"In 10 days, there'll be a ..." the clerk started to say.

"I don't care about 10 days, I care about today. I'm here to see my dog."

"Ma'am, the policy is ..."

"The policy is wrong," Rose said. "Listen, if you go out and murder somebody, you don't have to wait 10 days to get a visitor. So why should a little dog who weighs 20 pounds ..."

"Twenty-two," Bernie said from his seat.

" . . . have to be punished like that for doing nothing but saving his human companion from harm?"

"Ma'am, I don't make the rules here," the clerk said, showing the first sign of impatience with Rose.

"Well, who does?"

"I can have you speak with a supervisor."

"Good idea. I'll be over here, sitting next to Rip Van Winkle," she said, motioning to Bernie, who had already started to fall asleep in the chair.

A few minutes later, Bernie was startled by the sound of barking. A man with a German shepherd had walked in, causing the pit bull to strain at its leash and growl. Soon, both dogs were barking inches from each other's snouts.

In the commotion, Rose tugged on Bernie's pants and then bolted for a side door that led to an interior corridor of the building.

"Rose," Bernie said.

He caught up to her as she made her way toward the

kennel.

"Rose, what are you doing?"

"I'm going to visit my dog," she said.

"But Rose, you can't just …"

They were in the kennel now. Dogs stood up in their caged enclosures, looking through chain link at them, wondering if these were the people who were going to help them. Some dogs yelped. Others cried.

Rose found Lucky at the end of a row. His tail rapped hard against the concrete block wall of his pen when he saw them, and he made a high-pitch whine.

Rose would have climbed in the pen if the gate wasn't locked. So instead, she dropped down, pressing her face against the chain link, allowing Lucky to lick her over and over again.

Then she reached her fingers through and started rubbing him, starting with the scruff of his neck and then allowing the dog to move and pick his own favorite spots.

"Daddy's here," Rose told the dog.

"Rose, for cryin' out loud."

She ignored him. It was no use. So Bernie squatted down and found himself sticking his own fingers through the cage to touch the dog.

"We're going to get you out of here, Lucky," Rose said. "Don't you worry."

Then she turned to Bernie.

"Please hand me the foil package out of my purse."

"What is this thing, Rose?" Bernie said, handing over the warm package.

She unfolded the foil, and the aroma of broiled steak made Lucky's mouth hang open.

Bernie's too.

"A Porterhouse?" he said in disbelief. "That's like $7 a pound."

"No, actually it's $7.99 a pound."

She carefully slid the whole steak under the gate. Lucky

carried it to a far corner of the pen, then looked over his shoulder at Rose and Bernie.

"He's saying, 'Thank you,' " Rose said. "Now we can go."

■ ■ ■

Margo woke up with a knock on her door.

At first, she figured it was one of the Wonder Walkers telling her to hurry up or she'd be late. But then she looked at her alarm clock and saw it was 9:15. They must have gone to the mall without her by now.

She put on her bathrobe and went to the door.

"Sam."

"Oops. Looks like I woke you."

"No, that's all right. Come on in."

"I'm sorry. I tried calling, but there's something wrong with your phone."

"Yeah," she said. "I have it off the hook because of that radio guy."

They stood awkwardly in the doorway.

"My mom went on her walk. My dad left to price some repairs on the car, and I was just banging around the condo. I thought maybe if you didn't have anything to do this morning, we could . . . I don't know . . . do something."

They ate breakfast together in her condo.

"You don't want to turn on the radio and listen to what that guy's saying about you?" he asked as they washed and dried the dishes.

"No," she said. "I don't care what he thinks about me having a baby."

"I think about your baby a lot," Sam said.

"You do?"

"Yeah. Mostly I think about how your boyfriend could leave you alone like this. I just can't imagine anybody not wanting to be the father of your child. My parents told me about your boyfriend, Bill, and how he's hardly around. It makes me ..."

"Sam," she said, cutting him off. "Bill's not my boyfriend."

"He's not?"

"No," she said. "He's not the father of my child, either."

"No? Then who is?"

Margo put down the dishrag, faced Sam and shrugged.

"I don't know, Sam."

"I wish I could help you, Margo."

"You can."

She took his hand and led him to the bedroom.

31 All's quiet on the western Boynton front

It wouldn't be accurate to say that little happened to the folks from C Building during the next couple of days. But it was a period of relative calm.

Sam Hamstein and Margo Zukowski mutually agreed that a repeat performance in the sack would further complicate their already complicated lives. So, they restricted their growing fondness for each other to long afternoons at the Shady Palms clubhouse pool and evenings at Sam's parents' condo, where Sam, Margo, Bernie and Rose played board games or watched television.

With the weekend here and no shows to broadcast, Walter Wallbanger saw no excuse to remain in the hospital for a dog bite that, if the truth be known, didn't even hurt very much the day he got it. So Wallbanger checked out and spent the weekend thinking about how he could get another story about himself in the newspaper.

There were no stories about Shady Palms in *The Palm Beach Post* during these two days, a fact that greatly relieved Herb Troutman and the rest of the condo's board.

Margo, who took her phone off the hook because of the radio show, left it that way all weekend. She would later tell Bill she had forgotten it was off the hook. But that would be a lie.

She just liked the way it felt to have nobody bothering her.

The Wonder Walkers still walked, all of them but Jacqui Fisher. She was getting around on crutches now, and she spent a lot of time with her right leg propped up.

But despite her pain, Jacqui was happy. She had seen a change come over her son, Jake. And it was something she'd seen and felt before. Jake was in love.

Like all real love, it was a transforming experience.

Jake was too happy to look for another job. The former Señor Peppy at Kidz-a-Poppin' had grown content to mark time for a while. The only downside was that Craig was a lot busier than he was.

When Craig didn't have 24-hour duty at the fire station, he moonlighted as a house painter. So Jake had all day to himself before he'd get to see Craig.

But Jake didn't mind. Anticipation, after all, was half the fun. So Jake doted over his mother during the day and spent long afternoons at the swimming pool, where he discovered Sam and Margo, the only other people there under Social Security age.

"So when do we get to meet this Craig?" Sam had asked Jake one afternoon.

"Monday," Jake said. "He's finally taking a day off, and I told him, 'Craiger, you haven't lived until you slip on one of your tiny bathing suits and lie out among the fossils at the Shady Palms swimming hole.' I think I got him very excited about it."

Rose Hamstein had begun marking off the days on her kitchen calendar with big black Xs. After 10 Xs, she'd get her dog back. She didn't realize how much she'd miss Lucky. The first couple of nights he spent in the pound, she ended up sniffling into her pillow.

"Rose, you didn't even act this way when I left for the Army," Bernie had said.

"Yes, I did," she said. "You're just too old to remember."

Rose traveled alone now to see Lucky. She got stopped trying to sneak in on Saturday. The animal control officer turned her around and walked her back to the door.

Sunday, she made it all the way to the kennel. But she had just begun to pet her dog through the chain-link fence when she saw a pound employee. It was an unfamiliar face on duty this day, a young man who looked barely out of his teens.

Rose straightened up, about to plead her case. But the young man spoke first.

"I tell you what. I'll make this a little easier for you," he said. "But when I come back for you in 15 minutes, you've got to get out of here, or I'll get in trouble."

Then he unlocked the gate and swung it open for Rose. It was only then she realized what he had in mind.

"Thank you," Rose said, as she walked into the cage and sat there with Lucky, who ran excitedly in circles around her. The animal control officer closed the gate and walked off to euthanize another batch of unwanted dogs.

Bernie did his share of solo excursions that weekend, too. But not to the dog pound. On Sunday, he found himself driving through Atlantis again.

As he was winding his way toward Willow Bend Court, a lemon yellow Cadillac passed him, going the opposite way.

Bernie pulled into a driveway, backed up and headed in the opposite direction, following the Cadillac, which was now about a half-block ahead of him. He made out the "Jeb!" bumper sticker and knew he was following the right car.

He finally caught up with the Cadillac as it stopped at the exit of Atlantis. The driver was waiting for her chance to blend into the traffic on Congress Avenue.

Bernie eased his Camry inches from the Cadillac's bumper and tried to get a glimpse of the woman behind the wheel. But all Bernie could see was a head of strawberry blond hair. And that she was alone.

Looking through the Cadillac's back window wasn't the best way to identify anybody. But Bernie had a feeling it was Susan Plock.

He would have to ease his car next to her to get a real look at what had become of her.

Suddenly, the Cadillac made a left turn into the flow of traffic. He pulled up to follow, but had to wait for traffic before making the turn. The Cadillac faded into the northbound lanes.

He did his best to make up time. After a couple of miles, he
saw the Cadillac suddenly appear when a truck behind it exited
the road. The car was only a hundred yards or so in front of him
now.

He gunned the Camry and wedged between two other cars
in the left lane. Now, he was in good position. The Cadillac was
in the right lane, and he steadily gained on it.

Finally, he was inching up the left side of the Cadillac. It
wasn't until then that he thought, "Now what?"

Should he just look? Or should he wave and see if she rec-
ognizes him?

He pulled up alongside the Cadillac and turned his head to
get his first good look at his old girlfriend. He had a smile on his
face, and yes, he was waving. He even gave a little toot of the
horn.

The woman in the Cadillac turned to face him, and Bernie
saw that face again.

It was Susan Plock's face all right. The features were
unmistakable. And in an instant, he remembered it all. She
hadn't changed a bit.

But she didn't recognize him, that's for sure. The woman
in the Cadillac scowled at him, then gunned the engine.

Bernie sped up, pulled alongside her car again and tooted
one more time. She looked even more horrified now, and suddenly Bernie realized why Susan Plock looked so much like he
remembered her, and why she was now trying to get away from
him.

This wasn't Susan Plock. This was her daughter. He had
memorized the names of her children from that high school
directory. This must be Susan Plock's younger daughter, Sandra.

Bernie let his foot off the accelerator just as she sped up to
get away from him again, and the Cadillac seemed to launch

itself down the road.

"Ahh!" Bernie said to himself in disgust.

He made the next U-turn and headed for home.

He was still feeling foolish as he walked in the door, and he feared that his wife, who knew him so well, would look at him and say, "Bernie, what kind of nonsense have you been up to?"

But Rose's radar wasn't tuned to him that morning. Instead, she was thinking about her friend, Lois.

"Bernie, did you see Lois this morning?" she asked.

"Lois?" Bernie said, relieved. "No. Why's that?"

"It's odd," Rose said.

Yes, Lois was having an odd weekend. And of all the denizens of C Building, Lois was the one who was having the most eventful of times.

"I wonder if it has anything to do with that guy on the bicycle, Ricardo?" Rose asked.

"Lois with a man?" Bernie said. "Talk about your long odds."

"I don't know," Rose said. "Maddy told me Ricardo's been riding his bicycle to her place every day this week, and he ends up staying there longer and longer each time. And I noticed Lois hasn't referred to the guy as a Keebler elf since Thursday."

Bernie stuck his head in the refrigerator.

"I wouldn't worry about her," Bernie said. "Wherever she is, you can bet she's busting some guy's chops."

Bernie didn't realize how true his casual remark was.

Lois was someplace this morning busting some guy's chops.

But it wasn't Ricardo's chops.

And to be accurate, it wasn't the "chops" that were being busted.

It was a clavicle, and some lesser bones.

Yes, it would be one of the more exhilarating mornings of Lois' life.

32 Lois handicaps the race

"You can spend the night, but you've got to sleep on the couch," Lois told Ricardo.

It was Saturday night, and they had already split two bottles of wine over dinner. She didn't intend for him to spend the night. But it seemed easier to point him to the hide-a-bed than to load his bike in the trunk and drive him home.

"The couch would be wonderful," Ricardo said.

"We're not sleeping together," she said.

"No, of course not," he said.

She pulled a pillow out of the linen closet and handed it to him. When she retreated to her bedroom, she closed the door, and for emphasis, made as much noise as possible while locking it.

She got under her sheets and tried to go to sleep. But she felt too unsettled for sleep. No man had ever spent a night in her condo before. And although Ricardo was on the other side of a locked door, it was still close enough to make her realize she had let a man cross an invisible border she thought was impenetrable.

How did this happen? Was Ricardo special, or was she just becoming lonely in her old age? She thought she knew herself better than this.

Take that afternoon, for example. She could have gone shopping with Maddy, but she came up with a bogus excuse to be at home. The real reason was she figured that Ricardo would suddenly show up with his bicycle at her doorstep, like he had been doing all week.

And he did. For the first time, Lois invited him in for a cool drink. And that led to another. And then finally, the first glass of wine.

Ricardo had a fresh T-shirt and shorts rolled up in a bag on his bicycle. He told her about it just as they were finishing the wine.

"Now, why would you carry clean clothes on your bike?" she asked.

"Ricardo just started this week," he said. "Just in case."

"Just in case of what?"

"In case it was needed."

"It's the second door on the right," she told him. "The shampoo's on the shelf over the tub."

By the time he was showered and changed, she had begun preparing dinner.

"I'm making enough for two," she said. "If you'd like to …"

"Yes," he said, not even giving her a chance to finish asking him.

And now, dinner has led to this.

A soft knock on her bedroom door startled her.

"It's locked," she said.

"Ricardo is not trying to come in," he said. "Something occurred to Ricardo."

"What is it?" she said, not even bothering to come to the door. "And please stop calling yourself 'Ricardo.'"

"Yes. Ricardo … er, I … have a triathlon tomorrow in Boca Raton. It is one of those races I do. And I was wondering if you would like to go with me. To watch."

"What time?"

"The race starts at 7:30."

"I walk with my friends in the morning," Lois said.

"Oh, then it would not be possible," he said. "No problem. Goodnight. Sorry to bother you, Lois."

And then she heard him walk away and get between the sheets of his hide-a-bed.

Lois stared at the ceiling for a few minutes. Then she got up, put on a bathrobe, unlocked her door and walked into the living room.

Ricardo sat up in bed.

"So tell me," she said, crossing her arms. "How are you going to get to your race?"

"Not to worry," he said. "Ricardo will ride his bike there, then Manuel, my … friend, will come and bring me the rest of my gear."

Lois sat down on the edge of the hide-a-bed and looked at Ricardo.

"Ricardo, a few years ago, I had something called a mastectomy. Do you know what that is?"

He nodded.

"You're chasing after a woman with one boob. Don't be fooled by the packaging, sir. You're looking at damaged goods. I thought maybe it was time that you knew that."

He looked at her solemnly.

"Did you lose the left one or the right one?"

"What kind of question is that?"

"An important one."

"The left one," she said.

He smiled.

"Good. Ricardo only likes right breasts."

He leaned forward and kissed her on the cheek.

She stood up and walked to her room. Before she closed the door, she turned and said, "I'll take you to your race, Ricardo."

She didn't bother locking the door this time. In another minute, she was sound asleep.

■ ■ ■

By 7 a.m. Sunday, the parking lot at Spanish River Park in Boca Raton was full of cars with bike racks and young men and women preening in skimpy bathing suits.

"I don't see anybody our age," Lois told Ricardo.

"Oh, there are just a few of us left," Ricardo said.

A loudspeaker kept blaring race instructions to the athletes.

"I will be right back," Ricardo said, disappearing into the crowd.

Minutes later, he came back with a powder blue bathing cap in his hand and the number 817 written in black marker on his arms and legs.

"Ah, here comes Manuel," Ricardo said.

The Palm Beach butler pulled up with the Bentley, rolled down his window and handed Ricardo a gym bag. Ricardo spoke softly to Manuel and then said goodbye.

"He's some friend," Lois said.

"The best," Ricardo said.

Ricardo slung the bag over his shoulder and walked his bicycle to the racks where rows of others hung. As he and Lois made their way, racers looked up and greeted him.

"Uh oh, look out. Ricardo's here," they would say. Or "Ricardo, my man!" and then give him a big high-five. She could see them eyeing his bike, his leg muscles, his arms. And she saw their admiration and even heard one of them tell his friend, "What a stud."

A guy with the number "1" written on his arm stopped him.

"Hey, Ricardo, we missed you this week on the ride. Where you been?"

"Yes, Ricardo is trying a new bike route now. You got an aspirin for Ricardo?"

Scooter gave Ricardo three Advils, which he swallowed dry.

"Why does he have the number 1 on his arm?" Lois asked.

"Scooter is the defending champ. He is going to win the elite division today."

"And what about you?" she asked. "What are you going to win?"

"I usually win the masters division — that is guys over 40, and I always win my age group, which is 65 to 69. But I never raced with a head like this."

"The wine?"

He nodded.

"Sorry," she said.

"No, it was worth it. For sure."

The man on the loudspeaker was telling the athletes to head to the beach for the start of the half-mile ocean swim, the first leg of the race.

As Ricardo and Lois were walking through the darkened tunnel that connected the park with the beach, she heard a voice in front of her that nearly made her jump.

Because it was so dark in the tunnel, she just saw the man's shape. But there was no mistaking the voice.

"I told him, I know every lawyer in town, so you won't get very far with that," the man was telling the person next to him.

Lois grabbed Ricardo's arm and made him slow down.

"What is wrong?" he asked.

"That guy," she said softly. "The one with the black bathing suit."

"Harvey?"

"You know him?

"Like I said, there is not many left around our age."

Lois guided Ricardo to a bench.

"Sit down, I need to tell you something."

She told him the story of her third divorce and how her husband's lawyer had actually gone to the hospital in a white lab coat, posing as a doctor, to try to get her to sign away her rightful share of his wealth.

"This is terrible," Ricardo said, patting her hand. "But I do not understand why you are telling me this now."

"Ricardo, that lawyer was Harvey Shorter."

"Harvey?"

"Yes."

Ricardo looked down the beach at Shorter and shook his head.

"Do not worry, Lois. He is no competition for Ricardo. And today, Ricardo will take special pleasure in beating him again."

He stood up, feeling that surge of pre-race jitters.

She pulled his arm, making him sit down again.

"Ricardo," she said. "Beating Harvey Shorter in a race wasn't what I had in mind."

"No?"

"No. It would take something more dramatic than that. Something more lasting and personal."

"Lois, I do not know what you mean."

"Ricardo," she said, "for a year, I was too weak to do anything but save myself. Then I told myself to forget about it. It wasn't worth the aggravation. That it would be his word against mine, and I'd only lose. But I just found out recently he'd become a judge. It's a fresh wound again. And now seeing him here today just ..."

The announcer was calling out the names of notable local athletes who were racing, and Ricardo knew his name would be one of them.

"I have to go," he said.

"Ricardo," she said, clutching his hand one more time. "It would mean a lot to me if something happened today."

He ran down the beach now, getting to the cluster of athletes just as the announcer said, "And of course, what would a tri be without the great one, Ri—car—do Ver-aaaaa!"

Ricardo waved his hand over his head to the applause. But he looked back toward the tunnel and saw Lois still sitting on the bench.

"Ricardo has already qualified for a slot in next month's

Ironman Triathlon in Hawaii," the announcer said.

More applause.

Ricardo smiled, but it was a tight smile. He was too distracted now to be the pre-race showman he usually was. Instead, he grimly wet his toes in the ocean and then walked back to the group, moving through the ranks of bare shoulders until he was where he needed to be.

"Good luck, Ricardo," Harvey Shorter said, sticking out his hand.

Ricardo looked at Harvey now, imagining him in a white lab coat holding out a piece of paper.

"Good luck to you," Ricardo said, shaking the judge's hand and feeling a sickening sensation in his gut.

He wasn't sure if he was sickened more by Harvey, or by himself and the thought of what he was about to do.

The race began, and for the first time ever, Ricardo didn't even bother starting his stopwatch.

What's the use, he told himself? After all, this wasn't going to be a race he would finish.

33 Fresh wounds and old acquaintances

Judge Harvey Shorter's courtroom was dark the next day. The sign outside said all matters would be postponed until further notice.

It didn't mention anything about his broken clavicle, or that Judge Shorter was spending the day in Boca Raton Community Hospital flat on his back with his right side in a soft cast.

But what happened to Judge Shorter was far from a mystery. About 200 people, mostly spectators at Sunday's triathlon, had seen the terrible fall. And after hearing chatter over the police scanner about it, a photographer from *The Boca Raton News* got there in time to snap a couple of quick frames of the judge, bloodied and wearing only an aqua-colored Speedo bathing suit, as he was being loaded into the back of an ambulance.

The photo also showed a cluster of spectators watching the injured racer being carted away. The photo showed only the backs of the spectators, which was a good thing for Lois. Because if the photo had been taken from another direction, it would have shown that she was the only one in the crowd smiling.

Harvey Shorter saw her. Just as he was about to disappear

into the ambulance, his eyes locked on that smiling face. And through the pain, something had registered.

That face. He'd seen that face before. It was … It was …

Gone. The ambulance door closed.

Months later, Harvey would talk jokingly about his healing shoulder injury and about how in the delirium of fresh pain that day, he had hallucinated disagreeable images from his divorce lawyering days.

But on the day after his fall, he found nothing to laugh about.

Ricardo wasn't so jolly, either. He took a long run on the beach Monday morning, hoping it would clear his head. But it didn't.

The injury to Harvey had happened just as Ricardo had planned, and yet, it still surprised him that he actually had gone through with it.

He had to force himself to swim slowly. Normally, he would have gotten out of the water a good six minutes before Harvey. But he didn't want to be that far ahead. So, Ricardo stroked leisurely down the course, fighting his urge to stay up with the faster swimmers. Even so, he was still out of the water a couple of minutes before Shorter.

He remembered running up the beach after the swim and seeing the disappointed look on Lois' face. She didn't know his plan. She had probably figured that if he was going to do some-thing to Harvey, he would have stayed closer to him. But Ricardo had a better idea, an idea that would make his eventual act look less deliberate.

Ricardo was already out on the bike course by the time the winded judge pedaled away from the transition area.

Lois figured there was no way Harvey could catch Ricardo. Ricardo looked like a racer. Shorter just looked like an old man on a bike.

But about three-quarters of the way through the bike course, Ricardo intentionally popped his chain by a rapid sequence of shift changes. Once the chain became disengaged, he slowed to a stop, got off his bike and moved it to the grassy shoulder. For effect, he began cursing.

As other racers zipped by him, he bent down, pretending to have some trouble hooking up his chain. He continued pretending to fix the chain after he watched Shorter pedal by him.

Ricardo gave Harvey a lead big enough to last him until the end of the bike leg. When Ricardo got back on the road, he estimated that if he pedaled his hardest, he'd catch Harvey in front of the transition area, where Lois and everybody else was bound to be watching.

Ricardo had felt himself gaining on the judge, reeling him back, closer and closer. As he made the final 180-degree turn south, he saw the crowd up ahead and nobody between him and the judge.

Ricardo got up off his bike's saddle and began sprinting toward the transition area. Normally, he would have shouted "On your left" to warn a rider in front of him that he was about to be passed. But instead, Ricardo approached Shorter silently, just as the judge was about to make the right turn into the long downward slope leading to the bike racks.

Ricardo was in front of Harvey's bike before the judge even knew he was there, and then in one motion, Ricardo cut his bike sharply, as if he were in a hurry to get to the transition area before the judge.

With Ricardo's rear wheel only inches from the judge's front tire, the final devastating act was a simple quick tap on the brakes. The hesitating jerk of Ricardo's bike was all it took to wipe out the few inches of cushion.

Ricardo's sideswiping blow to Harvey's bike yanked the handlebars from the judge's grasp and began a wobble that would lead to his flying over his handlebars and the bike skidding out from under him.

The judge crashed hard on his shoulder and then went body surfing down the long asphalt slope of the transition area.

Spectators gasped. The band, which had been playing *Born to Be Wild* in the parking lot, saw the judge come slaloming right up to their amplifiers as the lead singer sang, "Fire all of your guns at once and explode into space."

Ricardo got off his bike and ran up to the judge, who was obviously in a lot of pain. Ricardo was relieved to see that he didn't kill him. A race marshal tapped Ricardo on the shoulder and notified him that he committed a clear-cut position foul and was being disqualified.

Ricardo nodded.

"Yes, Ricardo was clearly wrong," he said.

Without bothering to gather up his gear or look for Lois, Ricardo got back on his bicycle and pedaled out of the park.

He rode hard all the way up to Palm Beach, crouching low over his handlebars and not bothering to look up at the passing traffic.

The next morning, Lois told the Wonder Walkers the story over their cinnamon buns.

"And then what happened?" Maddy asked. "After the race."

"Nothing," Lois said.

"What do you mean, 'Nothing?' " Rose asked.

"I mean I haven't seen him since it happened," Lois said. "He just disappeared."

"Uh, oh," Maddy said. "You may have finally scared that man off."

"Nah," Lois said. "He'll be back."

After Wonder Walkers, she went to Publix and bought more groceries and three more bottles of wine. She vacuumed her condo, took a long hot shower and put a fresh bouquet of flowers in her bedroom.

As she changed the sheets on her bed, she noticed her fingers were trembling a little. She looked at herself in the mirror and applied more makeup.

By 2 p.m., there was nothing left to do but wait.

Ricardo must have been running late. He was usually there

The judge crashed hard on his shoulder and then went body surfing down the long asphalt slope of the transition area. Spectators gasped.

by 3.

At 4 p.m., Lois opened up the first bottle of wine.

"To settle my nerves," she told herself. "Just a bit won't hurt."

She finished the bottle an hour later, alone and now convinced that her friend, Maddy, was right.

■ ■ ■

Margo walked to the clubhouse pool that afternoon. As she got near, she could see Sam hadn't arrived yet, but Jacqui's son, Jake, was there, and so was his new friend, Craig, the guy Jake had been talking about so much. Jake was swimming in the pool, and Craig was stretched out on a chaise lounge with a ball cap slung low over his face to protect him from the sun.

When Margo reached the pool deck, Jake motioned her toward the reclining Craig, as if she would have trouble picking Jake's friend out from the clusters of retirees around them.

Margo plopped her bag down next to Craig's chaise and pulled up a chair.

"And so, you must be Jake's friend," Margo said.

Craig moved the ballcap from his face and squinted into the sun behind Margo's back. He extended a hand toward the blurry figure in front of him.

"Hi, I'm Craig Shelbourne," he said, as his eyes finally adjusted so he could see her face.

"Margo," she started to say.

"Zukowski," Craig finished.

He laughed. She didn't.

"Well, I'll be," Craig said. "It really is a small world. How long has it been, Margo? Almost a year now, isn't it?"

"Craig, listen I …"

"When Jake said he wanted me to meet Margo, I had no idea he was talking about you …"

Margo took a panicky look toward Jake and saw that he was climbing out of the pool and walking toward them.

"Craig, listen," she said, grabbing his arm. "You don't know me. Do you understand?"

"What? What do you mean I don't know you? I practically …"

"Craig, please. Trust me."

Craig looked toward Jake now.

"It has nothing to do with Jake," Margo said. "Please, I can't explain right now, but …"

Jake walked up, dripping water behind him.

"Hi, Margo," Jake said, plopping down on the end of Craig's chaise. "I see you two have already made your introductions."

"Yes," Margo said. "Craig and I were just getting acquainted."

Craig stared at her.

"If we're nice to Craig, he might tell us one of his paramedic stories later on," Jake said.

Margo reached for her sun screen, busying herself and trying to avoid looking at Craig.

"I'm thinking of one story in particular," Craig said, still looking at Margo. "But I don't think she'd want to hear it."

34 Margo, lost and found

Craig did tell the story. But it wasn't until hours later, after Jacqui had fallen asleep on the couch watching a silly movie they had rented. And after he and Jake had walked back to the pool and sat alone under the stars in the Jacuzzi.

"So," Craig began, as if no time had elapsed from when he was sitting there poolside with Margo and Jake. "About a year ago, I got an emergency call to a house in a nice neighborhood out in Wellington."

"Uh, huh," Jake said, slouching deeper in the water.

"It was one of those 'child having trouble breathing' calls," Craig said. "Which usually means a kid is choking on his food. Something like that. When we get to the house, I rush in, and there's this 6-year-old girl just blue in the face, and she's got vomit all over the front of her shirt.

"She's just there alone on the floor. The mother was screaming in another room, and the father's pacing around the house, cursing to himself. Like he's angry about something.

"I'm trying to do mouth-to-mouth and yelling, 'How long has she been like this?' and they're not even in the same room. After about 10 minutes, another paramedic taps me on the shoulder and takes over. But it's pretty hopeless. We know by now the little girl's not going to make it.

"So, I'm sitting there on the floor, panting, when I first see the marks on her body. It looked like she'd been beaten with a strap. Regularly. Some of the marks were fresher than others. She had welts all over her. Even a few cigarette burns on her arms.

"So, I leave the room and go looking for the parents. I find the father in the garage, smoking a cigarette and working on his bass boat. It said "Jimbo" in big gold letters on the back.

"I was so angry by then, I almost grabbed him and banged his head against one of the outboard engines.

"He just looked up at me and said, 'Nothing anybody could do.'

" 'May I use your phone?' I asked.

"He pointed me to the kitchen. I called the Sheriff's Office and asked that they send a homicide detective over there immediately.

"We were still there when the cops showed up. A couple of squad cars and a detective. I showed the detective the marks on the girl's body. By then, Jimbo was doing a little more talking.

" 'A father's got a right to discipline his kids when they lie,' he said.

"And I guess I snapped. I called him a murderer and said a bunch of things I shouldn't have said. He also said a bunch of things he shouldn't have said, a bunch of admissions that would help get him indicted for murder.

"Which was what happened. The autopsy concluded that the girl suffocated on her vomit. The mother said she saw Jimbo covering her mouth while he beat her with a belt. He didn't want the neighbors to hear. The next-door neighbor had already called the child welfare people twice on Jimbo.

"It seemed like a pretty air-tight case. The detective did a lot of legwork, getting statements from the neighbors, traveling to other states to interview Jimbo's other children — this was his second marriage — and making a pretty convincing profile of a deadly child abuser.

"But things unraveled. He hired a sharp attorney, who challenged all the incriminating statements Jimbo made. He wasn't read his rights yet when he blurted out those things to me. The detective hadn't done it yet, but it was more my fault for goading him into talking before all the formalities were taken care of. I should have known better.

"The judge threw out all his statements. The next thing we knew, his wife changed her story, saying she never saw Jimbo with his hand over their daughter's mouth.

"They mortgaged their house, which paid for the parade of medical experts they flew in for the trial, a bunch of prostitutes, if you ask me. They challenged the autopsy findings, saying the medical examiner overlooked a rare genetic illness the girl had, or that the marks on her were consistent with falls rather than beatings. They came up with competing accidental death scenarios.

"Jimbo cleaned himself up for the trial, too. The wife testified about what a model father he was. They had blown-up photographs of the girl smiling next to her parents at Disney World.

"But I knew he was guilty. And so did the detective. We spent days sitting outside the courtroom together waiting for our turns to testify.

"We both felt like we had screwed up the case. The detective kept saying that if only Jimbo had been given his Miranda rights from the start. And I kept saying that if only I could have controlled my temper, Jimbo might have made those same admissions after his Miranda rights were given.

"The first trial ended in a hung jury. The second one was a mistrial, because one of the jurors turned out to be a former legal secretary for the defense lawyer. The jury on the third trial deliberated for three whole days. And then it came back with a not-guilty verdict.

"It was a terrible day in my life."

Craig paused and looked up at the stars.

"That sounds awful," Jake said.

"It was."

"Was that the sad story you were going to tell Margo today?"

"Yeah," Craig said. "But I knew she wouldn't want to hear it."

"Not with her having a baby," Jake said.

"No, it's not that, Jake," Craig said. "It's something a lot stranger than that."

"What do you mean?"

"The detective in that story was Margo."

■ ■ ■

Bernie waited patiently for his wife to finish brushing her teeth. He wanted to talk to her, and he didn't want her to walk off in the middle of the conversation and start brushing her teeth.

So Bernie waited, watching her wipe her mouth, turn off the bathroom light and walk into their bedroom, where he was sitting in his pajamas on his side of the bed.

"What?" Rose said.

She had been in a lousy mood that night. Bernie had learned why earlier when he sat down to a dinner of steak salad, a sure indication that Rose hadn't been successful at slipping Lucky a prison meal that afternoon.

"We've got to talk," Bernie said.

"We talk all day," Rose said, walking by him and taking off her robe.

"We've got to talk about Margo," Bernie said. "Rose, I've been putting this off as long as I can, but I can't any longer."

"What about Margo?"

"She's been deceiving us, Rose."

"Bernie, Bernie," Rose said, climbing into bed and getting under the covers. "Has Herb Troutman been bending your ear?"

"Rose, she's a liar."

Rose noisily blew air out of her mouth.

"Rose, first of all. She's not from North Dakota. She's been living in West Palm Beach for years."

"How do you know that?"

"Stuart Fine said …"

"Oh, well, if Stuart Fine says something, then it must be true," Rose said in a mocking way. "Bernie, since when do you believe anything that weasel says?"

"OK, forget Stuart Fine," Bernie said. "But even if you do, tell me how do you explain this?"

"How do you explain what?"

"This afternoon when you were out, I tried to talk to Margo's boyfriend, Bill."

"Bernie, why would you do a thing like that?" Rose asked. "You're not trying to get Margo to move away from here are you?"

Now, she was sitting up and getting her Sicilian temper working.

"Please, Rose. Hear me out. The condo board offered her two months rent if she would agree to move out now …"

"That's ridiculous."

"… and I thought her boyfriend should at least know about it."

Bernie got up and walked around to Rose's side of the bed and sat down.

"So, I went to the Turnpike toll plaza in Lake Worth. That's where she said he worked. Remember that story she said about driving into the state and not having enough change and … "

"Yes, I remember. Go on."

At least Rose was listening now, Bernie thought.

"So I go there and ask for a guy named Bill. And they say there's nobody there named Bill, and there hasn't been a Bill or a William or a Willie who has worked there in the past year."

"So what does that prove?"

"That she made the whole story up."

"Maybe his name is Chester William or something like that," Rose said, "and he's known as Chester at work, but prefers Bill with friends."

"Rose, you're just being difficult."

"No, I'm not. You're just turning into a condo commando. Margo is a sweet child, and she doesn't need us to turn against her."

"I'm not turning against her," Bernie said. "I just think there's something she's hiding from us."

They heard the front door of their condo open and close, and then footsteps on their tiled foyer.

"Sam, is that you?" Rose called.

The footsteps approached, and their son poked his head in.

"Where've you been?" Bernie asked.

"Out," Sam said. "Was Margo here tonight?"

"I thought she was with you," Rose said.

Sam walked into the room. He seemed flustered.

"We were at the pool this afternoon, but she left early. She said she wasn't feeling well."

He sat on the bed.

"We had plans. I was going to meet her for dinner at the Shoney's. I sat there for three hours, but she never showed. I kept ringing her condo, but she wasn't there, either."

Sam paused. Bernie spoke next.

"In other news, Jasmine called you tonight."

"Jasmine?"

"Yes," Bernie said. "You remember Jasmine. She's your wife."

Sam rubbed his forehead.

"And to think, I thought that coming here would simplify my life."

He stood up.

"I'm afraid something's happened to Margo."

Bernie looked at his son and spoke.

"I'm afraid something's happened to you."

35 Margo's day job

That afternoon at the pool, Margo had told Sam the sun was making her woozy, and she needed to go lie down a while.

But it wasn't the sun that was bothering her. It was Craig Shelbourne, who sat there looking at her and trying to figure out why she was pretending to be a stranger. The game she had been playing at Shady Palms was coming to an end.

"I'll just meet you at Shoney's," she had told Sam. "I've got a couple of errands to run later on."

But she had known right then she wasn't going to meet him. She was going to her condo, to throw a few clothes, her spiral notebook and her service revolver into a suitcase and get away from Shady Palms.

She went to her apartment in West Palm Beach and called Bill.

"It's over, Bill," she said. "By tomorrow, everybody in that place is going to know I'm a cop."

"We'll have to move quickly," he said. "Margo, come in this afternoon. I'll get everyone together."

And so, 20 minutes later she walked into a big conference room in a nondescript state government building in West Palm Beach. As she walked in, a dozen male heads turned around and stared at her.

Bill Johnson stood up.

"Gentlemen," he said, "I trust you all remember Detective Zukowski."

The men nodded, a few of them having trouble keeping the sheepish grins off their faces.

The only time Margo had seen this group was the day before she had begun her assignment on FIST, the Florida Integrated Strike Team.

Her lieutenant at the sheriff's office thought it might be a good idea to get Margo away from murdered children for a while. FIST was an operation run by the Florida Department of Law Enforcement, which used its own agents as well as loaners from local jurisdictions.

In her interview, Margo had only a few questions for the FIST commander, Bill Johnson.

"What kind of work would I be doing?"

"We need a woman to do undercover."

"Drug stings?" Margo asked.

"No. You'd be going undercover in Shady Palms."

"Shady Palms? That old people place?"

"That's the place."

"So I assume this won't be about children then?"

"Definitely no children involved," Johnson had said.

But two months later, there she was, hoping she didn't look pregnant yet to the men who sat around the table. Johnson had been wrong. There was a child involved. Her child.

Margo looked at them, trying to remember a night she wanted to forget. They had said on that night two months ago that no new member could join FIST without the proper initiation.

They took her to a country and western bar on Okeechobee Boulevard and ordered tequila shooters. She was obviously going to be made one of the boys.

She could handle herself, she had said at the start. She would play along. But the tequila hit her faster than she imagined it would, and before she knew it, she was out of control.

She remembered being all over the dance floor, even though she wasn't much of a dancer. She remembered being sick in the parking lot as the other agents hooted and hollered.

She remembered throwing caution to the wind in a way she thought only silly 14-year-olds did. She remembered putting her clothes back on. But how and why she got them off was a mystery as puzzling as the identity of the guy who whispered in her ear and disappeared into the night.

As she looked around the table now, she wondered how many of these men had made jokes about that night, and how many felt any guilt leaving her in the condition she was in.

"As I explained," Bill was saying, "Margo's identity there is about to be discovered, so I think we need to move fast. What I'd like to find out from all of you is if we can move tomorrow."

Johnson went around the room. Tomorrow would be fine, the men said.

"What does tomorrow look like, Margo?"

Margo paged through her spiral notebook, checking for the names and times. She had begun making entries the day she started her part-time job at Loehmann's in the Shoppes of the Shady Palms.

"Tuesday," she said, looking at her paper. "Tomorrow's a busy day."

"That's good then," Johnson said. "How many do we have?"

"They start at noon tomorrow," Margo said. "Let's see, there's Miller, Friedman, Hinton, Crimble, Gilbert, Martin, Sorenson, Able and ..."

She paused, looking at the last name on her list. She looked up, and then back down at the names. She wiped the hair from her face. Then she read the final name.

"... and Hamstein."

■ ■ ■

More than 50 years ago, before any of the members of the

FIST unit were alive, Joseph Abrizzio was serving the apprenticeship for his life's work on the Lower East Side of Manhattan.

Abrizzio was physically big, which made him an asset in his line of work. And he had another thing going for him. He didn't mind killing people if that's what the job called for. It often did.

As a junior associate of a busy organized crime family, Abrizzio had to do a lot of the heavy lifting. Literally. There seemed to always be someone who needed to be taught a lesson or silenced. And by the time Abrizzio was out of his teens, he had become one of the most reliable go-to men in the Carrando crime family, which officially made him a member after an unusually busy five-homicide weekend.

What Abrizzio's capo liked so much about the young man's work was that his body disposal skills were superior. Lesser Mob enforcers would throw their victims in hastily dug shallow graves or toss them improperly weighted into nearby waterways. The bodies would be discovered, and it would invariably lead to some unnecessary heat.

But Abrizzio's work never surfaced. Nobody ever saw his people again. It was so impressive that one day his capo summoned him to his office — a table in the back room of a Mulberry Street social club — and asked the young Abrizzio what his secret was.

"I got a brother-in-law who works in Bayonne," Abrizzio said. "He's the night foreman at a dog food factory. Nobody knows nothin' but me and him."

Pretty soon, other mobsters just started calling Abrizzio by a name that would follow him through the rest of his life in New York.

Joey Alpo.

The dog food factory in Bayonne wasn't an Alpo factory. But accuracy was never the prime consideration in Mob nicknames. Ten years later, when the FBI first put Abrizzio's name in the Carrando family tree diagram, he was listed as "Joseph 'Joey

Other mobsters just started calling Abrizzio by a name that would follow him through the rest of his life in New York. Joey Alpo.

Alpo' Abrizzio."

By then, Abrizzio's brother-in-law was selling aluminum siding, and there were younger associates who did the heavy work. But Abrizzio was stuck with "Joey Alpo," which was fine with him. It was a name that inspired an impressive amount of deference.

Like many of his brethren, Abrizzio attracted frequent attention from lawmen, but nearly all of it amounted to little more than minor inconveniences. Until recently.

The 1980s were bad for people in his line of work. The feds were going after everybody. When they got John Gotti, Abrizzio figured it was time to switch gears and keep a low profile.

Abrizzio's niece, Rena, was the one who suggested he move to Florida.

"Uncle Joey, you could blend right in," she had said. "You and Aunt Mary would just be another retired couple down here."

So that's what Abrizzio did. No more Joey Alpo, he told himself. He even gave up his vanity New York license plate that said, "WOOF WOOF."

He paid cash for a $250,000 ranch house in suburban Boynton Beach, a huge place that faced a man-made lake. Abrizzio tried to be a model citizen. He recycled his garbage, shared the grapefruit from his tree and joined the neighborhood crime watch committee.

He was a good neighbor. Good and bored.

He needed a little action. Something he could do besides sitting around the house.

He supposed he could get a legitimate job, but in 75 years of life, he had never had a legitimate job, and he didn't think this would be the time to start.

No, he thought. Go with what you know. That meant murder, loansharking, bookmaking and extortion. Becoming a bookie seemed like the most benign of the possibilities. South Florida was full of people his age, and seeing the way they played the Lotto and Bingo, he knew they would give him plenty of action.

About a mile from his home was this huge condo called Shady Palms. It was full of old men who were bored and looking for a little diversion. He would befriend a few of the men there and get himself a little business.

Abrizzio would take their bets on football, baseball, basketball, hockey, boxing . . . anything they want. He'd pocket the vig, making his own little nest egg. His wife wouldn't know a thing about it.

That was a given. Mary didn't approve of Abrizzio's line of work. Ever since Gotti went down, she made him promise he would give up that life. She wanted him to become a bag boy at Publix. Imagine that!

Joey Alpo said he would think about the bag boy job, but meanwhile, he called up his niece, who was the day manager at a nearby clothes store.

"Rena, how about I pay you $50 for every day I come and sit in the front of your store?" Abrizzio said.

"Uncle Joey, I don't understand."

"That's good," he said. "It would be best if you continued not to understand."

He knew Rena could use the cash. And he also knew she had a kindred spirit for playing things a little fast and loose.

"And please," he told her. "Don't say a word to Aunt Mary."

And so the former Joey Alpo set up shop in the clothing store managed by his niece. It was a fool-proof arrangement, he thought.

But he didn't count on a federal prosecutor in New York who kept meticulous records on the Carrando crime family and managed to trace Joey Alpo's exodus to Florida. This prosecutor had alerted his counterparts in the Southern District of Florida. And when FIST was forming last year, Abrizzio's name was added as a potential target for the task force.

Joey, of course, had no idea. He thought Joey Alpo was something he had left behind in New York.

When the old men from the condos had introduced themselves, he never gave them his address or his phone number. He didn't even give them his last name. Instead, if they persisted, he had them call him by the name of the clothes store where they rendezvoused.

"The name's Joe," he would say.

"Joe what?" the nosey ones would ask.

"Joe Loehmann."

36 Wonder Walkers begin to wonder

Jacqui Fisher, with her sprained right ankle still wrapped, surprised her friends by showing up for Wonder Walkers on Tuesday morning. It was Lois' turn to drive, and at the appointed hour, Jacqui was standing in the parking lot leaning against Lois' car.

"I thought you were hurt," Lois said.

"I am."

"Can you walk?"

"No," Jacqui said. "But I can talk."

"Well, talking does seem to be the point, anyway," Lois said. "Climb in."

Jacqui couldn't stay away. Not this day. Her son, Jake, had told her the most fascinating story that morning. He had said, "Mom, Craig told me something last night about Margo, the pregnant renter, that you're not going to believe."

And so it was Jacqui's turn to tell her friends. She'd wait for them at one of the tables in the food court, and when they were through with their walking, she'd tell them between bites of sticky bun.

"She's a cop?" Maddy asked after Jacqui finished telling the story.

"A homicide detective," Jacqui said.

"So she's at Shady Palms doing an undercover murder investigation?" Maddy asked.

"Not unless it's a crime to die of natural causes," Lois said.

"It doesn't make sense," Maddy said.

"I said the same thing to Jacob," Jacqui said. "But he said, 'Mom, I'm just telling you what Craig told me.'"

Maddy wiped the icing off her plate before speaking.

"She has been secretive about herself," she said. "And that boyfriend of hers, Bill, I wonder if he's an undercover cop, too?"

"Maybe she isn't pregnant, either," Lois said.

Rose, who had been sitting in uneasy silence, spoke up for the first time.

"No, she's pregnant," Rose said. "I know that."

"Did you know she was a detective?" Lois said.

"No," Rose said. "Of course not."

"Well, I say we just flat out ask her," Lois said. "Say, 'What's a pregnant homicide detective doing living in Shady Palms and pretending to be somebody else?'"

"It's too late," Rose said. "Margo's gone."

"Gone?" they all said.

"Yes, gone," Rose said.

She was sure of that now.

"Last night, she was supposed to meet my son for dinner at Shoney's, but she never showed up," Rose said. "She wasn't in her condo, either.

"Then this morning, I thought I'd ask her to join us. But when I went by her condo, nobody answered the door. And then I looked in the lot, and her car wasn't there."

"You think she's not coming back?" Maddy asked.

"Maybe she knew we all were going to find out her true identity," Jacqui said. "And so she had to leave."

"But why?" Rose said. "It's not like there's some murder to investigate here."

"Maybe she's investigating some other kind of crime," Maddy said.

"Crime in Shady Palms?" Jacqui said. "Like what?"

"I don't know," Rose said. "But I've got a sinking feeling we're about to find out."

■ ■ ■

Joseph "Joey Alpo" Abrizzio had a late and leisurely breakfast in the Florida room of his home. He chewed the last of his eggs slowly as he watched the fountain spew in the man-made lake just beyond the rolling greenery of his back yard.

His wife, Mary, got up and started clearing the table.

"So when's your tee-off time?" she asked.

"Noon," he said.

"So hot to play golf. I don't know how you do it."

Joey didn't do it.

In fact, there had been only one time in his life when he had ever stepped on a golf course. And that was back some 35 years ago when he made a late-night pickup of a body on the 17th fairway. The body had more holes than the golf course. Joey took the corpse to the dog food factory, where the body, as Joey liked to say, "rested in pieces."

Truth was, Joey Alpo had no use for golf except as an excuse for his gullible wife, Mary, who actually believed Joey had given up a life of crime in exchange for hitting a little ball all over creation four times a week.

The worst part of his deception was the clothes. She went out and bought him golf clothes, expecting him to dress like the golfer he was supposed to be. At first, Joey thought of refusing. But he didn't want to make her suspicious. So he obliged, figuring it was the price he had to pay for continuing his life's work.

"I'd better get dressed," he told her.

He walked to their huge bedroom and opened his walk-in closet. The choices were all hideous. A row of bright-colored shirts and pants assaulted his sensibilities. He picked out a green shirt with yellow pants, while looking longingly at the side of his closet that was the real Joey Alpo. Black, black and more black.

He sighed and closed the closet door. He walked to the clothes tree and picked the golf hat that said "Pebble Beach" on it. The clubs he never used were in their bag by the utility room door leading to the garage.

"Be good, Mary," he said, walking out the door. "I should be home around 3:30."

Joey Alpo whistled as he put the clubs in the trunk of his Cadillac Biarritz and drove to the Shoppes of the Shady Palms for his day's work.

■ ■ ■

With all the commotion over Margo, Lois escaped getting grilled by her friends over what had happened to Ricardo. On a slower news day, the other Wonder Walkers would have sensed the uncharacteristic uncertainty in Lois' manner.

They would have been observant enough to ask her what was wrong. And Lois would have been unhinged enough to tell them, and yes, maybe even admit it was bothering her that the once hot-to-trot Ricardo Vera had disappeared in the moments after dispatching Harvey Shorter in such spectacular fashion.

"Why is he being like this?" Lois would have asked her chums. "It's as if he's angry at me, or disappointed in me."

But she didn't say this because her friends never asked. Margo had dominated their thoughts. Even Lois herself got swept up in the Margo drama, temporarily tucking her own troubles out of sight.

Soon, though, the Wonder Walkers were done for the morning, and Lois was back in her condo, thinking she couldn't take getting drunk for another afternoon while waiting for Ricardo not to show up.

The alternative was simple. If Ricardo wasn't trying to speak to her, she would have to try to speak to him. The problem was she had no idea how to contact him.

She didn't know where he lived. In the time they'd known each other, she didn't even have his phone number.

So she picked up her phone and dialed directory assistance.

"The last name is Vera," she said. "First name Ricardo. It's a West Palm Beach listing."

The operator paused for a second.

"I'm not showing a Ricardo Vera in West Palm Beach," she said. "I have an R. Vera on Palm Beach."

"Palm Beach?" Lois said. "No, that can't be the one. You sure you don't have one in West Palm Beach?"

The operator said she had three listings for "Richard Vera" in West Palm Beach.

"Yeah, it must be one of those," Lois said, taking down the numbers.

But it wasn't. All wrong numbers.

"Ricardo Vera?" one Richard Vera told her. "No, I'm Richard."

"I'm looking for a Ricardo Vera," Lois said. "He's in his late 60s, very athletic, not too tall."

"Doesn't sound like anybody I know," the guy said. "He's not one of the sugar baron Veras, is he?"

"Sugar baron?" Lois said. "Heavens, no. He's just a little guy who rides a bicycle a lot."

The bicycle. Of course. Why hadn't she thought of that earlier? Ricardo knew all those guys who ride bikes. That one he was talking to before the race — what was his name? Scooter, that's it — had asked him about the weekly ride they took.

She was sure Scooter would know how to find Ricardo. Now, how would she go about finding Scooter?

The newspaper. Ricardo had told her Scooter was going to win the race. Maybe the results were in the sports section. She dug through the pile of papers and found Monday's sports section, paging through it until she found a small story about the triathlon on Page 10C.

Ricardo was right. Trevor "Scooter" Lindsey had won. The story said Scooter worked at a local bike store. It didn't say which one, but how many bicycle shops could there be?

Plenty, it turned out. Lois found Scooter on the seventh call. Actually, she didn't find Scooter, she just found somebody who knew where Scooter worked, which turned out to be a bike shop she hadn't called yet.

By the time she heard Scooter's voice, she was both exhausted and exhilarated.

"Scooter?"

"Yes?"

"You don't know me, but Ricardo Vera is a friend of mine, and I was wondering if you know how to reach him."

"Ricardo? We're going for a spin later this afternoon."

"A spin?"

"On A1A," Scooter said. "Why's that? You want to join the pace line?"

"I well, uh . . . pace line?" Lois was envisioning some sort of country and western dance.

Scooter plowed on.

"Everybody's welcome," he said. "But let me just warn you, it's a real hammer ride."

"Where do you meet?" she asked.

"By the Ritz-Carlton in Manalapan. Know where that is?"

"Yes I do," she said.

"Two o'clock," he said. "We go south to the Hillsboro Inlet and then back."

"I'll be there," Lois said.

"Let me just tell you up front, if you get flicked, nobody's going to slow down for you."

"Flicked?"

"We've been known to cruise at about 27," Scooter said. "Just so you know."

"That won't be a problem."

"No problem? Cool," Scooter said. "What are you riding?"

"A Chrysler," Lois said. "And I've been known to cruise at about 80."

37 Bernie's back for more

The phone rang. Margo Zukowski was startled by the sound. After spending the first night in her West Palm Beach apartment in two months, she still felt disoriented.

Now where was the phone?

Before she got it on the fourth ring, it occurred to her it wouldn't be Rose asking her to come to Wonder Walkers, or Sam wanting to know when he could meet her at the pool. Those days were over. And those people were not her friends anymore. Not after today.

"Hello?"

"Good morning, Margo. Hope I didn't wake you."

"No, Bill. I've been up."

Much of the night, actually.

"I just want you to know we're going to be doing some press after today's bust," Bill said.

"What kind of press?"

"News conference, say about 4:30, which will give the TV stations time to get it on the 6 o'clock news," he said. "If everything goes to plan, we'll be taking down Joey Alpo by 3."

And Bernie, Margo was thinking.

"We're getting Suzie Ching," he said.

"Excuse me?"

"Suzie Ching, that crime reporter from Channel 5," Bill said. "We've decided to give her an exclusive and take her in with us when we take down Joey Alpo in Loehmann's."

"Why's that?" Margo asked.

"It doesn't hurt to throw some of those media people a bone once in a while," Bill said. "And besides, it will make some dramatic video and get us better play on the news."

"I thought you were going to arrest Abrizzio when he walked out of Loehmann's," Margo said.

"Yeah, we were, but then Suzie suggested …"

"The TV reporter is in on planning the bust?"

"No, Margo. It's just that when we gave her a brief sketch of what was going on, she just suggested it would make better video to actually surprise Joey Alpo when he's sitting there in the store with the last gambler of the day."

"Bernie Hamstein," Margo said.

"Yeah, that's the guy, Hamstein," Bill said. "We barge in there and take down Alpo and Hamstein at the same time. We're bound to get some interesting exclamations from that, don't you think?"

"I don't want to be there, Bill."

"That's fine. I understand. You don't have to be. You'll just be available for backup."

"Do you have to make a circus out of it?"

"C'mon, Margo. This is your big day. You've got nothing to be ashamed of. We're taking down a big-time mobster here. You've worked the hardest on this case, which is why I'm calling.

"I want you standing next to me at the news conference," Bill said. "You're the star here, Margo. And besides, with all the press you've been getting at Shady Palms, it's only fitting we clear things up. I can't wait to see what that buffoon on the radio is going to say tomorrow."

"Bill, if there's a way I can skip the news conference …"

"Skip the news conference? No way, Margo. What's wrong?"

What's wrong? Margo could fill his ears for five minutes about what's wrong. About betraying the people she had come to trust and, yes, love. But there was no use telling that to Bill. She knew the rules when she took the assignment. She just didn't know she could get attached to people inside a place like Shady Palms.

"Do we have to make such a big deal of it?" she asked Bill.

"It is a big deal," Bill said. "When we take down a mobster and nine of his associates on felony charges, it's a big deal."

"Felony charges?" Margo said. "Since when is gambling a felony?"

"Gambling isn't. But racketeering is."

"I thought only Abrizzio was going to be charged with racketeering," Margo said.

"Yes, but after our meeting yesterday, I talked to the prosecutor's office, and they wanted us to file racketeering charges against them all. You know, ongoing criminal enterprise. And these old guys, they weren't just betting for themselves. They were taking other people's bets, too."

"But it's not like they were making a percentage on it," Margo said.

"How do you know?"

"Bernie wouldn't do something like that."

"Besides," Bill said, "you charge those old guys with misdemeanors, and they won't be much help to us. But charge them with felonies, and we'll at least have their attention. The bigger the charge, the easier it is for the prosecutor to get them to roll over on Joey Alpo."

"So you're planning to call these old men mobsters?"

"We're still working on the language," Bill said. "Right now we're leaning toward 'Carrando crime family associates.' What do you think?"

"I think they're a bunch of old men from Shady Palms," Margo said. "Their idea of organized crime is taking extra packets of artificial sweetener from the local diner. That's what I think."

■ ■ ■

When Rose Hamstein got home from Wonder Walkers, there was a note on the counter from her husband.

"Rose — Be back this afternoon. Eat lunch without me. I've got some condo business this morning, then I'm getting an oil change for the car. I've defrosted a chicken for dinner. Love — Bernie.

P.S. — Sam's down at the pool."

Rose was disappointed. She wanted to tell Bernie about Margo being a cop. Oh well, it could wait.

The condo business Bernie was talking about was both official and non-official condo business.

The non-official condo business consisted of getting the weekly football bets in order. This was the day he would pay a visit to Joe Loehmann, so Bernie had to make the rounds to the other gamblers to make sure he had all bets and cash in hand.

Bernie liked the Raiders this week. And he was banking on the Eagles to cover the spread against the Giants. He was still toying with the idea of throwing another $50 on the Dolphins game, even though he knew it was folly to think he could predict the dizzying ups and downs of the Miami franchise.

He planned to mull over the Dolphins while driving to the official condo business he had that morning. Soon after Rose left for Wonder Walkers, Bernie had gotten a call from Troutman. The condo board president said Fine was ready to file the lawsuit against Margo and that before he did, he recommended they take a look at it.

Bernie knew Troutman was including him in this because he was hoping Bernie would give him a ride to the lawyer's West Palm Beach office. But Bernie had no intention of sitting in a car with Troutman for a 20-minute trip.

"Herb, I'll just meet you there," Bernie said. "I have to run some errands after the meeting. So, maybe it would be best if we take separate cars."

Bernie wasn't planning to get an oil change for the Camry, but this was a good excuse.

By the time he got out of the meeting with Fine and Troutman, it was nearly noon. There's no rush, he thought. Rose didn't need to go out that afternoon.

So Bernie stopped at a Greek diner, sat down at the counter and ordered a gyro with a side order of fries and coconut cream pie.

Then he stopped at one of those 10-minute oil change shops, but he had to wait nearly 30 minutes because the place was so busy. When he got out, it was nearly 1:45 p.m.

He looked at his watch. He still had more than an hour to kill before meeting Joe Loehmann.

He could go home, sit around for a while and then go to the shopping center. But if he did that, Rose was bound to waylay him with errands of her own. And Joe Loehmann didn't like it when Bernie was late.

Bernie figured he would be better off if he killed some time, went to see Joe and then went home. After all, it wasn't as if Rose was expecting him.

So Bernie began driving south on Congress, and before long, he turned off the busy road and into Atlantis. He drove slowly as he made his way to Willow Bend Court and the house of his former high school sweetheart, Susan Plock.

He slowed the Camry even more when he drove by her house. The Cadillac wasn't in the driveway this time. But another car was, a white Lexus with gold trim and "MD" license plates.

"That must be her car," Bernie said aloud to himself.

He drove around the block, trying to think about what he should do. By the time he got to Willow Bend Court again, his heart was pounding.

"Just get it over with," he told himself.

He pulled the car into her driveway, checked his hair in the mirror and then got out. He took a couple of deep breaths as he made his way up the winding brick walkway, climbed the three slate steps and rang the doorbell.

No answer. He waited a few more seconds, then walked back toward his car. On his way, he thought he heard a sound from the backyard. Maybe that's why she hadn't heard the doorbell.

He looked at the wooden fence on the side of the house. Oh, why not?

He opened the gate, closing it behind him, and then followed the narrow path of bricks past the air conditioner and toward the backyard, where the swimming pool was now visible.

He rounded the corner of the house and pasted a smile on his face.

But the yard was empty. The sounds had been coming from the backyard of the house on the other side of the fence.

He peered in a large back window of Susan's house, which revealed a sun room with Mexican tile and big wooden chairs with floral patterned cushions. He tried to imagine Susan sitting in that room, looking out on the still water of her kidney-shaped pool.

Then Bernie heard a sound behind him. It was the sound of footsteps on the brick pathway in the side yard. Bernie turned expectantly.

He was hoping it would be Susan.

38 Lois in the fast lane

Lois drove south on A1A looking for a line of cyclists. When she got to the town of Gulf Stream, she thought she saw a long patch of bright colors moving along the side of the road about a half-mile ahead.

She sped up, not bothering to notice the town police car parked under the canopy of Australian pines lining the road. In another minute, she could make out the eight bicycles in the group and see Ricardo, with his gray ponytail poking out of his helmet, somewhere in the middle of the line of riders.

She was about a hundred yards from the last rider when she noticed a flash of color in her rear-view mirror. The police car wasn't on the side of the road anymore. It was right behind her, and to give a little extra emphasis to the red and blue lights flashing on its roof, the officer was motioning with his finger for Lois to pull over on the big shoulder.

Lois complied, watching the line of cyclists disappear into the distance as the Gulf Stream officer got out of his car and sauntered up to her window.

"Do you realize how fast you were going, ma'am?" he asked.

"Do you realize this is the first time I've chased a man in years?" Lois responded.

'Whatever they're paying you,' Lois told the cop, 'is too much.'

The cop, who had been working the speed-trap detail for the past six months, had heard plenty of lines before. But never this one. He pulled his sunglasses down to get a better look at Lois.

"You're chasing somebody, ma'am?" he said before looking down the long empty road.

"I was until you stopped me."

"I don't see anybody to chase," the cop said.

"He was one of those guys on the bicycles that went by."

"Yeah, those bicyclists can be a problem," the cop said. "But it's not a good idea to try to run them off the road."

Lois shook her head.

"Whatever they're paying you," she said, "is too much."

The cop pretended he didn't hear that. He also stopped debating whether to let the woman go. Not after that remark. She was definitely getting the ticket now. He took his pad and pen out and started writing.

"License and registration," he said, holding out his hand.

Lois ignored the hand.

"Officer, take a look at me. How many more romances do

you think a person my age has left in her?"

He had never heard this question, either. Nobody caught going 42 in a 35 zone had ever tried this line of defense. This woman was either desperate or crazy. The cop began wondering whether he should call for backup, just to make sure.

"You can save your questions for the judge, ma'am."

Lois really surprised him with her next reply.

"For your information, young man, the judge is in the hospital."

And then she leaned her head out her window and said in a whisper, "And I put him there."

The cop reached for his radio, and in a voice that sounded unsteady to the dispatcher, he requested a backup. Thirty seconds later, the sound of the pounding surf to the east gave way to the wail of approaching sirens from more than one direction.

■ ■ ■

Margo's role in the takedown of Joey Alpo was minimal. She sat in an unmarked car with an agent named Trimble Hawkins two blocks from the Shoppes of the Shady Palms.

They were there as a safety valve. The plan was for other members of the FIST squad to make the arrests. Joey Alpo had his gamblers on a schedule that facilitated smooth arrests.

Because he saw only one man at a time and spaced his meetings every 20 minutes, the agents could make a series of individual arrests, nabbing each gambler soon after leaving the Loehmann's, and Joey Alpo would have no idea what was going on.

The FIST unit set up a command post in the delivery area of the shopping center. It wasn't visible from the road or the parking lot. As each gambler left the Loehmann's, he was approached by two agents in the parking lot, who flashed their badges and instructed the man to get into the back seat of a waiting unmarked car. The man was then driven behind the shopping center, where other agents were standing by to begin the arrest process.

If any of the gamblers somehow got away from the agents, Margo Zukowski and Trimble Hawkins were supposed to chase them, stop them and arrest them before they made it back to Shady Palms.

The idea was that everyone would be held at the command post behind the shopping center until the final arrests of Joey Alpo and his last gambler, Bernie Hamstein, were made at 3 p.m. Then the whole bunch of them would be paraded before the TV cameras as they were herded into a bus for transportation to the county jail.

Margo and Hawkins sat silently in the car, listening to the police scanner. The arrests were going off without a hitch. Four men were already sitting on the bus behind the shopping center. The fifth gambler was inside, ready to come out for the surprise of his life.

As the names clicked off, Margo put faces to them. She had seen them, even talked to some of them during her short stay at Shady Palms. The words "Carrando crime family associates" were laughable to her, except she knew some of the men would never recover from the shame they would face today.

Especially Bernie. His son, Sam, might laugh off the idea that anyone would call his father a mobster. But Bernie would be wounded, perhaps mortally. Margo remembered him telling her about how he became the most successful Big Top bread deliveryman.

"Some guys stole," he had told her. "They shorted the store on the delivery and then pocketed the extra money. Not me. Never. The store managers didn't even have to check my deliveries. They knew that if I said I was putting 120 loaves in their store, there would be 120 loaves on the shelves.

"It's important for a man to have his honor," he had told her. "Other drivers made more money than me. But nobody made more the right way."

Margo looked at her watch. In another hour, Bernie's

honor would be history.

"Mind if I turn on the radio?" Trimble Hawkins asked her.

Before she could say anything, he had country music blasting in the car. The voice of Garth Brooks mixed with the voice of Bill Johnson, relaying that the fifth gambler was now in custody and the sixth was in the store.

Margo reached over and turned down the music.

"What's a matter, honey?" Hawkins said. "You don't like country?"

She didn't like country, and she didn't like Hawkins.

Of all the FIST squad members, he was her least favorite. He was the one who seemed to delight the most in her wretched performance on the night of her welcoming party. He was the one who had insisted on that final bottle of tequila. And he was the one who had groped her the most on the dance floor.

"I just have a headache, that's all," Margo said.

Hawkins sat behind the wheel of the car, thumping his hand to the beat of the music.

"We're going to be doin' some dancin' tonight," he said.

Margo ignored him. She had already warned Suzie Ching. She'd heard the agents inviting the slinky TV reporter to their bust celebration party at the same Okeechobee Boulevard nightspot where they took Margo two months ago.

Margo had pulled the reporter aside back at headquarters.

"Don't let them make you drink tequila," Margo had said.

Ching had looked at her as if this was some sort of unreasonable request.

"I can handle myself," Suzie told Margo.

"There will be some handling," Margo said. "But you won't be doing it."

Ching and her cameraman were now waiting behind the shopping center at the FIST mobile command center.

And Bernie. What would Bernie say?

What would Margo say? No, she'd never be able to face the Hamsteins again.

Margo looked across the parking lot. She and Hawkins were parked in a convenience store lot, and there was a bank of pay phones just steps from the car.

She could call now and warn Bernie. It could get her fired. When Bernie didn't show up, Hawkins would rat her out and tell Johnson she slipped away to make a phone call while the bust was going down. There'd be no good way to explain it.

Margo thought for another minute, then did what she knew she had to do.

"Trimble," she said, "I need a big, big soda."

"Go ahead," he said, motioning to the convenience store.

"And I need some aspirin," she said. "This head of mine is just pounding. Could you do me a favor?"

"What's that, doll?"

Oh, he made her skin crawl. This would be easier to do than she thought.

"Could you please get them for me," she said. "The way my head is, just getting out of this air-conditioned car seems like something I won't be able to take."

She handed him a five-dollar bill. He frowned. Then he took the money, muttering something under his breath.

"Thank you ... doll," she said.

As soon as he was inside the store searching the shelves for aspirin, she slid over to the driver's side, put the car in reverse and drove out of the parking lot.

She rolled down her window, took the blue flashing light from the floor and attached it to the roof. The cars in front of her parted to let her get by.

C Building in Shady Palms was less than five minutes away. She hoped she wasn't too late.

39 Margo in motion

When Ricardo and the group of cyclists cranked through Gulf Stream again, they were heading north. As they rounded a corner, they saw a clot of cars and people on the southbound shoulder. Some sort of police action. Three squad cars with their lights on. Five or six officers. As the cyclists got closer, they looked up from their hunkered positions.

Ricardo, who was leading the pace line, didn't see the Chrysler until he was nearly past it. But there it was, Lois' car, sandwiched between two of the police cars. Lois, with her head back and her eyes closed, was sitting in the driver's seat.

Even though the Chrysler didn't appear to be damaged, Ricardo's first thought was that she had been injured in a crash. He signaled with his right hand that he was relinquishing his spot in the front of the pace line. As he moved his bike to the left and allowed the stream of riders to pass him, he announced, "Ricardo will catch up with you guys later."

"Equipment problems, Ricardo?" Scooter asked.

"No, everything is fine. You go. Ricardo needs to take care of something."

And so he let them go as he slowed and then made a U-turn, heading back to the cluster of cars. He stopped his bicycle on the shoulder and walked it up to the Chrysler.

"Are you all right?"

"I've been better," Lois said.

"What happened?"

By then Ricardo's presence had gotten the attention of the officers standing in a group in front of the car. The one who ticketed Lois walked back briskly, trying to shoo Ricardo away.

"Excuse me, sir," the cop said. "But do you mind stepping away from the car?"

"They're deciding whether they should let me go or take me to a loony bin," she said. "They're convinced I'm some sort of escapee from the South County Mental Health Center."

The cop was next to Ricardo now.

"Sir, would you please step back from the car?"

"What is the problem here, officer?"

"Sir, if you would …"

"This cop stopped me for speeding just as I was about to catch up to you and those other biking friends of yours."

"You were coming after Ricardo?" Ricardo said.

The cop asked, "Who's Ricardo?"

"He is," Lois said, pointing to Ricardo. "They think I'm nuts, Ricardo. Would you please straighten it out?"

Ricardo said he'd try.

"You stay here," he told her.

So Lois sat in the car, watching as Ricardo stood in the cluster of officers. First, the officers spoke to him, then Ricardo seemed to be doing quite a bit of talking, motioning with his hands and occasionally glancing back at Lois. Then some officers asked questions, and he answered them. Whatever was going on seemed to be working.

One by one, the officers got in their cars and drove away. When it was just the Chrysler on the side of the road, Ricardo walked back and leaned against the driver's side door.

"Well?" she asked.

"You are a free woman," he said.

"You saved me again."

"It looks that way," Ricardo said.

"What did you tell them?"

"That you are loco. That we have been married 40 years and that you become disoriented whenever Ricardo goes for his afternoon bike ride. And sometimes, you panic and come looking for me."

"And hallucinate about hurting judges?"

"Yes," Ricardo said, a small smile forming around the corners of his mouth.

"That is the worst part about your degenerative illness, the way your imagination can get the best of you."

Lois shook her head.

"The worst thing about your story is that part of it is true," she said. "I did panic and come looking for you."

"Ricardo also told them you were one of the most difficult people in the world to love," he said. "And that is also true."

Lois reached out and rested her hand lightly on his forearm.

"I drove after you this afternoon to say I'm sorry, Ricardo. I shouldn't have asked you to hurt Harvey Shorter. At first, I was real happy that you did it. But then I realized that getting back at Harvey wasn't as important as seeing you again."

Ricardo smiled.

"You mean that?"

"I mean it."

"Good," he said.

"If there's anything I can do to make it up to you, Ricardo, you just name ..."

"There is something," he said, cutting her off.

He loaded his bicycle in the trunk and hopped in the passenger seat.

"Where are we going?" Lois asked.

What Ricardo said next made her regret her offer.

"To the hospital," he said.

■ ■ ■

Margo had nearly reached Shady Palms when the police radio in her car burst to life.

"716, this is 701."

No sense answering, Margo thought.

"716, this is 701."

It was Bill Johnson's voice.

"Margo, what's going on? Trimble just told me you drove away from your post and left him at the …"

She reached over and turned off the radio. She was at the front gate of the condo complex now. The blue light was still flashing on the roof of her car when she stopped and waited for Hector to walk out of his guard shack.

Hector smiled at her.

"Good afternoon, Detective Zukowski."

"Let me guess," Margo said. "Everybody in Shady Palms already knows I'm a detective."

"There are probably still one or two who haven't heard that rumor today," Hector said.

After he opened the gate for her, she sped through the complex, ignoring the speed bumps. She pulled into the lot of C Building and ran inside, taking the stairs when the elevator wouldn't arrive after a single press of the button.

By the time she knocked on the Hamsteins' door, she was out of breath.

Sam answered the door.

"Hey, it's Detective Zukowski," he said. "Are you here to investigate the disappearance of a woman who was supposed to meet me for dinner last night?"

She ignored his sarcasm.

"Where's your father?" she asked.

"Aren't you supposed to flip me your badge before you ask questions?"

"Sam, is your father here?"

By then Rose had walked up behind her son. Margo could see the hurt in her face.

"Look who's back, Mom," Sam said.

"Rose," Margo said. "Is Bernie here?"

"Why's that?" Rose said. "Are you here to arrest him?"

"No, Rose. I'm here to help him."

"Well, he's not here," Rose said.

"Where is he?"

"Out."

"When will he be back?"

"Why do you need to know?" Rose said. "Margo, until today I thought I knew you, but I'm not sure anymore."

"Bernie's going to be arrested in a little more than 30 minutes, unless I can warn him off," Margo said.

"Arrested?" Rose shrieked. "What for?"

So Margo told them. She hit the high points. Joey Alpo. The weekly meetings at Loehmann's. And her own role as undercover detective in the FIST operation.

"Dad's tied up with a mobster," Sam said in amazement.

"I couldn't let him get arrested," Margo said. "Not after what you've done for me."

"Well, you surely waited until the last minute," Rose said.

"Tell me I'm not too late."

"I don't know," Rose said. "He's been out all day running errands. I thought he'd be back by now. But maybe he's planning to go to the Loehmann's before he comes home."

"I'm sorry, Rose. I really am."

Rose retreated to the kitchen and began maniacally chopping two cloves of garlic into a watery paste.

Margo followed Sam to the patio.

"So, is your pregnancy a scam, too?" Sam asked.

"No."

"Who's the father?"

"I don't know."

She told him the story of her night at the country and western bar.

"So why don't you just get an abortion?"

"Because I can't. I just can't bring myself to do it. I was adopted, Sam. My biological mother didn't want me, but she gave me away at birth to somebody who did. And that person became my mother in all the ways that a mother is real. So, I figure I owe my baby at least that much."

"You're giving the baby away?"

"No."

"Look, you can't raise a child alone," he said, placing a hand on her shoulder.

"Sam, you don't need me to complicate your ..."

"Just don't disappear on me again. Please."

Three o'clock came and went. Sam and the two women sat wordlessly in the condo. They'd take turns standing up and walking by the window to look out.

At 3:15, the phone rang. It was Jacqui, wondering if Rose had seen the unmarked police car in the parking lot. Rose said she couldn't talk and hung up.

At 3:17, the phone rang again. Maddy wanted to know about the police car, too. Rose said she couldn't talk and hung up.

A minute later, the phone rang again.

"This must be Lois," she said.

But Margo could tell instantly from Rose's expression that it wasn't.

"It's Bernie," Rose said. "He's been arrested."

40 Bernie on ice

Bernie Hamstein had never even seen the Palm Beach County Jail before. It was bigger than he imagined. And cold. Freezing cold. All the guards wore jackets.

"Does it have to be this cold in here?" Bernie asked while he waited in a holding cell.

"Keeps the body odor down," a guard told him.

Bernie had just called Rose. He had expected she would go nuts when he told her he had been arrested. But she had surprised him, acting almost as if she had expected it.

Of course, he didn't tell her the nature of his arrest. He said he couldn't talk. Just to come and bring money for a bail bondsman. How much money? He wasn't sure. He was still getting booked.

Rose, of course, would flip out when she found out why he was arrested. There will be hell to pay, Bernie told himself.

"And Rose," he had said to her before hanging up, "bring a sweater."

Rose got her friend, Maddy, to take her to the jail.

"I would take you," Margo had said. "But I can't. I've got to return the unmarked car."

"Are you going to be in trouble?" Sam asked.

"Don't worry about me. Worry about your father," Margo

told him.

Rose grabbed her son's arm.

"She's right, Sam. Come with me."

Forty-five minutes later, they pulled into the jail parking lot.

■ ■ ■

Susan Rosen was in her husband's office when the receptionist told her she had a phone call.

"Hello?"

"Yes, Mrs. Rosen, this is Officer Smits from the Atlantis Police Department."

"Yes, Officer Smits."

"I'm just letting you know I arrested a prowler at your house this afternoon."

"Oh, my."

"I've spotted the guy a couple of times earlier this week casing the neighborhood. When I got him this afternoon, he was in your back yard, looking in a window."

"Is everything all right?"

"I got him before he had a chance to get inside," the cop said. "There's something else you ought to know. Your daughter, Sandra, got a look at this guy and said she's certain he's the same guy who was following her the other day."

"Oh, no," the doctor's wife said. "Do you think our family is in danger?"

"It's hard to say," the cop said. "This guy wasn't armed, but that doesn't mean anything. So far, I've got him booked on a prowling charge. But that's not going to keep him in jail for long."

"Where is he now, officer?"

"He's being processed at the jail. If there's a way we can stick him with stalking or attempted burglary, we'll upgrade the charge. But right now, we don't have enough."

Susan Rosen exhaled loudly into the phone. Her hand holding the receiver started to tremble.

"Anything else you can do, Officer Smits, will be deeply

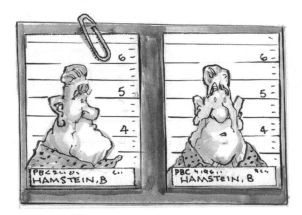

Bernie Hamstein finds himself in the Palm Beach County Jail, where it's freezing cold – but not as cold as the reception he expects to get from Rose when he explains why he got arrested.

appreciated," she said. "And thank you for being so observant."

"No problem," he said. "I'll keep you posted."

She was about to hang up when the cop stopped her.

"Oh, one more thing," he said. "I realize this is a dead end, but when I confronted this character, he claimed he knew you. All the burglars use that excuse. It's the oldest in the book. This guy didn't even know your name. He kept calling you Susan Plock."

Susan Rosen wondered who would be calling her by her maiden name.

"Officer, what was the name of the person you arrested?"

She could hear Smits shuffling through a bunch of pages.

"Here it is, right here …Hamstein. Bernard is the first name."

"Bernie Hamstein," she said in amazement.

"Yeah, Bernie Hamstein. That's it. Do you know him, Mrs. Rosen? … Mrs. Rosen? … Are you still there, Mrs. Rosen?"

■ ■ ■

Bernie signed his name.

"That's it?" he asked.

"That's it," the clerk said. "It's called an O.R. bond. You're free on your own recognizance."

"I don't have to post bail?"

"Your signature is your bail. Just don't miss your court date."

"No, no. I won't."

Bernie made his way out of the jail and smiled as he stepped from that fluorescent meat locker into a sunny, humid Florida afternoon.

And there were Rose, Sam and Maddy coming toward him.

"Bernie, they let you out!" Rose said, hugging him.

It was sometime during that hug that Bernie realized another woman had come up from the opposite direction and rather than walk by them, she just stood there, looking at Bernie.

"Bernie?" she finally said. "Is that you?"

Rose stopped hugging her husband and turned around to see who was talking to him.

"Yes?" Bernie said, still trying to make the connection.

"It's me," the woman said. "Susan."

"Susan?" Rose said.

"Susan!" Bernie said.

She wasn't like he had imagined at all. She was …old. Like him. What was he expecting? Probably someone more on the lines of her daughter, the one he had seen in the car the other day. Her daughter was the Susan Plock he knew. This woman standing in front of him was another South Florida senior citizen. She was about as much like Susan Plock, the teenager, as he was like Bernie Hamstein, the teenager.

"You haven't changed a bit," Bernie told her.

Rose and Susan were facing each other now, both struggling to make the connection.

"Susan Plock?"

"Rose Cangelosi?"

They both looked at Bernie.

Susan spoke first.

"I'm so sorry about what happened to you, Bernie," Susan said.

Sam, meanwhile, had taken the jail forms from his father's hand and read them.

"Dad, it says you were arrested for prowling?"

"Prowling?" Rose said. "I thought you were arrested with Joey Alpo."

"Who's Joey Alpo?" Susan said.

"Yeah, who's Joey Alpo?" Bernie said.

"Where were you prowling?" Rose asked.

"In Susan's back yard," Bernie said.

"Why were you doing that?"

"I don't know. Curiosity, Rose. I just got an old school directory from Mort Granger, and in browsing through it, I saw that Susan lived here. And then I find out you've been seeing her husband for years."

"Bernie," Rose said indignantly, "in all the years we've been married, I've never seen another man!"

"Oh yes, Rose," he said. "I know for a fact you've taken your drawers off for this guy."

Bernie had a little smile on his face. Sam was getting flustered.

"Mom?"

"I don't know what he's talking about. Your father's nuts."

"Her husband is Dr. Rosen, your gynecologist," Bernie said.

Rose slugged her husband on the shoulder.

"You did pretty good for yourself, Susan. Leaving Bernie for a gynecologist," Rose said. "And Jerry's a nice guy, too."

Bernie plowed on.

"So I just thought it would be nice to see Susan again, just to say hi," he said.

"You miss your old girlfriend, Bernie?" Rose said.

Both women were looking at him, and for that moment, Bernie wished he was back in jail.

"No. It was just something to do ... I don't know. I just wanted to see what became of her. I know it's a stupid thing. It just started out as a silly idea, but the more I thought about it, the more it grew."

"I think he's unhappy with me," Rose told Susan.

"No, it's nothing like that," Bernie said.

"Maybe it's the dog," Rose said. "We just got a dog. You may have heard of him. He's the one in quarantine at the pound for biting that obnoxious talk-radio guy."

"No, it has nothing to do with the dog," Bernie said.

"I don't listen to talk-radio," Susan said.

"Remembering Susan made me think about the way I was when I was a teenager," Bernie said. "That's all. About what it was like to be young. It's the being young I miss. Not you, Susan."

"Romantic, isn't he?" Rose said.

"I'm sorry for scaring your daughter," Bernie said to Susan.

"She'll have a funny story to tell someday," Susan said. "And this handsome young man here is your son?"

"Yes, this is Sam. He's my youngest. Rose and I have three boys."

"Your son, Jerry, is just like his father," Rose said. "A real sweetheart."

Susan pulled out her wallet.

"I've got a picture of the whole family here," she said.

Rose, not to be outdone, went for her wallet pictures, too.

Sam just realized something.

"Let's take a break from *This Is Your Life* for a second here to recap the criminal activities of the day," he said.

They all stopped and looked up at him.

"Dad, you were arrested for prowling in your old girlfriend's yard at approximately what time?"

"About 2 o'clock."

"So then, I take it you missed your 3 p.m. appointment at Loehmann's," Sam said.

"Hey, how do you know about that?"

"Dad, in another couple of hours the whole county is going to know about it," Sam said.

"What are you talking about?"

"Organized crime. The Mafia. The little old guy you've been using for a bookie is a lifelong soldier in the Carrando crime family. They call him Joey Alpo because he used to make bodies disappear by turning them into dog food."

Susan Rosen said she really had to be going.

"I'll see you in court," she said.

"Oh, yeah," Bernie said.

"I think I should be able to work out a deal where your sentence would consist of you and Rose coming over for dinner one night," she said.

"That'd be great, Susan," Bernie said before looking over at Rose, who was staring at him.

When Susan was out of earshot, Rose finally spoke.

"I hope you're not thinking you made a mistake 50 years ago."

"Rose," Bernie said, throwing an arm around her, "how could you think of such a thing? Can you imagine that, Sam? Can you imagine me with anybody but your mother?"

Sam shook his head.

Maddy, who had been memorizing it all for future telling to the Wonder Walkers, finally spoke up.

"I think we best be getting out of here," she said. "There's a bus full of gray-haired prisoners coming, and it would be awful if they all step out and start asking Bernie why he didn't show up."

So, the four of them walked quickly to Maddy's car while the bus stopped near the sallyport.

Maddy drove where they could get a better look. Bernie craned his neck from the back seat to see eight of his Shady Palms neighbors and one old mobster walk off the bus in handcuffs.

One of the men looked toward the car, prompting Bernie to sit back and slide down in his seat.

"Let's get out of here," he said.

41 Harvey and the visitation

Harvey Shorter heard voices in his hospital room. But he was too doped up to care. He had just gotten his afternoon intravenous cocktail of mind-numbing painkillers, and he was beginning to ride that wave of bliss when he became aware that two people were standing over his bed.

The man was wearing cycling clothes, and he was talking to a woman who was somewhere on the bandaged side of Shorter's face. He'd have to turn his head to see her. But what was the sense? These weren't real people anyway, Shorter told himself. These were people from his dream world.

"Harvey, are you there?" Ricardo asked him.

"Mmm," Harvey said.

"We are here to apologize for what happened Sunday," Ricardo said. "It was not an accident."

"Mmm," Harvey said, then he started to laugh.

Lois looked at Ricardo.

"I don't believe he's with us," Lois said.

Lois didn't believe she was there, either, standing next to Harvey Shorter. Well, at least he was the one in the bed this time. When Ricardo had told her they needed to go to the hospital to make things right with Shorter, she had first laughed and then told him, "No way."

"Then it is something Ricardo will have to do alone," he had told her.

"Fine," Lois had said. "You go up there to his room to apologize. But leave me out of it. Harvey Shorter hurt me, and Sunday, I hurt him back. I've got no regrets. Men are pigs, and that guy's one of the biggest porkers on the farm."

Ricardo had looked at her sadly.

"Is Ricardo a pig?" he asked.

She looked away from him.

"A person cannot live a happy life and be angry," Ricardo said. "We must deal with our anger and move on. We must apologize."

"No," she had said, "you must apologize. I must wait in the car."

Ricardo took her hand and started to say something but stopped himself.

"If you tell him, he'll have you charged with a crime," Lois said. "He's a judge."

Ricardo shrugged.

"Ricardo will apologize and pay his medical expenses," he said.

He got out of the car and started toward the hospital, with the cleats on his cycling shoes clacking against the pavement. She watched him disappear into the building, then she rapped the palm of her hand on the dashboard, opened her car door and stepped out.

She caught up to him by the time he had reached the elevator.

He looked at her, surprised.

"Sunday, you did something for me that bothered you, but you did it because you cared for me," she said. "So, here I am. You're not a pig, Ricardo."

He kissed her on the cheek.

"It is the only way to make things right with him ... and

us," Ricardo said.

But now that they were in Shorter's room, Lois wasn't sure she could say anything to him. The judge was looking pathetic, his whole left side in traction.

"Harvey, can you hear me?" Lois said.

"Mmm" Harvey said.

"This is Lois, Lois Rodgers. You knew me as Lois Brockman. Remember me?"

"Mmm."

"Harvey, I told Ricardo to cause an accident during your race," she said.

"Mmm."

"It wasn't a good idea," Lois said.

That was as close to an apology as she would come. She looked up at Ricardo, who was beaming.

He reached out his hand to her, and she took it. Both their hands were stretched over Harvey's body, and for a second, Harvey focused on those clasped hands and thought somebody was performing last rites on him.

"Mmmm! Mmmm!" he said, urgently.

"Yes, it is understandable that you are angry," Ricardo said.

About that time, Lois heard the voice on the television suspended from the ceiling near her head.

The newscaster was talking about arrests of Shady Palms residents. Lois dropped Ricardo's hand — right on Harvey's bandaged chest.

"Mmmmm!"

Then she walked back a few steps to get a better look at the TV.

The words "Exclusive Story" flashed on the bottom of the screen as an unsteady camera showed agents and Channel 5's Suzie Ching striding into the Loehmann's at the Shoppes of the Shady Palms and confronting a silver-haired man sitting in one of the chairs up front.

The silver-haired man stood up.

"What's going on here?" he said.

And before the agents could even flash their badges and announce the arrest, Suzie Ching had a microphone to his face and a question in the air.

"Do you deny you are Joey Alpo, the ruthless mobster who chopped his victims up into dog food?"

Lois turned up the volume on the set.

"Mmm," Harvey said.

The judge was free-falling now, in and out of consciousness. He kept turning the words "dog food" over and over in his head, trying to figure out what dog food had to do with the two people standing over his bed. Somebody was apologizing. Apologizing about dog food?

Oh, this was some dream he was having.

"Come, let us go," Ricardo said.

■ ■ ■

Margo didn't attend the news conference. When Bernie called the condo to say he had been arrested, Rose rushed off to the jail, leaving Margo mumbling apologies in her wake.

What next?

Margo drove past Hector the gate guard without even acknowledging his wave. If only there was something she could do for Bernie. But she knew it was too late.

He'd be getting booked on a felony racketeering charge. His name and picture would be on the TV news and in the newspaper.

She was in a spot of trouble herself.

Bill Johnson would want a full explanation. She had abandoned her post, stranded her partner and potentially damaged the operation. There would be an internal affairs investigation, at the very least. She'd be suspended, perhaps without pay.

Margo knew she'd have to face the music, but there was no sense in rushing to her own execution. So she drove the unmarked car to her West Palm Beach apartment. She wet a wash rag, rolled it up and put in on her forehead as she stretched out on her bed.

When she woke up, the room was shadowy and the sun was well on its way to the horizon. She looked at the alarm clock near her bed. It was already 6 o'clock. She reached for the remote control and flicked on the TV.

There was Bill Johnson, explaining to the cameras what a success the operation had been.

Then the words "Team Coverage" flashed on the screen, and a reporter was standing on the front sidewalk of a large home.

"It was in this house in this quiet suburban Boynton Beach neighborhood where the reputed gangland figure lived. Neighbors here were shocked to learn ..."

Margo wondered when neighbors would ever be anything but shocked.

The "Team Coverage" logo flashed again on the screen, and it was Suzie Ching, standing in front of the entrance to Shady Palms.

"And it was here," she said, "behind the walls of this quiet condominium community ..."

"Quiet? Hah!" Margo said. "You live there and see how quiet it is, Suzie Ching."

"... where the other Carrando crime family associates lived ..."

"Hah!" Margo said again.

"... raking in millions of dollars in illegal sports betting every year from their unsuspecting neighbors."

Margo turned off the TV when the station started to show the mug shots of the arrested men. She didn't want to see Bernie that way.

She sat up in bed and thought for a moment. Maybe there was still a way she could help Bernie.

After all, they really weren't after Bernie. They were after
Joey Alpo. They'd be eager to make plea deals with Bernie and
the others. And the quicker the deal, the easier it'd be to make.

That's it, she told herself. What she needed to do now was
make sure that Rose and Sam got Bernie a lawyer right away.
And not just any defense lawyer. She needed to get him Ross
Davidson, a well-known wheeler-dealer. Davidson could work
out a sweetheart deal for Bernie by tomorrow.

Charged by the thought of helping, she dialed the
Hamstein condo. She knew it wouldn't be easy talking to Rose
and Sam again. They might even hang up on her. But this was
important, and she was willing to take a little bit of abuse if it
meant helping them out.

The phone rang three times before somebody picked it up.
"Hello?"

"Sam?" Margo said.

"No, this is his father."

"Bernie?"

"Yeah."

"Bernie," she said, "what are you doing home?"

"Chopping rappini."

Margo could hear Rose asking, "Who is it?" and Bernie
answered, "It's Margo."

"I thought you were arrested?"

"I was," he said. "But they let me out."

"I'm so sorry, Bernie," she said.

"You're sorry? What about me? Getting arrested for prowling at my age."

"Prowling? You mean you weren't at the Loehmann's this
afternoon? I thought you ..."

"No, I'm not a Carrando crime family associate," Bernie
said. "Which is too bad. You know, my father always told me that
if I married an Italian, I'd get recruited into the Mob. I guess I
missed my chance."

"Oh, Bernie, I can't tell you how relieved I am …"

"Margo," Bernie said. "Why don't we finish this conversation over dinner tonight. Chicken parmigiana with the rappini on the side. Have you ever had rappini? It's basically Italian collard greens. Rose sautés it with lots of garlic. Margo? … Margo?"

"Yeah, I'm here."

"What's a matter? You got a cold?"

42 An evening at Ricardo's

"What now?" Lois asked.

"Let us go to my place," Ricardo said.

Before they walked out of the hospital, he excused himself, saying he had to make a quick phone call. She wandered into the nearby gift shop.

"Manuel," Ricardo said. "Dinner for two tonight. On the patio by the sea wall."

"The lady, sir?"

"Yes, with the lady."

"Very well."

"Blacken the grouper the way you do, Manuel."

"Yes, sir."

"And Manuel …"

"Yes, sir."

"You will play your violin while we eat?"

"If you wish, sir."

"Yes, Manuel. Ricardo wishes to hear your violin tonight."

After Ricardo hung up and found Lois in the gift shop, she had a little smirk on her face.

"You got the girlfriend stashed?" she asked.

"Pardon me?"

"The girl in your apartment. The one you didn't want me to

see," Lois said. "C'mon, Ricardo. I wasn't born yesterday."

Ricardo thought about protesting vigorously. But instead, he merely smiled.

"Ah, you have found me out," he said as he began walking her to the car.

Lois looked at him, trying to measure whether he was serious. Every time she thought she had him figured out, he surprised her.

"I don't know what I'm going to do with you," she said.

"For now, taking me home will do," he said.

On the way north, Lois made mental images of Ricardo's place. She had him pegged for a no-pictures-on-the-walls bachelor pad with stacks of frozen dinners in the freezer and a pile of dirty clothes in the corner of the bedroom.

He insisted she take the beach route along A1A, and while they were going, he rolled down his window and nearly stuck his head out to gulp air like a dog.

"Would you rather I take your bicycle out of the trunk, and I'll just follow you there?" Lois asked.

Ricardo hesitated for a second before answering, "No, no. That is quite all right."

When they got past Lake Worth, she told him to let her know when to turn west. When they passed the Southern Boulevard crossing, she asked, "Are you sure you don't turn there? That's how you get to West Palm Beach, isn't it?"

"Yes," Ricardo said. "That is how to get to West Palm Beach."

"So, why didn't you have me take that road?"

"Because we are not going to West Palm Beach."

"But you told me you lived in West Palm Beach," she said.

"Ricardo told you that?" he said, with a little smile curling on his lips. "Now, why would Ricardo say a thing like that?"

They drove into the north end of Palm Beach, and Lois suddenly realized there was nowhere else to go. If they kept going north, they'd run into the inlet.

"You live in Palm Beach?" Lois asked.

"Turn ahead," Ricardo said. "At the next break in the hedges."

The hedges were enormous and broken only by the width of a long winding driveway that connected the road to a three-story estate nestled nearly a quarter-mile away on the ocean.

When Lois pulled into the driveway, she looked at Ricardo in alarm, thinking for sure he had made some mistake.

But Ricardo just smiled.

Then she saw the Bentley parked in the driveway, and Manuel, the man who had come for Ricardo the day he got the flat tire, was walking out of a small servants' quarters on the north end of the property.

Ah, so that was it. Manuel and Ricardo were household servants here. That made sense.

Manuel was walking toward Lois' car, and as soon as she turned off the ignition, he was there, opening her door.

"Welcome, Mrs. Rodgers," he said.

"Hello," Lois said.

Ricardo, who had pulled his bicycle from the trunk, began to walk to the main house.

"Ricardo," Lois said, a bit flustered. "What are you doing?"

"It is not good to leave a bicycle like this outside. The salt air is very bad for it."

"No. I mean, what are you doing, going in that house?"

Ricardo shrugged and held out his arm.

Something clicked with Lois. It was that phone call when she was blindly calling numbers trying to reach Ricardo. One of the Richard Veras had asked her if perhaps she was looking for one of the sugar baron Veras. And she had laughed, saying "Sugar baron? Heavens no. He's just a little guy who rides a bicycle a lot."

Now, she looked at Ricardo.

"Why didn't you tell me you're a sugar baron?" she said.

They were walking together toward the huge house.

Ricardo had one hand on his handlebars and the other around Lois' waist.

"That would have ruined things," he said.

Later that night, when the last strains of Manuel's violin had blended with the last of the wine, and a big yellow moon made its belated arrival, Lois sat back in her chair and looked at Ricardo.

"I think I could sit like this forever," she said.

"No, you cannot," Ricardo said, before he hopped over the sea wall and began taking off his clothes as he ran toward the ocean. He stopped only once to look back at her from the beach.

Lois was surprised, but then again, she had learned to expect surprises when it came to Ricardo. But what really shocked her was what happened next — when she found herself stripping, jumping over the sea wall and following Ricardo's footprints into the darkness leading to the watery horizon.

■ ■ ■

Much to her surprise, television reporter Suzie Ching spent the night in the Palm Beach County Jail.

She tried to explain to the arresting officer that it was a big, big mistake. But after too many rounds of tequila shooters with the celebrating FIST members, it was hard to understand her objections.

"You see, officer, I've been out drinking with other police officers and I was ... oh, my..." she said.

But even if she had been more coherent, it wouldn't have made much difference to the trooper, who found her speeding and weaving between lanes on Interstate 95.

To make matters worse, she couldn't walk in a straight line, began the alphabet in reverse with "Z, Y, M, C, A" and ended the night tooting a 0.21 on the breath test.

Margo, who read a small account of the TV reporter's drunk driving arrest in the newspaper two days later, said, "Well, at least you didn't get pregnant, Suzie."

■ ■ ■

Later that week, Sam Hamstein stood on a small stage with the bright lights blinding him. It seemed like forever since he'd performed in a comedy club, and he was glad for the chance.

At the last minute, a feature act canceled at the Comedy Corner in West Palm Beach. Sam got the job to fill in. One night only. Two shows of about 30 minutes, just enough to get the crowd ready for the headliner.

He had some new material he wanted to try out. As his eyes adjusted to the lights, he looked over to the table where Margo was sitting.

He didn't tell her about his new material. He thought it best to let her hear it this way, from the stage.

"It's good to be here," he told the crowd. "Life's been hard for me lately. I fell in love with a woman cop. Tough woman. Her idea of foreplay is saying, 'Feet apart and spread 'em.'

"When we go for a romantic drive, I look at the scenery, and she checks to see whether the other cars have expired registration stickers."

Sam looked out at Margo's table, but all he could see was her silhouette.

"I'm thinking about getting engaged," Sam continued. "But so far, I haven't been able to find a doughnut small enough to slip on her finger."

When the scattered laughter died down, he heard a voice from the darkness.

"Are you really thinking about marrying me?"

It was Margo. The crowd laughed, thinking this was part of the routine.

"Yes," Sam said, "after I divorce my wife, of course."

The crowd laughed again.

"What about the baby?" Margo asked.

Even bigger laughs.

"Package deal," Sam said.

The guy operating the spotlight swung it around to Margo's table, and suddenly the audience saw her sitting there, tears streaming down her cheeks.

The laughter stopped. There was an awkward silence, and then a couple of people began to clap their hands. Others joined in. Soon the whole place was applauding, showering them in a thunderous ovation.

■ ■ ■

The next morning, Bernie and Rose drove to the county's Animal Care and Control facility.

"I'm here for my dog," Rose said, giving the receptionist her best no-nonsense expression. "His quarantine is over, and I want him back."

Bernie stood behind her, pretending to read a sign on the wall.

When a worker finally brought Lucky out to them, the dog yelped with joy. Rose squatted down and let the mutt lick her all over her face.

"C'mon, let's get out of here," she said to Bernie, "before they change their minds."

On the way back to the condo, the dog sat between them, resting parts of his body against both of them.

"Let's take him right to the condo office, Bernie," Rose said. "I can tell, he lost some weight in the pound."

Sure enough, Lucky was 19.6 pounds, according to the scale in the condo office.

"I told you this was no 20-pound dog," Bernie said triumphantly to Herb Troutman, who kept staring at the scale and wishing for an extra half-pound that wasn't there.

After they left Troutman, Rose patted Lucky on the head and whispered, "Now, you can have your steak."

Lucky obviously didn't understand English. If he had, he wouldn't have set such a leisurely pace back to C Building.

Which was fine with Bernie.

It was Rose's idea to walk to the condo office for the weigh-in. She had skipped Wonder Walkers that morning to go to the pound. So she thought a walk would be good for all three of them.

"You know, I was thinking," Bernie said, as C Building loomed ahead of them.

"Yes?"

"It's going to be nice now that things around here will be getting back to normal."

Just then, a car horn tooted, and they turned to see Sam, who didn't spend the previous night in their condo.

"Mom, Dad," Sam said through the opened window. "I've got some great news."

43 The end ... and the beginning

Despite overwhelming evidence, a Palm Beach County jury found Joseph "Joey Alpo" Abrizzio not guilty on all charges. Joey Alpo, followed outside the courthouse by his four attorneys and a throng of TV cameras, had only one brief comment before he got into a waiting black Cadillac.

"All I gotta say, ladies and gents, is it looks like the prosecution didn't cover the spread."

The New York Post ran a story of the mobster's acquittal the next day, under the headline: "Alpo out of the can."

The prosecutors blamed the acquittal on a series of evidentiary rulings that went against them. The trial judge, Harvey Shorter, had excluded some key evidence, they complained.

Shorter, who had recovered fully from his triathlon injury, never recovered from the Joey Alpo case. He was soundly defeated in the next election.

The Shady Palms residents arrested on gambling charges were convicted, each of them accepting plea bargains for a little community service and testimony against Joey Alpo, which as it turned out didn't matter.

On the night of Joey Alpo's acquittal, the FIST law enforcement squad ran up a $1,758 bar bill at a Military Trail strip club. This might have gone unnoticed by the public had not the group's leader, Bill Johnson, bitten a stripper on the rear end during a table dance. Johnson took early retirement shortly after the stripper's lawsuit became the lead story on *Hard Copy*.

Walter Wallbanger might have made great sport of all this, but by the time the story had emerged, he was selling refrigerators again. The indisputable truth of Wallbanger's *Search for Truth* was that his show had lousy ratings. The radio station replaced the Wallbanger show with an advice doctor, who doubled the ratings in the first week she was in his time slot.

On the second week, someone firebombed the advice doctor's car in the station's parking lot. No one was charged, though the police narrowed the suspects down to a disgruntled former postal worker, a neo-Nazi and a United Nations conspiracy theorist. After the bombing, the advice doctor never returned. So, in desperation, the station aired elevator music — which got even higher ratings than Wallbanger and the advice doctor combined.

Jake Fisher moved out of his mother's Shady Palms condominium and into Craig Shelbourne's apartment in suburban Lake Worth. Jake, however, still spends a lot of time visiting his mother. And he and Craig are frequently seen lounging around the clubhouse pool in their skimpy Speedos, much to the chagrin of many Shady Palms residents.

Jake found an acting job, too, working with the Burt Reynolds Institute for Theatre Training. His stint there was brief, though. On the night of his first performance, the theater closed because of money problems. Jake is waiting tables on Clematis Street these days.

The Wonder Walkers still gather every morning at the Boynton Beach Mall to hash out each other's lives and eat sticky buns. Once in a while, Margo joins them. But mostly, it's just the four women, Rose, Jacqui, Lois and Maddy.

Mort Granger is causing a stir again with his *Shady Palms Gazette*. The paper has been harping on Johnny Fox's lax accounting practices with the Shady Palms Players, which is now doing a production called *Bright Lights, Big Condo* — a collection of original show tunes written by Shady Palms residents.

Herb Troutman still runs the governing board of condo presidents, but he has hinted he may be ready to step aside.

"I'll believe that when I see it," Bernie said.

The rest of the football season passed rather quietly in Shady Palms. Without the weekly betting, the games themselves seemed boring to the men. Many of them couldn't even see the point in watching a game when they didn't have any money riding on the outcome.

One Sunday afternoon when the Dolphins were at Indianapolis, Bernie clicked off the set in boredom and called up four of his friends to meet him at the clubhouse. Within a half-hour, they had a decent poker game going. The next week, another table of guys joined them.

These days, the clubhouse looks like a casino at times.

"It's going to happen again," Rose warned her husband. "You guys are all going to get yourself in trouble again."

Bernie doesn't think so.

Lately, he's been feeling lucky.

The prowling charge filed against him when he was arrested in Susan Plock's back yard was finally dismissed. The only time he saw Susan again was that day in court. They exchanged pleasantries, but he could tell she was just as eager to get away from him as he was from her.

That, of course, didn't stop Rose from hounding him about Susan.

When he'd say he was going out for a while, she would sometimes say, "Going to see Susan Plock?"

It was something Bernie would have to live with.

So was Lucky the dog.

Lucky was part of the family now, sleeping with them, sitting under the table while they ate and whimpering whenever they left the condo without him. Bernie still liked to grumble about the dog, but the truth was, he had become just as fond of Lucky as his wife was.

"Bernie!" Rose would say as he tossed another piece of meat in Lucky's bowl. "You're going to make him fat, and then somebody will complain we have an overweight dog again."

Actually, that was precisely Bernie's original plan. Even if he had to be the one to make the anonymous complaint. But nobody complained, and over time, Bernie felt like feeding the dog, not to cause trouble, but because he liked making Lucky happy.

In October, Ricardo Vera placed first in his age group at the Ironman Triathlon in Hawaii, finishing at a time of just under 11 hours. The racing conditions were great that day, and as he ran the last hundred yards to the finish line, he saw Lois standing there holding a lei to drape over his shoulders.

When they got back to Florida, he asked Lois to move into his Palm Beach mansion with him. Lois said she would.

But by the next day, she had changed her mind.

"I'm sorry, Ricardo," she said. "But I think I belong at Shady Palms. I'm a Wonder Walker. I'm not one of the beautiful people."

And so, you can still see Ricardo riding his bicycle into Shady Palms a few afternoons a week, pedaling past Hector the gate guard and over the speed bumps toward C Building.

Margo Zukowski was suspended for two weeks without pay for abandoning her post during the Joey Alpo arrest. The remainder of her assignment with FIST was canceled, and she returned to the sheriff's office, where her position on the homicide squad had already been filled.

"I can put you in the burglary unit," her boss had said.

When Margo frowned, he added, "Other than that, the only options are road patrol and the training office."

"What would I do in training?" she had asked.

"Dreadful stuff," he said. "Teaching crime prevention to senior citizens in condos."

She smiled.

"I'll take it," she said. "I think I have some experience in that field."

As for Sam Hamstein, he imagined that divorcing his wife, Jasmine, would be a lot tougher than it was.

"That's fascinating," was what Jasmine had said when Sam unloaded the news that he had fallen in love with a pregnant woman in his parents' condo complex. To Sam, Jasmine said "fascinating" the same way she might have remarked about an aberrant strand of DNA molecules.

Bernie made up for Jasmine's clinical coolness.

"What!" Bernie had said. "You're taking on a pregnant woman … with somebody else's kid …and you're telling me to calm down. You don't even have a steady job."

"I'm a comedian, Dad."

"Like I said, you don't even have a steady job."

"I thought you liked Margo."

"I like a lot of people," Bernie said. "I like Mrs. Goldbloom in 39C, but that doesn't mean I think you should shack up with her."

Rose was better about it.

"Shut up, Bernie, you old fool," she said. "Our Sam is going to be living in Florida now, and we're going to have a new grandchild."

Sam moved in to Margo's West Palm Beach apartment, and he did get regular work traveling the comedy club circuit around the South.

It was while he was on one of those trips through Alabama and Georgia that Margo went into labor. She was visiting Bernie and Rose at the time, and when her contractions became unbearable, she looked up at Rose and said, "It's happening."

Bernie, in a panic, ran over a small ficus hedge on his way out of the parking lot. But he got Margo to the hospital in time.

Rose was in the room with Margo when the baby was born. Bernie preferred to pace the lobby. When Rose walked out of the delivery room to find him, he was conducting an animated lecture on condominium law to a custodial worker who appeared to be dozing.

"Oh, Bernie," she said, running up to him.

She hugged him and began crying on his shoulder.

"Rosie, Rosie, what's wrong?" Bernie said.

Suddenly, he had the sinking feeling something had happened to the baby, or to Margo, whom he actually liked a whole lot more than Mrs. Goldbloom in 39C.

"Tell me everything's OK, Rose," Bernie said. "Please, tell me everything is OK."

His wife, the woman he had shared so much with all these years, held his face in both hands. He could tell just from her expression that it was only joy that had made her so emotional. Yes, everything was OK.

"Oh, Rose," he said, in a way that made him feel he had expressed in that single name the entire mystery and purpose of life itself.

"Wait till you see him," she said, dragging Bernie across the lobby.

"A boy? It's a baby boy?" Bernie said.

When they got to the room, Margo was holding the infant and watching him sleep against her.

Bernie walked to the side of the bed and put his index finger in the infant's hand.

He thought he should say something, but he didn't trust his voice.

Then he heard Margo's voice.

"His name is Bernie," she said.

At first, Bernie thought she was talking to her baby, telling him the name of the old man who was probing his tiny hand. But when Bernie looked at Margo, he saw she was looking at him, not the baby, when she spoke.

"His name is Bernie?" Bernie said.

"Yeah," Margo said, "you got a problem with that?"

That night, he and Rose took one of their old sheets, wrote "It's a Boy" on it and hung it over their balcony in C Building. It was the first time in Shady Palms history that the birth of a child was announced in such a fashion.

Three residents complained to Herb Troutman about it, and within 10 minutes, Bernie got a call to take the sign down.

"Bernie," Troutman said, "I don't have to remind you it's against the rules in Shady Palms to hang anything from the balcony. If you are allowed to get away with this, it will set a dangerous precedent that will ..."

Bernie hung up the phone.

"Who was that?" Rose asked.

She was lighting candles in their bedroom and putting on the silky thing she brought out of her closet once a week, even though this wasn't the usual night.

"That was nobody," Bernie said, moving closer to her.

"Hey, can't you wait till I light these candles ..."

A Hamstein family portrait: Bernie and Rose with the surprising additions to their lives at Shady Palms.